Losing My Soul

Barbara Joe Williams

Amani Publishing, llc

Barbara Joe Williams

Tallahassee, FL

Amani Publishing, LLC
P. O. Box 12045
Tallahassee, FL 32317
(850) 264-3341

A company based on faith, hope, and love

Visit our website at: **www.barbarajoe.webs.com**

Email us at: **amanipublishing@aol.com**

ISBN, 9780983366645
LCCN, 2013900414

Cover creation by: Diane Bass

Prologue

"I'm telling you, the Lord can bring you from a mighty long ways. I was lost in a world of sin. Y'all don't hear me!" Belinda Taylor shouted, holding the microphone in her right hand. She was in front of the podium at a modest-sized, non-denominational church in Dallas, Texas, pacing back and forth in a gold-textured, two-piece skirt suit with a pair of matching leather high–heeled, pointed-toe pumps. The congregation was on fire this morning, and every member present was standing on their feet clapping for the newly ordained minister as she delivered her first sermon.

Belinda paused for a second, wiping the perspiration from her brow, gathering her thoughts before continuing. Placing one hand on her hip, she straightened her back, and looked out over the crowd of almost three hundred people. Smiling at their happy faces, she said, "This time two years ago, I was married to a doctor, and we had two fine children. I had a three-story, seven-bedroom house. I had a maid to do the cleaning and the cooking. I drove a brand new Mercedes Benz. I owned the finest clothes, jewelry, and perfume money could buy. I traveled to all the exotic places I wanted to visit. But how many of you know today that I was drowning in sin! How many of you know today that sin was suffocating me, and I was slowly losing my soul! Hallelujah! God delivered me! Yes, He did!" Belinda shouted, pumping a fist in the air. Tears were streaming down her face like water from a broken faucet, but that didn't stop her from praising Him.

The applause was too loud for Belinda to continue. She stopped, listening to the praises coming from the Abundantly Blessed Church members shouting out to her from every corner of the building. Leaning to one side, she said, "You see, I had low self-esteem because I didn't know Jesus. I thought that having a successful man validated my existence. I thought that being wealthy would bring me happiness. But all it brought me was a twenty-year marriage filled with pain. Yes, I lived with heartbreaking hurt for all that time simply because I didn't know any better. It was all because I didn't know Jesus!" Belinda shouted, returning to the podium. She opened the Bible resting on the stand and turned to one of her favorite passages, Genesis 1:1-3, and read:

In the beginning God created the heavens and the earth. The earth was without form, and void; and darkness was on the face of the deep. And the Spirit of God was hovering over the face of the waters. Then God said, "Let there be light;" and there was light.

"Amen. I'm so thankful for the light today! You see, when I first accepted the Lord as my Savior, I picked up this Bible and this was the first verse that I read," she stated, shaking her head in disbelief. "Y'all just don't know how much I've been through. My marriage almost killed me because I wanted to hold on to a man who didn't even know how to love, let alone be married. While he was running around sleeping with other women, I was running behind him trying to destroy every woman that he touched. Then, I was happy when he came home to me. I was grateful for the crumbs and the leftovers. And I could keep on keeping up with the Joneses. But all of that eventually changed. All of that changed about two years ago after a devastating turn of events. You see, some of you know that I've served time in prison, but most of you don't know how I got there or how I got out," she said, pausing to look at the concern on many of the members' faces who had returned to their seats. Belinda closed her eyes and recited a silent prayer. This wouldn't be an easy story to tell, but she had to get it out...

1

(Belinda's Life)

"I'm Jessica Robinson. Thank you for joining us for this evening's edition of the late news on KDFW-Four Fox, in Dallas. It's Wednesday, July fifteenth." Belinda pressed the off button on the television remote control and slammed it on the nightstand. She hadn't been listening to the bubbly, brown-eyed newscaster anyway. Belinda was completely caught up in the latest electronic book she'd recently downloaded to her Kindle Fire, a novel by Zane, one of her favorite erotica authors.

Reclining in her California, king-sized, canopy bed on a mountain of soft pillows wearing her sheer, red nightgown, Belinda turned a page in the titillating novel she'd been reading for the past two nights. Lately, reading erotica by the popular author had become her way of relaxing during the evening hours, especially when her husband, Dr. Desmond Taylor, claimed to be working late at the office doing medical research. If she couldn't get any hot sex for herself, she could at least read about other women who were. A lot of readers criticized Zane, but Belinda didn't blame those women for doing their thing. Shoot, she was proud of them.

Two more hours passed before Belinda stopped reading again. Realizing it was about time for Desmond to return home, Belinda wanted the house quiet so she could hear his sorry, philandering behind whenever he came tipping in during the middle of the night. He normally made it home before the sun rose. There had only been a few occasions where Desmond had felt grown enough to stay out all night with his mistress. After witnessing Belinda's violent behavior, he made a conscious effort to be home by three o'clock in the morning whenever there was a need to "stay over" with another woman.

Belinda clicked off the night lamp at the first sound of the alarm system beeping to signal that her long, lost husband was finally entering the house. Throwing some of the pillows on his side of the bed, she slumped down, and pulled the covers snugly around her shoulders. Undoubtedly, Desmond wasn't expecting her to be up this time of night waiting on him anyway.

Glancing at the digital clock on the night table, Belinda didn't want to hear what his excuse was for coming in at one-fifteen in the morning, so she turned her back away from his side of the bed and pretended to be asleep. Belinda had a good idea where he'd been until this hour, but she wasn't in the mood for listening to yet another lie from his smooth lips.

Silently, she waited as he neared the bedroom entrance. Belinda heard the doorknob turn and click as Desmond eased the door open. She could sense him peeping in to see if she was still up, but Belinda didn't dare move a muscle.

Tiptoeing into the bedroom with his Italian leather loafers in his hand, Desmond had his clothes draped over his arm as he lowered himself to the right side of the bed. Placing his suit on the Queen Anne chair beside his bed, Desmond eased underneath the satin covers, and thanked the Lord that Belinda was pretending to be asleep again. He surely didn't want to argue with his wife tonight regarding his whereabouts, not that she would be bold enough to ask. Desmond was his own man and as long as he paid all of the bills, he called all of the shots, and he didn't have to answer to anyone, especially the woman he'd been married to for the past nineteen years. If Belinda didn't understand their key that she'd copied from Desmond's extra key ring last week would come in handy in the morning. It was time to let this wench know who was living large and still in charge. "Nobody messes with my man, dammit. Nobody. I can't wait to see the look on her face in the morning…"

2

(Belinda's husband)

Dr. Desmond Taylor welcomed a new day because a new day meant new conquests for the smooth-skinned dermatologist. As a fourth generation doctor, he had acquired everything in life that he'd set out to obtain. A thriving medical practice, a seven-bedroom estate, all the designer clothes and shoes his walk-around closet could hold, a convertible Porsche Boxster, a loyal wife, two intelligent children, and a sexy mistress. Now, it was just a matter of enjoying all these fine things he'd accumulated and finding new ways to keep his libido stimulated. He was truly a man's man, the kind who thought with the wrong head when it came to attractive women.

Sliding his long arms into the gray jacket of a Kenneth Cole suit, Desmond smiled at his reflection in the full, body-length mirror. He had to be able to see himself in all his glory every morning before exiting his plush bedroom. His good looks came from the combination of an African-American surgeon, David Taylor, and his Caucasian wife, Eileen. And since he was their only child, Desmond became the product of a wealthy environment which centered on fulfilling his every desire instead of just fulfilling his human needs. With his overly attractive features, he'd had his choice of women since his teenage years. And yes, there had been more women than the well-educated man dared to try counting, but only the superfine ladies were added to his account.

"Good morning, Dez," Belinda said, standing in the

doorway of his dressing room, watching him admire himself. She had on a silk robe covering up her size eight body.

Desmond didn't turn around; he glanced at his wife's reflection in the mirror. "Good morning," he replied, straightening his printed necktie, pretending like the sound of her voice wasn't irritating him.

"I know you had a late meeting last night, but I was hoping you could make it home for dinner tonight around seven o'clock." Belinda leaned one shoulder against the doorframe, placing a hand on her hip. "I've already asked Ms. Rodriguez to make your favorite meal. She's going to the Fresh Market to buy the pork chops this morning, organic brown rice, and fresh asparagus tips. And if you're really good, I'll ask her to make your favorite chocolate tower truffle cake for desert." Belinda grinned, remembering her husband's addiction to the dark substance.

Desmond grinned inwardly, but he wasn't swayed by his wife. "That sounds delicious. But I'm afraid that I won't be having dinner with you all tonight." He moved to the leather bench in his closet, sat down on the soft cushion, and slipped on a pair of size eleven loafers.

"Why not?" Belinda asked, sounding perturbed. "You don't usually work late two nights in a row, Dez. Besides, I've already asked Ms. Rodriquez to stay longer today so that she can serve us tonight."

"Well, you should have asked me first, B," he snapped, looking in her direction. "Why are trying to pull this crap on me? You know I can't be home for dinner every night. In fact, I won't be home tonight at all. I'm driving down to San Antonio with Maurice after work to catch a Spurs game."

"And since when did you two plan this?" she asked, stepping into his immense closet space. Belinda knew exactly where this conversation was headed.

"Actually, Maurice just told me about the tickets yesterday. I don't know how he was able to swing them at the last minute, but you know how much we wanted to see them play again. I can't pass on this." He stood up, walking towards Belinda, trying to sport an honest face. "We're going to stay over at some hotel and drive back in the morning," he said, walking past his wife.

Biting down on her bottom lip, Belinda could taste the blood seeping into her mouth. Only Dr. Desmond Arnez Taylor could make a Harvard-educated woman this damn angry with his exaggerated lies and blatant deceitfulness. She knew he was planning to meet with his skank mistress at her apartment tonight, drive her down to San Antonio, cruise the Riverwalk, and screw her puny brains out at the Elixir Hotel. Only she wasn't about to let that happen. After she finished having an impolite conversation with Ms. Bridget this morning, he'd be coming home to enjoy the flavors of their specially prepared dinner. Belinda licked her sore lip, imagining the taste of the smothered pork chops replacing the bitter taste of blood on her tongue.

Squatting on the bench where Desmond had just sat, Belinda could still feel the warmth from his buttocks. It reminded her of the heat she used to feel in their marriage bed. Only they hadn't had sex in almost two months, and she knew her husband well enough by now to know that meant he was having sex with someone else. Not that he'd tried to hide it; the scent of other women could sometimes be smelled on his Calvin Klein's underwear from across the room.

Belinda bent over, pressing her face against her palms. She didn't like having to eliminate Desmond's mistresses year after year, but if she wanted to maintain her splendid lifestyle, what else was she supposed to do? She couldn't fathom the idea of sharing him with another woman. And since her flawed strategy for divorcing him last year hadn't worked out, Belinda was out of options. Besides, she'd become accustomed to the pleasures associated with being married to a prominent physician, like spending her days with pampered rich friends getting spa treatments, being invited to upscale events, having lunch at five-star restaurants, traveling to exotic islands, shopping overseas for designer clothes, and fulfilling her pointed-toe shoe fetish. No, she couldn't do all that as a divorced mother living month-to-month on a measly alimony check.

Belinda wasn't going to be like her ex-girlfriend, Nina, who was stupid enough to divorce her wealthy husband, Dr. Mayfield, thinking she'd be able to maintain her lavish lifestyle. Well, when they left divorce court that overcast day, Nina walked away with a few million dollars, but he slithered away with everything else—the houses, the cars, the prestige, the children, and all their friends. Not one housewife in their circle of friends ever called Nina again, including Belinda. She was determined not to have the same fate.

That was it. Belinda was psyched now. Raising her head, she leaped off the bench, smiling to herself. It was time to get up, get dressed, and get prepared to seal her marriage for a few more months. Maybe another year, if she was lucky.

Desmond had his sun visor down, blocking the beaming light from his emerald eyes. With the drop-top back, he welcomed the wind blowing through his short wavy locks on such a heated day. Today was going to be a scorcher in more ways than one for him. The humidity was rising outside along with the pressure between his thighs. Listening to the beats of Usher singing about "them papers," Desmond blocked out the sounds of the city. He envied Usher for having the courage to divorce that chick and wondered how much it had cost the brother.

Speeding down the highway in his two-seater Porsche, he weaved in and out of traffic like a teenager on a joy ride.

Sucking his teeth like he had a bad taste in his mouth, Desmond recalled the conversation he'd had with Belinda this morning. He hated how much she got on his nerves, especially when she sweated him about his whereabouts.

He tried to change his ways after his wife had gotten enough backbone to present him with an ultimatum last year. Somehow, he was able to keep up the façade of being a happily married man until Bridget Hunter literally landed in his lap on a flight to Los Angeles. Desmond was headed to a convention being hosted by the Dermatologist Association of America at the University of California. Bridget had been fortunate enough to be walking past him when the plane hit an air pocket in the clouds, abruptly landing her on top of his groin. And that's where she ended up before the night was over, on top of him again. Only neither one of them had on any clothing the second time their bodies collided.

His cell phone rang, rudely interrupting his pleasant thoughts of Bridget. "Hello, baby," he answered, grinning, without checking the caller ID. He was positive that it was Bridget returning one of his recent phone calls.

"Hi, Desmond." He dropped the childish grin from his face at the sound of Belinda's nagging voice. "I was just calling to remind you that we're confirmed to attend the Richmond's dinner party tomorrow night at seven o'clock. So you need to be home by five for us to make it on time."

"I know this, Belinda. Why are you calling to tell me that?" he quipped, glancing at his frowning face in the rearview mirror.

"Because, I don't want you and Maurice to get caught up in San Antonio after the game and think about spending another night down there. You need to come on back."

"Fine, it's a one night trip. I'll see you before five tomorrow." He clicked the button, ending their conversation, and tossed the cell phone in the passenger's seat. He didn't have time for Belinda's pettiness. If she wanted to pretend like she didn't know what time it was, then he'd play the game to. That's what being a playa was all about anyway.

Sometimes, Desmond wished that he'd let Belinda divorce him so he wouldn't have this constant drama in his life. After all, he'd never loved her from day one; she was just the most logical choice at the time since he wanted to get his hands on all that money. His studious parents had set-up a twenty million dollar trust fund for Desmond to receive at the age of thirty, but the catch was that he had to be married by that time or receive a much smaller fraction of the matured value. As hard as he'd tried to talk them out of this ridiculous set up, neither one of them would budge for their overly spoiled son. It was the same type of arrangement that his grandfather had made for Desmond's father, and he wasn't about to break the tradition.

Belinda wasn't the most attractive woman he was boning, but she certainly was the most dependable. He believed the dark-skinned woman with the pretty almond-shaped eyes, right upbringing, and aggressive attitude would always have his back no matter what. And he was right about that—Belinda was a personal investment that had paid out handsomely over the years. She enjoyed their extravagant lifestyle and would protect it at all costs. He figured Belinda would sell her soul to the devil to keep what their material possessions. In that respect, they truly were soul mates.

Desmond also knew that Belinda had confronted several of his mistresses in the past and frightened them away from him. But he surmised that if they were weak enough to leave him behind her scare tactics, then they didn't deserve his good sexing anyhow. And it didn't matter because, usually, by the time Belinda figured out who the other woman was, he was tired of her and anxious to move on to the next unsuspecting victim. So she really just saved him the trouble of having to break it off with a weakling.

Returning his thoughts to Bridget's tempting body, Desmond slid a hand over his crotch area and licked his lips. "Now, I can do whatever I want to do. I've got the power in this relationship and B has always understood that I have to be number one. So why should I rock the boat by divorcing her, paying for a high-priced attorney, and upsetting my kids? She's got me covered; she knows how I am, but she's smart enough to keep quiet and enjoy the good life. It's not like she's going to do better. What's the net worth of a single black woman these days, maybe five dollars? And that's being generous."

3

(Belinda's Opponent)

"It was a good day! It was a good day!" The sound of Ice Cube's loud rapping could be heard throughout the complex as Bridget Hunter whipped into an open parking spot. It wasn't an upscale apartment building, just a moderately-priced facility with a unit that suited her limited needs. She wasn't home in between flights long enough to be worried about where she'd lay her head a couple of nights a week. This one-bedroom deluxe apartment with a balcony in the back provided a lovely atmosphere for entertaining her private guest.

Climbing out of her red Smart Car convertible, Bridget pointed the remote control and clicked the button to lock both doors. She was the proud new owner of the Mercedes-Benz engineered vehicle. Her boyfriend laughed at her last week for buying it, but when Bridget saw how surprisingly roomy it was with four safety airbags and forty-one estimated miles per gallon on the highway, she was sold on more than the price.

With a computer bag slung over one shoulder, she used both hands to roll two large suitcases down the sidewalk. Bridget's face blushed at the thought of her new boyfriend, Dr. Desmond Taylor. She'd never dated an African American doctor before now, but as fine as he was, she would have dated him if he was a forty-six-year-old street sweeper. Having a doctor on her arm was just an added perk. It didn't matter that he was sixteen years her senior. The only thing about him that slightly bothered Bridget was that she suspected him of being married. However, as long as no one was getting hurt, she reasoned that if his wife couldn't keep him satisfied, then it wasn't her problem. "He couldn't be too happy at home if he's always coming to visit when I'm in town. I mean I could see if he was just seeing me sometime. But we've been getting it on every night I'm home. And I'm sure tonight won't be any different. I mean he's already called me twice this morning wanting to meet me at my place. I guess seven days away gave him plenty of time to miss me. And I plan to show him what he's been missing after I slip into the silky lingerie I purchased in Italy," she thought.

"Hi, Bridget. I see you've made it home. How was your last flight?" Mrs. Tremble asked as she mounted the stairs, a bag of groceries in each hand. She was the retired nosey neighbor from across the hall.

"Oh, it was great! I loved everything about Milan. It's one of the most beautiful places I've ever been. But it was much colder there than it ever is in Dallas."

"Goodness, I know you're happy to be home then. I hate cold weather."

"Yes, I am. Thanks for keeping an eye on my place. Can I help you with those bags?" Bridget asked, standing outside the door to her apartment with a key in her slender hand.

"No, that's okay. It's nice of you to offer, though. You've got enough to handle yourself," the elderly lady replied, eyeing the leather luggage beside her neighbor's black pumps.

"Yeah, I guess you're right about that. I just thought maybe you had some more bags downstairs that you needed help with or something."

"Nope, this is it."

"Okay, I'll be by to visit you later on," she said. "I had a long exhausting flight. Right now, I just want to get out of this uniform and into a long hot bath so I can take a decent nap." Bridget wiggled the key in the door. She pushed it opened, releasing a sigh of relief.

"That would be nice. I saved you some of my special homemade lemon pound cake as a welcome home present," Mrs. Tremble said, stretching her neck to see what Bridget was doing.

"Well, it might be a while before I can make it over there," Bridget replied, holding the door open with one hand. She rolled one bag inside, propping the door open with her tiny butt.

"Take your time. I'm not going out again today," Mrs. Tremble responded, opening the door to her apartment. She admired Bridget's neat uniform, as well as her long term career as a flight attendant. "We'll talk later today. I've got to go watch my soaps anyway."

"Okay. If I don't make it today, I'll see you tomorrow. We can watch the soaps together and eat cake," Bridget stated, pulling the second suitcase inside.

"Yes, dear, that's a splendid idea. Just call me when you wake up and let me know what you decide. Is that handsome boyfriend of yours coming by today?" Mrs. Tremble asked, smiling slyly.

Bridget blushed. "Ah, yeah, he might be by later. So I probably won't see you until tomorrow."

"That's what I thought," Mrs. Tremble replied, closing her door.

Pushing her straight, honey-blonde hair to the side, Bridget stepped through her apartment door on the second floor of the north eastside complex. It had been a long flight from Toronto to Dallas, and she hadn't seen her place or her man in over a week. "But all of that is about to change," she thought, pulling both suitcases further inside the foyer. "When he sees what I have in store for him, he'll be begging me not to leave again."

Upon entering the apartment, Bridget thought she

smelled an unfamiliar fragrance lingering in the air. "Maybe Mrs. Tremble was in here spraying air freshener or something when she checked on my apartment. I've got to open a window and let it air out in here before Desmond comes over."

"Hello, Bridget. It's nice to finally meet the heifer who's been screwing my husband," Belinda stated calmly. Sitting in a chair with her arms folded across her chest, she was wearing a tailored, navy business suit with a white silk blouse, a pair of St. Germain high-heeled matching pumps, and carrying a Gucci purse. Belinda sounded like the mean witch from a Grinch fairytale.

Bridget turned around so fast at the sound of the unexpected voice she almost tripped over her suitcase. Gasping for air, she grabbed her small chest, and leaned against the wall. With bulging eyes, she managed to ask, "Who the hell are you, and what are you doing in my apartment? How did you get in here?" Surveying the small confines, her eyes darted towards the door and then back to the intruder.

"I let myself in with my key," Belinda said, standing up. In the blink of an eye, she was standing between Bridget and the closed door. She held up the key for Bridget to view. "Or should I say that I let myself in with my husband's key," she added, smirking.

"I don't know what you're talking about. I'm not dating a married man. Please get out of my house right now before I call the police." Bridget scanned the room, searching for the cordless phone set.

"Oh, I'm not leaving until we get a few things straightened out, and you can count on that. What makes you think that I'm going to let you call the police anyway?"

"Well, you can't stop me." Bridget rushed toward the telephone resting on top of the sofa table.

"I wouldn't touch that if I were you," Belinda snarled at

her as she snapped out a six-inch switchblade. "I should cut your throat for boning my damn husband. You white wenches are always running behind our men. You think I haven't had to take out poor white trash like you before?"

Stopping dead in her tracks, Bridget stared into Belinda's anger-filled, brown eyes. "I told you that I'm not dating a married man. I'm sorry if your husband is cheating on you, but it's not with me." Bridget tried her best to sound convincing. She'd only suspected that Desmond was married; she hadn't taken the time to confirm her suspicions. Now she was wishing that she had.

She guffawed. "You expect me to believe that! I've got proof that you're humping my husband. Does the name Dr. Desmond Taylor mean anything to you?"

"I—I don't..."

"Shut up! Would I be here holding a knife on you if I wasn't sure that you're the one?"

"I didn't know! Believe me—I didn't know that he was married! Now just put the knife down, and let's talk about this like two calm adults," she said, taking a small step backwards. "I promise you that I'll never go near him again. He didn't tell me that he had a wife. I mean it—I won't see him again!"

"You're just saying that to keep me from cutting your lily white throat. I'm nobody's fool, so just give me one reason why I shouldn't kill you right now," Belinda snarled, pointing the knife right beneath Bridget's pointed nose. Belinda could smell the fear emanating from the heifer's sweaty body, and thought, "That's what she gets for fooling around with a married man."

Bridget held up both palms as she carefully chose her next words. "One thing I know is that you don't want to go to prison for murder, not over a man. No man is worth losing your freedom for. Now I don't know you, but I can see that you're hurting, and you've probably been hurt many times before. I'm telling you that I'm not your enemy. I despise men that cheat on their wives. I was married for four years when I found out my husband had been unfaithful to me starting with our wedding night."

"Oh, so you want me to feel sorry for you. Desmond and I have been married for nineteen years and trifling whores like you keep trying to take him away from me, but I've got something for you today," she grunted, inching the knife closer.

"Stop!" Bridget screamed, waving her hands in the air like she was signally for a plane to land. "Think about what you're saying. I'll do whatever you want me to do, just lower the knife, and I'll listen to you. I'll call Desmond right now," she cried, glancing at the telephone. "I'll tell him that I know he's married and it's over, and I never want to see him again. I swear it!"

Belinda looked into Bridget's tearful eyes and felt that she'd done what she'd come to do — put the fear of God into this tramp. So, Belinda relaxed a little bit, and began lowering the knife to her side.

At that very second, the telephone rang on the sofa table. Checking the caller ID from where she was standing, Belinda noticed that it was her husband calling from his cellular phone. Knowing that Desmond was on his way to have an afternoon rendezvous with his mistress, Belinda involuntarily reacted. Her right eye started jumping and the right side of her face began twitching with uncontrollable anger.

Noticing the immediate change in Belinda's facial expression, Bridget decided to make a quick move towards her opponent. She grabbed Belinda's wrist and squeezed it with all her strength. "Drop the knife, witch," she sneered.

"Not on your life," Belinda retorted, looking like a crazed woman. She wasn't about to let this skinny, white girl get the best of her.

"I'm going to teach you a lesson like I taught the last one who fooled around with my man." Bringing her arm down with force, Belinda elbowed Bridget in the stomach forcefully enough to knock the wind out of her for a second.

When Belinda raised the knife, Bridget lunged for her wrist again. With their bodies pressed together, they began struggling for possession of the weapon as the telephone continued ringing in the background. Forcing her body against Belinda's, Bridget pushed until Belinda fell backwards and dropped the knife. Pouncing on top of Belinda, Bridget tried to hold the mad, black woman down, but she wasn't strong enough. Belinda slung Bridget off her like she was a five-pound bag of potatoes. Both women were grunting and gasping for breath as they continued rolling on the carpeted floor, pulling at each other's clothes and hair until one of them managed to clutch the knife.

Without hesitation, Belinda pushed the sharp blade into Bridget's stomach and felt a warm gush of blood splash against her midsection. Screaming in gut wrenching pain, Bridget's eyes rolled upwards, and she collapsed backwards. Her long, blonde hair covered most of the pain on her face as she grunted like a pig being slaughtered.

Belinda stumbled to her feet, feeling woozy, and looked down at her rumpled jacket with two buttons missing and a white blouse soaked in Bridget's blood. Through blurred vision, she tried to focus on the ghastly victim sprawled at her feet. Belinda gasped in horror at the knife protruding from Bridget's side. The blood was gushing from Bridget's tiny body onto the off-white carpet like a miniature water sprout.

"Please, help me," Bridget begged, trying to pull the knife out of her side. "Don't leave me like this."

Giving her a totally blank stare, Belinda shook her head a couple times trying to clear up the dizziness she felt. The pounding of Belinda's heart was making it difficult for her to process the severity of the situation. With blood dripping from her hand, Belinda stood still as the room continued to spin. She had to think fast.

Grabbing her Gucci bag, she stumbled towards the front door without looking back at the bloody woman on the floor. Belinda cracked the door, and stared right into the face of Mrs. Tremble.

"What's going on in here?" the elderly woman asked, shaking at the sight of Belinda's blood-stained clothes. "Who are you?"

"Get out of my way, old lady," Belinda demanded, barreling past Mrs. Tremble. Clutching the keys in her hand, all Belinda heard as she dashed down the hallway were bloodcurdling screams.

"She killed Bridget! Oh, my God, she killed Bridget!"

4

(Belinda's Getaway)

It was almost noontime. Coasting down the road, listening to a smooth jazz station, Desmond wondered why Bridget wasn't answering her house telephone. He figured she would be home by now and wondered if she was still at the airport.

He dialed her cellular phone number, but she didn't answer that line either. "That's okay. I'll be there in a minute, and I can let myself in if she hasn't made it home yet. Maybe there was a delay in her flight and she didn't have her cell phone turned on. Anyway, I can be in bed, butt–naked, waiting on her when she arrives," he thought.

Desmond grinned at the thought of climbing into Bridget's queen-sized bed and waiting on his vixen to walk through the bedroom door wearing her uniform jacket with a short skirt showing off her slim legs. He imagined the smile on her blushing face from seeing the outline of his body beneath the satin sheets.

Thinking about the sexual things they'd done in the past, Desmond wondered about future love sessions with his latest conquest. One of the benefits of dating a white woman was that they were usually more amenable to doing freaky things in the bedroom. That's why Desmond liked a variety of female lovers and coined himself the International Lover Man, but he was particularly fond of those of the Caucasian persuasion. And Ms. Bridget was definitely ready for anything and everything that he'd imagined doing with her toned body the last time they had mated over a week ago.

The Playboy bunny lookalike, who hadn't disappointed him in bed yet, really had his mind going.

"I rented a porno movie for us to watch tonight. I'm going to do to you whatever the woman in the movie does to her man," she cooed, popping in a DVD with an interracial couple doing the nasty. With a title like, *Going Deep*, Desmond knew he was in for a treat on that particularly warm evening.

"And I'll return the favor, you can count on that," he replied, leaning back on the blue sofa, preparing to watch the movie on the fifty-inch television screen in front of him. Eyeing Bridget's narrow behind in a floral printed thong with a matching lace brassiere, Desmond licked his lips as thoughts of passion invaded his consciousness.

As soon as the hot and heavy action heated up on screen, so did the comparable activity in the living room. With his eyes fixated on the television set, Desmond watched two brothers sex a blonde-haired beauty on a yacht surrounded by cool blue water. He imagined himself being one of the well-endowed men floating to ecstasy with the buxom female. With that in mind, he and Bridget changed from one erotic position to the next, and the way they went at it for twenty minutes straight, it definitely didn't take them long to finish the first round of sex.

Making their way to the bedroom, they were both ready for the second round of loving. The movie was still playing on the big screen, only they didn't need the excitement that it provided anymore. Since they were both fully aroused, they fell across the bed together, clutching each other. This was the type of ecstasy that every man dreamed about, a woman willing to put her warm mouth in all the right places.

Desmond didn't have to worry about Bridget hounding him to spend time with her because most of the time she was busy traveling. She was only in town about two or three days out of the week. That was plenty enough time for Desmond to get his grind on with her, and then go home to rest up for a few days while he played daddy and hubby with his family. In other words, he had the best of both worlds and was proud of it. With Bridget's undemanding lifestyle, he might be able to carry on like this until he decided to retire his special married player's card.

Returning his mind to present day, Desmond concluded that this was just the type of extended lunch break he needed today. "As soon as I finish my good deed, I can return to work and let Bridget catch up on her rest the remainder of the day. Then, I'll be back this evening to drive her down to San Antonio so we can do it all night long," he surmised.

Turning into the six-story, red-brick apartment complex, Desmond thought he glanced the back end of a silver Mercedes that looked just like Belinda's car speeding away. Thinking that it couldn't possibly be Belinda, he turned his thoughts back to Bridget and the rendezvous he had planned for them. Across the seat from him were a dozen long-stemmed, yellow roses, the new Maxwell CD, enough seafood pasta for four people, and a cold bottle of wine.

Parking beside Bridget's Smart Car, Desmond shook his head at the mini version of a vehicle. Still, he smiled to himself, thinking that she'd made it home safely. Climbing the stairs two at a time with his goodies in tow, he stopped cold in the doorway of Bridget's apartment on the second floor. The sight of her bloody body on the floor clinging to the arms of Mrs. Tremble caused Desmond's blood pressure to escalate.

"I called nine-one-one. The ambulance is on the way!" Mrs. Tremble shouted.

"What happened?" Desmond asked, dropping everything on the floor as he dropped to his knees beside his lover.

"I don't know. I heard screaming. When I came over to check on Bridget, I saw a black woman running out of here looking like a crack head."

They could hear the siren from the ambulance approaching the unit. Desmond cradled Bridget's head in his arms and asked, "Who did this to you?"

Staring up at him in pain, with her last ounce of courage Bridget whispered, "Your wife."

Desmond gasped. Remembering the Mercedes he'd just seen speeding away, Desmond cursed Belinda for ruining his day. He knew his wife was dangerous, but she'd never gone this far to eliminate a mistress.

"Don't worry, Bridget, you're going to be fine. And I promise you that she's going to pay for this."

The second the ambulance driver sped off with Bridget in the back, Desmond sped off in the opposite direction. He cursed his wife all the way home.

5

(Belinda's Arrest)

Belinda was speeding and trembling so much that she almost rear-ended two automobiles on the way home. Finally, she jerked the car into her driveway at their prestigious Northwood Heights address, slammed the stick into park, and bolted from the silver Mercedes. Her hair and mind were a total mess as she fumbled with the keys to the front door. Balancing on wobbly legs, she finally managed to loosen the bottom lock and the deadbolt. After fumbling with the alarm system and punching in several incorrect numbers, she remembered the code within the last five seconds of the alarm being activated.

Rushing down the long hallway, she stripped out of her clothes as soon as she entered the master bedroom. Belinda threw every designer piece she had on into the huge fireplace, including her expensive underwear. She made a beeline for the shower, turning on the hot water at full blast. Belinda wanted to get the blood off her body right then since most of it had dried on her skin in the July afternoon heat. She hated the feeling of the icky blood and the smell was nauseating. Belinda wanted to burn the clothes, but decided to wait until after she was cleaned up.

As the hot water poured down her face and the shower began to steam up, the reality of what had transpired began to consume Belinda. She cried out, "Oh, God, what have I done? Jesus, please don't let her be dead. Just please don't let her be dead. I know that old lady had to call an ambulance. Why is this happening to me? I just wanted to scare her so she would stop running around with my husband. Is that too much to ask? Why did she have to grab me like that? I wasn't going to hurt her. Please, please, let the ambulance make it there before she dies…"

At least thirty minutes had passed; Belinda was still in the shower sitting on the floor with her knees to her chest. With the water pooling around her naked body, she was all cried out. Suddenly, she heard the bedroom door slam with such force it made Belinda jump as the walls shook around her. The sound of Desmond screaming her name could be heard throughout the entire three-story house, causing the walls to vibrate.

"Belinda! Where the hell are you! Get out here now!"

Turning off the water, Belinda slowly stepped out of the shower and wrapped a blue towel around her shaky frame. Entering the master bedroom with a scared look on her face, she saw Desmond sitting on the side of the bed facing her. His elbows rested on his thighs while he cried into his hands.

"What have you done? What have you done? Have you completely lost your mind?" he asked, gazing up at his wife through colossal tears.

Frozen at the sight of her husband's composure, Belinda pretended not to process what he was implying. "I don't know what you're talking about, Dez, I've been in the shower for the last hour. What's going on?" she asked, walking away from him. Reaching for her navy silk bathrobe at the foot of the bed, she tied the wrap around her waist, and continued to avoid Desmond's penetrating stare.

That's when Desmond stood up and bolted over to the fireplace. Pulling out her blood-stained clothes one piece at a time with trembling hands, he shot daggers at Belinda with his eyes. "This right here is what I'm talking about. How could you hurt Bridget like that?" he asked, holding her silk blouse in one hand.

"I—I don't know anyone by that name," she stumbled. "I've been home all day."

"Like hell you have! Don't lie to me, Belinda! I saw your damn car leaving the scene of the crime! I know you found out about Bridget and me! Now why did you try to kill her?"

Belinda couldn't deny the guilt any longer; she had to release her feelings. "Because I love you, Desmond! I've always loved you, and I can't share you with anyone! I just went over there to scare her skinny ass, and she attacked me! Things just got out of hand!" Robbed of all of her remaining energy, Belinda collapsed on the bed, holding her side as if she'd been stabbed like Bridget.

"How did that happen? Tell me exactly what happened!" he demanded. Desmond's eyes and face were burgundy red. Every vein in his face popped with each word he shouted.

Belinda tried to sit up in bed but settled for leaning her head on a raised arm. Between gasps, she gave Desmond a blow-by-blow description of what occurred between her and Bridget less than an hour ago. Looking up at him through tear stained eyes, she asked, "Is she still alive?"

"Yes, Bridget is still living. She's at the Dallas Memorial Hospital in surgery right now. You better pray that she makes it," he stated coldly, walking towards the bedroom door.   Summoning the last strength she had in her body, Belinda flung herself at Desmond's feet and begged, "Oh, Dez, I'm sorry. Please, don't turn me in to the police." Squeezing his pants leg, she buried her face in the smooth fabric. "I'm sorry. I didn't mean to hurt anybody." Desmond shook his leg like he was shaking off a rat, and headed towards the door. He swung it open, waving a hand in the air.

"Officers, you all can come in now." Desmond eyed the short police lieutenant rushing into the bedroom. He stepped into the hallway surrounded by more police officers and proceeded towards the front door. Belinda was on her own from now on. He wouldn't lift a finger to help her regardless of how much she begged him.

Scrambling on the floor, Belinda sobbed even harder after she realized that the police had been right outside her bedroom door the entire time she and Desmond had been talking. Lieutenant Warren, a dark man with a neatly trimmed moustache, gave her a disgusted look as he spoke.

"Mrs. Belinda Taylor, you're under arrest for the attempted murder of Bridget Hunter. You have the right to remain silent..."

"No!" Belinda screamed. "Dez, please, come back. Help me! Don't leave me this way!"

6

(Belinda's Calls)

"Desmond, I know you're getting my telephone calls. I need you to come get me out of jail," Belinda bellowed into the telephone receiver. This was her fifth attempt at contacting her wayward husband. Undoubtedly, he was at the hospital right now holding the hand of his wounded girlfriend.

Belinda visualized his long body bent over Bridget's bed as he prayed for her recovery. She wanted Desmond there comforting her after all she'd been through for him. Belinda needed him more than she ever had before.

Slamming the telephone back on the receiver, Belinda cursed herself for ever going to see Bridget Hunter this morning. Now, she didn't know if the young woman was going to live or die. She didn't know if she would be charged with murder, attempted murder, manslaughter, or what. All Belinda knew for sure was that her husband of nineteen years had abandoned her in jail to be with his latest mistress.

Picking up the telephone again, Belinda reluctantly dialed her parents' eastside estate. She was fortunate that her father, George Hines, had retired from his commercial landscaping business and moved her mother to Dallas from Detroit, Michigan, two years ago. Being a wise investor, he was financially able to move to the warmer climate for health reasons and his wife needed to be near their only daughter and grandchildren for mental reasons.

Mr. Hines was delighted to play golf in comfort almost every month of the year at the prestigious golf course right in their backyard. The years of living in the Michigan cold had almost crippled him with a severe case of arthritis. When his physician suggested retirement and a southward move, his wife started making arrangements the next day. Belinda hadn't given much consideration to their move in the past, but now she realized what a blessing it turned out to be.

Although Belinda hadn't been a doting daughter or visited her parents regularly, the teenagers, Justine and Jesse, saw their grandparents almost every day. They were the highlights in their grandmother's life.

It was definitely time to let her parents know what was going on in her failed life. Belinda questioned herself, "How did I go from being a Harvard Business School graduate to being arrested for attempted murder?"

As soon as the recording that announced she was calling from the facility stopped, Belinda began. "Hi, Mom. You can see I'm calling from the county jailhouse. I've been arrested, and I need you and daddy to come bail me out."

"Oh, no, baby! What happened?" Julia asked. She'd been sipping on a Coke and almost dropped the glass at the sound of Belinda's panic-stricken voice. She'd never imagined that her daughter would call them with this type of news. Obviously, there had to be some type of mistake. Mrs. Hines was aware of her daughter's volatile temper, but Belinda had never called from jail before.

"Mom, it's really a long story, and I just want to get out of this nasty place. Would you please tell Daddy to come get me out of this disgusting hellhole right now?"

"Your father is at the golf course, baby. I'm going to call him on his cell phone and let him know where you are and what you need. I'm sure he'll be there as quickly as he can. Don't worry, he'll get you out." Mrs. Hines reached for a pen and paper so she could write down the precinct details.

"Thanks, Mom. I'll explain everything once I'm released from here. Just tell Dad to hurry," she added, sobbing into the telephone receiver. "I can't spend the night here, and Desmond isn't coming to get me out. He's only worried about his little whore."

"Belinda, try to calm down. We'll be there real soon. Do you need me to bring you anything?"

"No, I just need my Daddy," Belinda sobbed.

"All right, all right. I'm hanging up this second." Julia pressed the end button down for a second, and then dialed her husband's cellular phone number.

Before nightfall, Belinda walked out of the Dallas Police Headquarters a temporarily free woman with her parents and newly hired attorney, Francine Smith. Fortunately, her case had been arraigned after speaking with her attorney and entering a "not guilty" plea. Belinda was scheduled to report back to court for a jury trial on Wednesday, October thirteenth, at nine-thirty a.m.

The local television news reporters were there waiting in full force at the entrance of the huge building. Belinda was blinded by the flashing lights as picture after picture was snapped. Even the camcorders from the major television stations were there to document her release from jail. Steadily holding both parents by the hand, she followed the attorney's lead outside into the evening heat. Every reporter in the Dallas metro area seemed to be waving a microphone in Belinda's crumpled face asking painful questions.

"Mrs. Taylor, were you trying to kill Bridget Hunter?" one reporter asked.

"Mrs. Taylor, did you plead guilty to attempted murder?" another reporter asked.

"Where's your husband, Mrs. Taylor?" a female reporter asked.

"Please, please, let us by. My client has no comment to make at this time," Attorney Smith stated, pushing through the crowd. She was a tall, commanding woman known for handling high profile cases with a strong media presence. However, the questions kept being swirled directly at her client. Belinda wanted to respond to each one of them, but decided to heed her attorney's advice. With that in mind, she pressed her lips firmly together, and walked straight to the waiting car.

George and Julia Hines walked with their heads bowed as they promptly escorted their daughter away from the loud crowd. Belinda felt like a hobo crossing the street between the two of them wearing a pair of wrinkled pants and a knit shirt she'd hurriedly pulled on at the time of her arrest. Her mouth felt pasty, she could smell the dragon fire from her own breath, and the whole city was there to witness her frightening decent into darkness.

Opening the back door on the driver's side, Mr. Hines helped Belinda inside his black Mercedes Benz Five-hundred. As they were pulling away, Mrs. Hines turned to her daughter and asked, "Are you hungry, sweetheart Would you like for your father to stop and get you something to eat?"

"No, Mom, I'm not hungry. I couldn't eat anything if I tried. Have you all heard anything from Desmond?" Belinda's eyes wavered between her two parents in the front seat. Holding her stomach, she nervously awaited their answer.

"Why, no, we haven't been able to reach him at all. He hasn't returned any of our telephone calls," Julia replied. "Oh, sweetheart, you look like you've been crying for hours on end. I'm so sorry you had to spend all day in that dreadful place."

"Don't worry about it, Mom. I just want to get home and see about my children. Desmond probably hasn't left the side of his precious mistress since she was rushed to the hospital this morning." Lowering her head, Belinda said,

"You know, I didn't mean to hurt her, Mom."

"I know you didn't, baby. I know you're not capable of hurting anyone. This is all a misunderstanding, and your attorney is going to get you out of this mess so don't you worry about a thing. You have the best female criminal lawyer in Dallas. It takes a woman to defend a woman."

"Oh, God, I just wish that this whole episode could absolutely disappear," Belinda mumbled, dropping her face into her hands. "If only she hadn't tried to take the knife away from me, none of this would be happening. I just pulled out the knife to scare her, and then she had to go reaching for it like a stupid b..."

"Belinda," her mother said, coughing into her hand. "Let's not talk about this right now, darling. I don't want you getting upset again. You're almost home now, so try to concentrate on how happy the children will be to see you again." Julia glanced at her husband's stern face, which was almost as dark as the vehicle he drove, sitting up straight as he gripped the steering wheel tightly with both hands. He hadn't spoken a word since they'd left the jailhouse. Undoubtedly, he was very disappointed with his daughter right about now and chose not to risk saying the wrong hurtful thing to her.

Belinda spent the remainder of the ride home with her head against the padded headrest listening to gospel music coming through the crisp-sounding speaker system. She didn't care much for this type of music, and it was certainly never played in her home, but even she recognized the melodic voice of the popular recording artist, Yolanda Adams, singing one of her latest singles. The relaxing harmony caused Belinda's mind to wander to a time when she and Desmond were a happily married couple; to a time when she believed that her husband loved her as deeply as she loved him. But that had to be so long ago there was no way to pinpoint when their lives really began to change. She couldn't even remember the name of the woman with whom Desmond had the first affair that she'd become aware of.

However, Belinda still remembered the horror on the woman's face when she confronted her about sleeping with a married man. She'd left the woman's one-bedroom apartment with a smile on her face, happy to have her marriage still intact, only to find out less than a year later that her marriage would never be a complete circle of love again. That was truly the beginning of her downward spiral into the pits of hell.

Staring at her parents in the front seat, Belinda wondered how her mother had survived all her father's philandering ways without ever raising some type of a ruckus. In all the years she'd known her parents, she'd never known them to have one argument related to his infidelity. The only memory Belinda had of her mother complaining about her father's betrayals was the summer she turned ten and her auntie Karen came to visit them from Chicago. Belinda had gotten up to use the restroom in the middle of the night and on the way back to her room, she heard her mother crying in the kitchen. Tiptoeing towards the doorway, Belinda peeped in and saw Julia sitting at the round table blowing her nose into a tissue while Aunt Karen stood over her holding a steaming teapot.

"I'm telling you right now, you need to let this woman know what time it is so she'll leave your husband alone," Aunt Karen said, pouring hot water into a cup. "Some of these hussies need a hole stomped in their neck so they know who not to mess with."

Julia dried her red eyes and sniffed, "I can't beat every woman who speaks to George. It's up to him to let them know his marital status."

Aunt Karen returned the teapot to the stove, sat down, and placed an arm around her sister. "Now that's where you're wrong, child. You know men are weak, and we have to have their backs. If you give this woman a good beat down, I promise you, she'll leave your man alone."

Shaking her head, Julia replied, "Karen, that's nonsense."

"You can call it whatever you want to," Karen responded with attitude. "All I know is after I beat down a couple of them horny wenches, the word got around that my man was off limits, and we haven't had that problem in years."

"I just don't see that as a reasonable way to handle things in a marriage." Julia placed her face into hands.

"Well, you're the one sitting here crying at two o'clock in the morning because your husband ain't home. So you can take my advice or keep crying yourself to sleep every damn night." Aunt Karen chuckled, turning towards the doorway. Her angry eyes landed on Belinda's young face and narrowed as if to say, "Your mama is crazy, but you better heed my words, little girl."

Belinda never forgot the harrowing look in her aunt's eyes or the meaning behind it, which became her philosophy of marriage. "I guess I should have been Aunt Karen's child because her strategy for maintaining a marriage made more sense to me. Momma buried her head in the sand and was content to keep quiet as long as the bills were paid, and she never had to work a day in her life. But Aunt Karen taught me a different way to handle things that night. I never want to be sitting at the kitchen table crying over my man because he was spending the night with another woman. Momma just waited for Daddy to get too old to fool around on her. Well, I couldn't wait that damn long for Desmond to wake up and be true to me. I had to follow Aunt Karen's advice to save my relationship," she thought.

Belinda's thoughts were jarred as she felt the car slowing down. It was barely at a complete stop before Belinda swung the back door open. Rushing up the steps of her lavish estate, Belinda's heart was beating faster than a speeding bullet as she fumbled to find the correct key. After several minutes of trying various keys, she gave up in desperation.

"There must be something wrong with my key. It's not opening the door," she moaned, pressing the doorbell several times.

Waiting for the housekeeper to answer her calls, Belinda shifted from one foot to the next. She ran her fingers through her tangled hair as she frowned at her disheveled reflection in the painted stain glass surrounding the doorframe.

Belinda prayed that none of the neighbors were watching them arrive. She knew how awful she looked and couldn't wait to get inside her house.

Ms. Rodriquez, the housekeeper, cracked the door open enough for Belinda to peek inside over the security chain.

"Yes, ma'am," the housekeeper said, greeting her solemnly.

"Hi, Ms. Rodriquez. For some reason I couldn't find the right key to the front door. Can you let me in, please?"

"Ma'am, I'm sorry, but I have strict instructions not to let you enter the house," Ms. Rodriquez said, running a quivering hand down her neatly pressed uniform. She knew first-hand how outrageous Mrs. Taylor could behave when agitated. Belinda had verbally unloaded her frustrations on the mild mannered housekeeper at least a dozen times in the last year. "Dr. Taylor said to pack up all of your things and have them delivered wherever you'd like, but I'm not to let you inside under any circumstances."

"What the hell are you talking about? Woman, I live here! You better open this damn door before I stomp it in!" Belinda had that crazed look again. Raising her foot, she gave the door a swift kick.

As she continued shouting obscenities at the maid, Ms. Rodriquez slammed the door shut; immediately secured the other two locks and shouted, "I'm going to call Dr. Taylor if you don't leave here."

Julia hopped out of the car and hurried up the steps with

her husband trailing behind. Pulling Belinda by the arm, Mrs. Hines pleaded, "Come on, baby, you can come home with us until we get this worked out."

Belinda yanked her hand back and started banging on the solid wood door with both fists. "Oh, hell, no! That Spanish wench better let me in my damn house right now! She done forgot who she's working for!"

"That's enough," George Hines stated, grabbing Belinda's right hand in midair. "You're only embarrassing yourself by standing out here like this knocking on the door like a mad woman. Get in the car now! We'll take you home with us. I'll track down Desmond and get to the bottom of this myself." Mr. Hines gave Belinda that look he'd often given her as a child when he meant serious business. Knowing she'd better tone it down, Belinda resorted to crying, a trick which normally worked on her father when she was a little girl. It was her special way of manipulating her parents to get her way for as long as Belinda could remember. If flying off the handle and throwing a temper tantrum didn't get the desired results, she'd quickly resort to tears.

"I just want to get in my house," Belinda cried. "This is not right, Daddy. She's worked for me for over ten years; now she's treating me like a stranger. It's not right."

"I know, I know, but you've got to let me handle this," Mr. Hines replied, pulling Belinda into his arms. "This'll be over soon."

Reluctantly, Belinda followed her parents back down the long driveway. She turned to get one last glance at her gorgeous, three-story, red-brick mansion before entering the luxury vehicle. Narrowing her eyes in the sunlight, Belinda saw Ms. Rodriquez peeping through the front curtains holding the cordless telephone to her right ear.

Belinda stared straight into her horror-filled eyes and flipped the bird at the lady she used to like. "Now tell

Desmond about that while you're telling him all of my business on the phone, you wicked witch of the south. You better be gone by the time I get back in my damn house. And that's a fact!"

7

(Belinda's Attorney)

Sitting in the attorney's office on the eighth floor of a high-rise, downtown office building, Belinda could see for miles on the clearest day they'd had all week. Surveying her surroundings, Belinda felt like she was sitting in an upscale museum instead of a lawyer's office. She was impressed with the décor of the impeccably designed interior. Obviously, Attorney Francine Smith had good taste, or expensive taste to be more accurate. From the solid wood desk, to the extra wide credenza, to the antique pieces strategically placed throughout the office, to the custom-built bookcases done in mahogany, Belinda could tell that Attorney Smith was well paid for her legal expertise. She'd come highly recommended based on a thirteen-year career with an outstanding record as a criminal lawyer. Ms. Smith was one of the best in her field, and she was lucky to have a team of excellent attorneys on her side. Still, Belinda hope that she was good enough to get her out of this predicament. You couldn't stand not being able to see her kids everyday or the way this situation was affecting her retired parents.

Just the honest realization of what her parents were going through shattered Belinda's heart. She could see how much her parents had aged since she'd been living with them. Neither one moved as quickly as she remembered before all this happened. When her father wasn't hobbling around the golf course, he was shuffling around the house, lecturing Belinda about her life, and all the mistakes she'd made in her marriage, like his was perfect.

One day, Belinda became really worried about her father. She noticed him leaning over the kitchen sink experiencing shortness of the breath, but he wouldn't admit it when Belinda tried to help. He blew her off by saying, "I'm fine. You're worrying for nothing. I just need to get some fresh air." And with that being said, he left the room, and headed outside, walking towards the golf course.

Her mother's face had so many worry lines, Belinda wouldn't be able to recognize it if it wasn't for those soft, caring eyes. Several times, Julia Hines had scared Belinda because she'd have a faraway look on her face like she didn't know where she was or who Belinda was. Then, she'd snap out of it and appear to be fine. But it made Belinda wonder if her mother was experiencing the early signs of Alzheimer's because she could never remember where she left her car keys or placed the cordless telephone. She didn't really get out much except for going to church for Friday night prayer meeting and Sunday morning service.

"Other than that, all Momma does is drink Coke, watch television, read Ebony once a month, and Jet magazine once a week. I bet she has at least a million of those magazines between the house and garage. I'll never understand why she's keeping all those back issues. I know they think I'm heartless, but I feel for them. I really do. I wish Desmond would come to his senses and let me come home," Belinda thought.

"Are you all right?" Mrs. Hines asked, tapping her daughter's leg.

"Yes, Momma, I'm fine," Belinda responded, touching her mother's hand.

Belinda looked over at her father, but he was staring out the window, looking down on downtown Dallas. She guessed that he never got around to having that man-to-man talk with Desmond after all.

Every single thing Belinda thought she owned was in

Desmond's name. Therefore, she'd been denied access to all of her bank accounts and credit cards. If it wasn't for her parents' wealth, she'd be in dire straits right now. She hadn't been allowed to enter her home or see her children in almost three months since this fiasco began. Every time she called their house, the answering machine clicked on and no one ever returned her telephone calls. The children weren't even allowed to visit their grandparents since Belinda was living there.

She wasn't sure whom she hated the most, Desmond or that slut, Bridget Hunter, for ruining her life and marriage. But Belinda was so grateful that the wench hadn't died or else she'd be facing charges for first-degree murder with no chance of parole instead of a much lesser offense.

Checking her make up in the mirror of her MAC pressed powder compact, Belinda admired her face and perfectly relaxed straight hair just grazing the shoulders of her gray-striped, suit jacket. Crossing her legs, Belinda snapped the compact shut and placed it back inside her matching gray leather purse. Waiting patiently for the attorney to return, Belinda began to worry about what could be taking her so long. Before her thoughts could go any deeper, Belinda heard the office door opening.

"Sorry for keeping you all waiting so long." Ms. Smith entered the room tugging on her navy suit jacket with her hair pulled back into a bun. The pale look on her sunken face told Belinda that her case wasn't looking good. No, it wasn't looking good at all.

"I was on the telephone with one of my associates regarding your case. It seems that you've been offered a deal by the district attorney's office."

"What type of deal are you talking about?" Belinda asked, trembling. This was exactly what she'd been praying for, some good news.

"Well, if you plead guilty to the charges of assault and

battery with a dangerous weapon, you could get a five to ten year conviction and possibly be out of prison in six to twelve months with good behavior. How does that sound?"

"Ha!" Belinda eyed the attorney like she'd been asked to jump into the blazing fires of hell. "It sounds like a joke. What is my other choice? I don't plan on going to prison at all. That's absolutely not debatable," Belinda stated firmly. That was the last thing on her mind. There wasn't any way that she'd survive any time incarcerated. That was for the lowlifes. She was paying top dollar to keep out of the prison system.

Belinda crossed and uncrossed her legs several times before finally sitting still. Staring into Francine's dark eyes, she anxiously awaited the attorney's response.

"Your only other option is to plead not guilty and take your chances with a trial by a jury of your peers. If you're convicted, you're looking at spending five to ten full years in jail. Remember, this is Texas. You'll have to do every day of your time," Francine stated. After a brief pause she continued, "It's your decision to make, but I recommend that you take the plea bargain, do the six to twelve months, and serve the rest of the time on probation. Based on my experience, jury trials are very risky, especially in cases like this. They have a very strong case against you, Mrs. Taylor. Even your own husband is willing to testify against you."

"But—but they can't make Desmond testify, can they?" Belinda asked, looking worried.

"No, they can't, but like I said, he's willing to do it, and that means they have the right to call him to the stand."

Belinda called Desmond a vile name for being willing to testify against her after all she'd done to protect their marriage.

Aggressively shaking her head, Belinda sighed, "I don't think I can do a year in prison let alone five years. You have to get me out of this. Isn't there some way that you can get the charges reduced so that I don't have to go to prison?" she begged.

"Listen, Mrs. Taylor." Attorney Smith began, leaning in close to her client. "The charges have already been reduced lower than I would have ever gambled that they would be. You entered Ms. Hunter's apartment carrying a concealed weapon. You ended up stabbing her and almost killing her during a physical altercation. It's going to be your word against hers which will make it very hard to prove. You were an angry wife going to confront her husband's lover with a concealed weapon in your purse; that's not going to go over well with a jury on any level. And I'm sure the prosecutor will try to stack the jury with women who may not sympathize with you. Now, I suggest you take the twenty-four hours that they're giving you to think about this and seriously weigh your options."

"Is there a guarantee that I will be released in less than a year if I plead guilty?" Belinda asked, praying silently.

"No, that's not guaranteed. We can't guarantee anything when it comes to a criminal charge like this. We're taking a chance either way we go. But more than likely, if you stay out of trouble, we can file a petition for you to be released on probation after six months. Now, you probably won't get approved for release on the first try so it's important that you remain a model prisoner, and we can possibly have you out in twelve months."

Belinda couldn't stop the tears from cascading down her jittery cheeks. She hadn't even considered the possibility of going to prison for stabbing the woman that tried to wreck her marriage. After all, she was only defending herself after the mistress attacked her. How could she be going to jail for that? How could this be happening to someone of her stature and wealth? What would her high society friends think of her having a criminal record? How would she ever face her children again? The questions went on and on in

Belinda's mind until she felt like her brain was going to explode right there in the attorney's upscale office. Belinda asked herself, "Why is this happening to me? Why is this happening to me? Why can't we just make this go away?"

Two days later, Julia Hines pulled a white handkerchief from her black patent leather purse and balled it in her hand. Judge Jamerson, a heavyset man with graying edges, had just returned to his seat behind the bench and was about to announce Belinda's sentence. She'd known from the very first day Belinda called from that jail exactly how things would play out. "Lord, please, have mercy on my child. Forgive her for everything she's done. Her father and I should never have let her get away with those temper tantrums whenever we said no to her. Belinda grew up thinking that anytime she snapped on someone, she'd get her way. Father, it's our fault for letting her think that she didn't have to conform to the rules."

Wiping the tears flowing down her rosy cheeks, Mrs. Hines squeezed her husband's knuckles with all of her might. Being the strong man that he was, George Hines kept his tired eyes on the judge, silently praying, too, that the court would have mercy on his only child. He'd been on his knees most of the night sending up the timber to God's ears. Now it took every ounce of strength in his body to remain still and listen.

"Mrs. Taylor, you are hereby sentenced to five years in the Texas State Prison System based on the charge of assault and battery with a dangerous weapon. Since you have pleaded guilty to the charge, your case will be up for review in six months. At that time, your case will be reviewed for parole based on good behavior. So I advise you to be a model prisoner until such time."

Judge Jamerson stared down his thin nose at Belinda as he struck the gavel. Shuffling through the papers on the bench, he was ready to call the next case. He didn't feel any sympathy for a woman who had almost killed another woman over a cheating spouse.

Belinda didn't realize her entire body was shaking uncontrollably until Attorney Smith placed her arms around her shoulders. Slinking down into the hard chair, Belinda could barely hear the attorney speaking over the thumping of her heart.

"It's going to be okay, I promise you. We'll have you out of there on time. You won't have to spend more than a year in prison, at the very most. Just do this and move on."

Belinda wanted to curse out her attorney. Looking over her shoulder at Mrs. Hines, she could hardly see for the tears clouding her sore eyes. Julia had her head down crying into a handkerchief, but her father's eyes stayed dead on her. Then, she looked across the courtroom with disgust at Desmond, sitting up straight in a brown Armani suit like he had a reason to be proud. The sorry bastard even had the nerve to have his whore by his side, holding onto his upper right arm. Belinda wished that she could wipe that smug look from the white wench's face as she was lead out of the courtroom between two armed guards. Nothing could have ever prepared her for this day, absolutely nothing. But as bad as life seemed that day, the worst was yet to come.

8

(Belinda's Prison)

The sound of the steel metal door clanking closed at Datesville Women's Prison reverberated throughout Belinda's vibrating body. Although she was only one-hundred and fifty miles from Dallas, each time the door slammed shut, Belinda felt as if she'd just entered the gates of eternal hell more than a trillion miles away. Knowing that she would never get used to that penetrating noise, Belinda tried to send it to the furthest recesses of her mind.

Slumped against the cold prison wall, Belinda had both arms folded over her queasy stomach. For someone accustomed to eating five-course, gourmet meals on a daily basis, prison food was like scraping the bottom of a garbage can outside a Chinese restaurant. Most of the time, the food looked so sloppy, Belinda couldn't tell what it was. Dog food probably would have been a better choice given the options they had on the menu.

"Hey, are you all right?" Yvette Riley, her cellmate, inquired in a husky voice.

"Sure, I'm fine. I'm just a little sick from dinner, if you can call it that."

Yvette guffawed. "You're funny. But, hey, you'll get used to it," she stated, stroking her short, blonde hair that was desperately in need of a touch-up. Stretching her petite body, Yvette reclined against the lumpy mattress, remembering a picture of her three kids she'd just received from home. In the four months that they'd shared a cell, neither woman had said very much to the other.

Making her way to the adjacent single bed, Belinda eased down on the worn green blanket. Trying to recall what the mystery meat of the day was, she felt it rising up her throat, burning like fire, compelling her to rush to the dingy toilet bowl in the corner of the room. After regurgitating every morsel she'd swallowed a few hours ago, Belinda reached for the small sink, pulled her thin body up, and rinsed the stench from her mouth.

Then, she slowly undressed and changed into her only sleeping gown. Folding up her dirty, white uniform, she placed it into the cotton laundry bag at the foot of her bed. It was impossible to stay clean working the late shift in the galley kitchen, which was a job she detested to the utmost.

"You know, I'm married to a doctor. Now look at me—I can't even get a decent meal." Belinda stretched out on her narrow cot and buried her tear-stained face in the flat pillow she'd been issued.

"It's hard in here, but you have to stay busy by reading and exercising. Most of the guards respect us as long as we respect them, except for Officer Kelly. She's been reported several times for mistreating people, denying our phone call privileges, and being verbally abusive, but they haven't suspended her yet."

"Yeah, I hate it when she's on duty, and I know she doesn't like me. I don't know what her problem is." Belinda recalled the face of the guard with the dirty, blonde hair and a thick southern accent.

"Her problem is that she doesn't like black women. And she especially doesn't like you because she thinks you're trying to be uppity."

"I think the truth is that she doesn't like dark-skinned women like me, but she'll tolerate a light-skinned woman like you," Belinda said, pointing to herself and then to Yvette. "Well, I told her off yesterday. I'm tired of her thinking she can talk to me any kind of way and get away with it. After she cursed at me, I told her if I ever get out of this prison cell, I'll mop the floor with her fat ass. She grunted at me like a pig and smiled with her crooked teeth."

"You can't let her get to you like that. I just try to ignore her most of the time, but if I didn't pray every day, I'd go insane." Yvette clasped her hands together and shook them.

"You sound like my mother. She's always talking about the power of prayer. I don't see the point. What good is prayer going to do me sitting in a damn prison cell?" Belinda asked, lifting up on one elbow.

"I pray for my children. I need them to stay strong and remember that I love them. I'm doing the time, it's not gonna do me," Yvette said, pointing to her chest, sounding proud of her new declaration. "Yes, I was wrong for writing all those bad checks, but I was only trying to provide for my babies. What else was I supposed to do with two small children and a baby that needed milk?"

"You could have gone to social services and applied for welfare or some type of assistance. Isn't that what they're there for?" Belinda asked, snarling at the young lady.

She bristled. "You talk like a real rich woman. I guess when you have money, you don't have to worry about where your next meal is coming from. Don't you think I applied for everything that there was, but they kept telling me that my minimum wage job at Burger King disqualified me from receiving any benefits. Not to mention that I wasn't getting child support from any of my babies' daddies. Anyway, that's how it is for us po' folks."

"I didn't mean to insult you. I was just wondering if you tried to get any help," Belinda stated, rubbing her stomach, hoping that she wouldn't die from food poisoning in a prison cell.

"Yeah, I tried everything I knew how to do except for selling drugs. And I wasn't about to go there. But thank God I only have to do about six more months, and I can kiss this cell good-bye. My attorney says the next time I meet with the Parole Board, I should be approved for release since I've been an ideal prisoner." Yvette smiled to herself at the thought of her impending freedom.

"How do you manage to stay sane in this place? It's driving me crazy being cooped up in here," Belinda whined, rolling over on her back, clutching the blanket to her chest. Ever since her first night in the drafty cell, Belinda had high hopes that she'd be released before her designated time.

"Prayer is the only thing that brings me any relief. You need to go to church with me every Wednesday evening. At least, it'll get you out of this hole for an hour or so. The pastors are really nice. This one lady minister is off the chain. Her name is Reverend Dana and she tells it like it is. They have several different ones who take turns coming each week, but it should be her turn to come this Wednesday. Would you like to join me?"

"Huh, I don't think so. I stopped believing in God and all that prayer stuff a long time ago," Belinda responded, a slight attitude in her tone. "If there was a God, then He would have sent someone to release me the first night I stepped into this dungeon instead of leaving me here like someone shipwrecked on Hell's Island. I'll never forget the despair I felt that night. Every time the useless guard walked by, I thought they were coming to let me go, coming to say they'd made a mistake, and I could go home to my family. But that was asking too much of God."

"What! Are you telling me that you don't believe in Jesus?" Yvette asked, sitting up in her bed. She'd never met anyone who didn't believe in the powers above.

"That's exactly what I'm telling you. If I believed in all of that religious mumbo jumbo, I wouldn't be here in the first place, now would I?"

"Well, I believe in Jesus, but it's my behavior that has caused me to be here. I should have gone to my church and asked them to help me instead of trying to get over by bouncing illegal checks. I just called myself having too much pride to ask for anything, and this is what happened," Yvette said, wringing her hands. She glanced around the jail cell, shaking her head.

"You don't have any family that could have helped you? What about your parents?"

"Girl, my parents are long gone, God rest their souls. My father was killed when I was eleven months old after he got into an argument with someone at a nightclub. My mother raised me on her own until she passed away about six years ago when I was twenty-one years old. However, she was a God-fearing woman who took me to church with her every Sunday morning. I've been on my own with three kids for the past six years. And since I dropped out of high school in the tenth grade, none of my jobs have paid a dime over minimum wage."

"That's sad, Yvette. That's really sad," Belinda whispered.

"Will you two biddies shut the hell up and let the rest of us get some sleep in here!" an angry voice rang out in the dim night. Even whispers sounded loud when all was quiet in the cold building.

Without saying another word, both of the women rolled over in their cots, pulled the blanket over their tired shoulders, and waited for sleep to claim their active minds.

Belinda's thoughts briefly wandered back to Yvette's statement about attending church. "At least it would get me out of this cell for an hour every week, and it would probably look good to the parole board if they saw that I was attending church on a regular basis. I've heard before that everybody who goes to jail pretends to find Jesus long enough to get released. I'm willing to try anything to get me out of this Godforsaken place. Maybe I should try Jesus, or at least pretend to."

As Belinda began drifting into unconsciousness, an image appeared of a time when she and Desmond were happy and completely in love, if such a memory was possible. So much time had passed since they'd known true passion, Belinda wondered if it had ever truly existed or if it had just been a figment of her imagination.

Either way, Belinda longed for the extravagant life she'd once shared with a famous dermatologist. Although she hadn't heard a word from Desmond or the kids since her incarceration, Belinda remained hopeful that she would have her family together again. That was the only thing that kept her sane and trying to survive each dreadful day. Belinda reasoned that Desmond could have his other women and enjoy himself while she was away, knowing that when she returned, she'd be ready to do battle with anyone standing between her and their renewed happiness. Yes, it was going to be a joyful reunion as long as she wouldn't have to kill anyone to have it.

9

(Belinda's Divorce)

Hanging her head in disgust, Belinda contemplated how she was going to survive another six months in jail. Her parole hearing this morning hadn't gone quite as she'd hoped, and now all seemed to be lost until the next review. With excruciating pain in her heart, Belinda thought she'd never see daylight again. She cursed the racist committee in her mind and yearned to choke each of them to death.

Attorney Smith had advised Belinda not to get her hopes up for the hearing today. "Hardly anyone ever gets paroled their first time up," she'd declared. Belinda heard her concern, but she strongly believed that the odds were in her favor. After all, she'd been a model prisoner, avoiding other inmates, working in the kitchen every day, going to church every Wednesday night, going to the library to check out Christian-related books, and even pretending to pray with the pastors that ministered with them on a regular basis. She was planning to cry and act deeply remorseful about her crime, telling the committee members how she'd let the love for a deceitful man drive her to the brink of insanity. So, why wouldn't they approve her release? Because that's just wasn't the way the system worked.

"Mrs. Taylor, we are pleased with your progress at this time. You seem to have adjusted well to your new surroundings. Therefore, the board recommends that you work on a parole plan with your attorney, which will be reviewed at our next session in six months. At that time, if your good behavior has remained consistent, you may be released on parole with a community service requirement," Ms. Broward, the parole committee chairman, reported. Belinda stared through her fake tears at the woman's thin red lips in disbelief as she pronounced each word. It sounded like her voice was traveling through a tunnel in the ocean trying to reach the seashore.

Realizing what the chairperson had just announced, Belinda wanted to spit into her pale, wrinkled face, and slap those rosy cheeks. Instead, she wiped the conjured tears from her eyes as she spoke.

"Thank you, Ms. Broward, and the committee, for seeing me today," she began, making eye contact with each of the three men and three women on the panel to show her sincerity. "I want you all to know I regret my actions that landed me in prison. I wish I could go back in time and change everything that happened on that dreadful day. I promise you all that when I'm released, nothing like this will ever happen again." With that being said, the fake tears she'd been shedding turned into real ones exploding down her face.

"Thank you, Mrs. Taylor. We're glad to see that you have some sorrow regarding your behavior. Hopefully, you will continue towards a positive rehabilitation."

Rising from her chair facing the six committee members, Belinda fought to maintain her composure. She wanted to scream at each of them that they were out of their stinking minds, but Belinda walked out in silence, biting her tongue so hard it hurt.

Later, sitting on the side of her cot, Belinda fought against the tears she felt rising to the surface. Yvette had also warned her that this would probably happen, but Belinda had hoped against hope that she would be one of the lucky ones to get paroled in six months. After all, hadn't she been an ideal prisoner and done everything she'd been told? It just seemed like the pain would never stop. Everything about the place made her ill. Even now, the smell of female sweat mixed with piss-stained, toilet fumes was causing Belinda's stomach to turn. And the fact that she'd been assigned to kitchen duty the last month certainly hadn't helped her appetite or the everyday queasiness.

"Mail call!" Officer Kelly yelled.

As much as Belinda disliked the guard, she jumped off the bed at the sound of her loud voice. It was her favorite time of day. Not that she had a lot to look forward to besides a letter from her Mom saying how much she missed Belinda and how things were going to get better once she was released. But right now, that would give Belinda some comfort considering her earlier disappointment. Anything related to her former life would be sincerely appreciated.

The guard handed Belinda a letter and kept stepping.

"Hey, what's this?" Belinda mumbled, opening a letter from Desmond's attorney, Mr. Whittle.

Speed reading through the document, Belinda's mouth dropped in shock. Once she reached the end, she walked back to her cot and flopped down. This time, Belinda went back to the beginning of the paper and started reading out loud at a much slower pace. Obviously, she'd misread something or maybe her brain was too scrambled to comprehend all the legal terminology. This couldn't possibly be a final divorce decree from the love of her life, Dr. Desmond Taylor. But as the reality of the news began to register, Belinda's mind was filled with questions. "How can this be? How can he possibly divorce me without my knowledge? Why didn't my attorney contact me? This can't be legal."

Reading the document again and again, Belinda used every curse word imaginable. She even made up a few of her own to swirl around the empty cell. The anger consuming her at this point caused Belinda to throw the papers against the cold wall thinking, "How can my life possibly get any worse? I have to contact Attorney Smith and my parents to see what's going on. Maybe this is Desmond's way of trying to hurt me some more. There's no way he'd ever divorce me."

"All right, it's time for you to report to kitchen duty," Officer Kelly barked. Belinda hadn't even heard her heavy footsteps walking down the corridor. It was almost five o'clock, and she was working the five to ten P.M. shift all week.

"I need to make a phone call. I need to call my attorney," Belinda stammered.

"Well, that's too bad. You'll just have to wait until tomorrow. Right now, your services are requested in the mess hall. So let's go," the guard demanded, banging her club against the steel bars. "Get the lead out!"

"It's really important. I just got these divorce papers from my husband's attorney, and I need to know what's going on," Belinda pleaded, holding up her divorce decree. "Can someone divorce you while you're in prison without your consent?"

"Lady, please. Did you think that rich man was gonna stay with your incarcerated butt? It won't do you any good to call your attorney. Now move it," she demanded.

Belinda turned away from the officer and rolled her eyes up to the high heavens, but she dutifully complied with the guard's demand. It was definitely going to be a long five-hour shift.

After gathering the papers from the floor, she hurriedly stuffed them back into the envelope, and shoved them underneath her lumpy mattress. She'd have to call Attorney Smith first thing in the morning to find out how this happened. Belinda's mind just wouldn't let her conceive the thought of divorce. She'd done too much to save their marriage.

This was the last place Belinda wanted to be tonight. The

coldness of the kitchen matched the coldness in her heart. Luckily, with so many thoughts running through her mind, the time had flown by and Belinda's shift was almost over. She didn't know where the evening had gone; she was just glad that it had passed as quickly as it did. The only thing left to do was sweep up the place, and then she'd be done. Grabbing the broom from the closet, she headed to the back of the kitchen to wrap up her final chore.

Bent over the broom sweeping, Belinda's mind was in a world of its own, a place where she was free and living at home with her husband and children.

Oblivious to the activity going on around her, Belinda didn't notice the three inmates watching her until she heard a deep voice break into her concentration.

"Hey, ain't you the rich heifer we been hearing so much about? The one who thinks she's better than everybody else up in this joint?" one of them asked, glancing over at her two companions who both began to snicker.

"Yea, the one too good to talk to us little ole inmates," another one said.

Belinda stopped sweeping, looked up, and quickly surveyed the situation. Her heart leaped into her throat at the first sight of them. This was just the crowd she'd fought so hard to avoid since coming to this horrendous place.

"I don't want any trouble, so just leave me alone," she said, standing her ground. Not a muscle in her body moved.

Belinda didn't know anyone by name and had made a point to stay to herself. She didn't want to know anyone, and she didn't want anyone to know her besides her cellmate, Yvette. So far, no one had bothered her, and Belinda was fine with that. But she felt uncomfortable with the way these three butch-looking inmates were eyeing her. She searched the room for Officer Kelly knowing that the mean woman would never come to her rescue.

"Just who the hell do you think you talking to? I make

the rules around here, baby," the leader stated, easing closer to Belinda. She was much smaller than the other two in her entourage. "Now, we can play this either way you want. You can walk with us to the supply room real nice like or we can drag your po' tail back there."

Picking up the broom by the handle, Belinda held it out like a weapon, daring the enemy to come closer. The threesome glanced from one to the other and laughed.

"Oh, we're scared of you," one of them said, simulating a quiver.

When Belinda looked away to see if a guard was coming, the three rushed her and one of them snatched the broom out of her hand. She opened her mouth to scream but one of the women slapped her across the face so hard she went blind for about two seconds. When she was able to see again, one woman had her by each arm as the ring leader watched them drag her in the back room with a dish rag stuffed down her throat.

"Now, what were you trying to say? I can't hear you?" one of them teased, holding a hand up to one ear.

While they held her struggling body, the leader of the pack punched Belinda in the midsection. She doubled over from the pain, causing the two sidekicks to release her arms. Belinda sunk down onto the cold, hard floor moaning.

One of the sidekicks grabbed a hunk of Belinda's hair, jerked her head back, and sneered, "You're about to get taken down a peg or two, baby."

Belinda could hear someone softly calling her name. The only problem was that she couldn't tell if she was dreaming or not. Either way, she had difficulty responding to the light voice until the stale medicinal stench of the infirmary drifted through her nose, causing Belinda to wake up coughing. Raising a hand to her mouth, she felt a stinging sensation in her left arm. Belinda looked down at her vein to find a needle sticking in it, which was attached to an IV unit.

"Welcome back." She heard the tender voice say.

Lifting her head, Belinda eyes bulged as she stared at the red-haired lady standing over her bed holding a vial in one hand.

"Where am I?" she asked, touching the bandages on her head. Belinda felt a flash of pain shoot through her forehead, cheeks, and the bridge of her nose like she'd never known.

"You're at the prison's clinic. I'm Dr. Carter, and I'm the one who examined you last night. Just try to relax," she said, patting Belinda's shoulder. "I'm going to raise your bed a little bit so you can breathe better," she said, pressing the lever on the side of the bed.

As the bed rose, the pain from Belinda's head seemed to flow down through the rest of her body. She held her stomach while her eyes darted around the tiny examining room observing the rest of the scarce surroundings. It was just the two of them in the room with the door closed. Dr. Carter placed the vial into a container on the bedside table and took Belinda by the hand.

"Now that you're awake, I need to check your pulse," she said, squeezing Belinda's wrist.

"What happened?" Belinda asked, searching the doctor's eyes. "How did I get here?"

Dr. Carter sighed, looking away from her patient as though she didn't want to answer. Releasing Belinda's hand, she picked up a clipboard holding a chart and scribbled something on it. Turning to Belinda, she said, "One of the guards found you half-naked and passed out on the floor in the kitchen supply closet. Do you remember anything?"

Some of the incident came flowing back to Belinda. She remembered the thugs cursing at her, punching her face, and kicking her bare butt before she blacked out from the pain and embarrassment.

"What did those freaks do to me? Oh, my God!" Belinda cried, beginning to panic. She raised her head as high as she could. "Did they molest me?" Belinda asked, remembering the broom.

"Calm down," the doctor replied, patting Belinda's hand. "Based upon my examination, I didn't see any signs of molestation. They told me you were found lying on the floor with your pants and underwear around your ankles, but you weren't penetrated."

Breathing a sigh of relief, Belinda eased her head back against the pillow and asked, "Can't you just give me something for the pain, doctor?" she begged, holding her stomach.

"Ms. Taylor, you have some internal bruising around your lower intestines, and that's probably what's causing your pain right now. I'm going to give you something stronger for that in a minute. Can you tell me what all you remember happening in the galley?"

"Why? What good would it do?" Belinda asked, releasing her anger on the doctor. "All I know is that three inmates confronted me in the kitchen, stuffed a dish rag down my throat, and pulled me into the supply room. I don't know who they were, and at this point, I don't ever want to know. It's not like the prison system is going to reprimand them for their behavior. Why don't you ask that sorry Officer Kelly? Wasn't she supposed to be on duty?"

"Yes, she was, and she's going to be dealt with. But if you're willing to identify them for Warden Thomas, I'm sure she'll handle this by making sure they're prosecuted for their actions. You weren't sent here to be violated by anyone. The guards are supposed to provide some level of protection while you're here." Belinda was a little moved by what seemed to be sincere concern from Dr. Carter, only it didn't change how utterly disgusted she felt.

"This whole system is a joke! The guards don't give a

damn about anybody. Hell, they probably paid that bastard off to get to me. Now, if I nail them for what they did, then the other demented members of their gang will attack me again. And next time, I might not live long enough to tell anything. I may not be used to prison life, Doc, but I'm nobody's fool. I'll pass on your good prison protection."

"I'm sorry that you feel this way," Dr. Carter replied, stashing both hands into her crisp white jacket pockets. "I'll give you a prescription for some pain medications. You're welcome to come back to see me again tomorrow if you need anything else, okay. I'm going to step outside for a second while you get dressed. I'll make arrangements for you to meet with a counselor."

Belinda was laughing now like a mad woman. Slapping her thigh, she said, "That's funny, Doc. Is that one of the special services provided by the prison system? Doesn't everybody in here get abused one way or another?"

"I understand how you feel," the doctor replied, folding both arms across her chest." That's why it's important for you to get counseling. You may not want to confront your attackers, but you need to confront yourself."

"Thanks for your concern, but I'll handle this my own way," Belinda uttered, turning to face the wall.

"Well, it's mandatory that you attend at least one counseling session after an incident like this. After that, it's your choice whether or not to continue. We have an experienced female counselor who'll be very sympathetic to your situation. Just remember, we're here if you need us." Grabbing her clipboard and the vial containers, Dr. Carter took one last look at Belinda's back and headed towards the door.

Holding her breath, Belinda was waiting to hear the door close behind Dr. Carter. That's when she leaned over the side of the bed and heaved until her stomach was empty, and her throat was raw. Tears streamed down her bruised face. There was nothing she could do to hold them back. There was nothing she wanted to do to hold them back. All her life, Belinda had been a strong woman, not afraid of anyone or anything. If she thought that coming to prison was the worst experience of her life, this was certainly the most humiliating thing she'd ever experienced. No one had ever violated her body. She was the one who violated other people for trespassing on her territory. Belinda asked herself, "Was I wrong for trying to protect my property? Am I truly helpless now? Who can help me in my hour of need? Maybe I do need to see a counselor?"

10

(Belinda's Screams)

Yvette kissed her youngest daughter's picture, changed into her white nightgown, and sat down on the side of the cot. She had to get one more look at her beautiful child before the lights went out. "I'll see you soon," Yvette murmured, sliding her fingers across the child's face. Kissing the picture again, Yvette glanced at the empty cot across from her, and wondered about the disappearance of her cellmate. Belinda hadn't returned from her kitchen duty last night, and Yvette hadn't seen her all day long.

For some reason, she wasn't tired. Sleep was the furthest thing from Yvette's mind. There was an uneasiness that prevented her from relaxing the way she normally would. Maybe it was the rumors she'd heard circulating around the cell block. It seemed that three prisoners were bragging about beating up some high society chick in the galley last night. And from the way they were talking, she was roughed up mighty good. Yvette had been incarcerated long enough to know that most rumors turned out to be true, especially when it came to acts of violence. She'd warned Belinda to be careful and watch her back at all times.

Yvette had tried to get more details about what happened, but figured it was best not to ask any questions. She kept her mouth closed and her ears opened while they were in the television room last night. Although she heard the whispering and giggling in the back, Yvette didn't dare turn around to see who was talking. But she was worried about her cellmate.

Yvette could hear the guards marching down the shallow hall, the jingling key chains sounding almost as loud as their steps. They stopped at her cell. The steel doors were parting. She looked up to see Belinda standing between two guards. The scowl on Belinda's face, along with the swollen left eye, told Yvette that her deepest fear was now reality. She wondered how she'd ever convince Belinda that there was a God after this incident.

Yvette stretched out her arms, hoping to embrace the friend she'd made. She wanted to comfort Belinda and let her know that no matter what she was going through right now, God hadn't forgotten nor forsaken her.

"No, please, don't touch me. I just want to go to bed, go to sleep, and forget this whole thing ever happened," she whispered, holding up one hand, halting Yvette's steps towards her. Belinda eased down fully dressed, closed her eyes, and balled up into a fetal position.

Yvette reached for the green blanket at the foot of the bed and pulled it up around Belinda's shoulders. "I'm sorry," she whispered.

Seconds later, the lights were turned out. They were both alone in the darkness with their separate pains. Yvette rested her head against the flat pillow and pulled the blanket up to her chin. Listening to Belinda crying in the dark, Yvette tried to imagine what her cellmate had been through in the pass twenty-four hours. Shaking her head, Yvette accepted the fact that her imagination could never stretch that far. So she pressed her hands together, and thanked God for keeping her out of harm's way during her incarceration. Finding Jesus was the best thing she'd ever done.

Knowing that she couldn't physically comfort Belinda, Yvette slid out of the bed and got down on her knees, preparing to pray.

Belinda had finally stopped crying when she heard Yvette getting out of bed. She assumed that Yvette was heading for the toilet in the corner and covered her ears to block out the sound. One thing she hated about prison life was the lack of privacy when using the bathroom. They didn't even that the privilege of pissing in private. That was purely inhumane treatment.

But to Belinda's surprise, Yvette hadn't gotten out of bed to use the toilet; she'd gotten out of bed to pray. And not only was Yvette praying for herself, but she was praying for Belinda and asking God to wrap His loving arms around her, to provide her with loving protection, and give her the strength to forgive those whom had hurt her in any way. Then, Yvette closed out her prayer by referencing a Scripture having something to do with faith, hope, and love.

"Good night, Belinda," Yvette whispered.

She didn't respond. Belinda didn't know what she was supposed to say, so she pretended to be asleep. This was a first for her. She'd heard people praying in church before, but she'd never had anyone to specifically pray for her salvation. Belinda asked herself, "Why is God tormenting me this way? How could a good Savior let so much pain happen to me in one day and then have someone praying for me like this? I wish she'd hush because there's no Jesus or justice in this God-forsaken place. If it was, I wouldn't be hurt up like this."

The following morning, Belinda was allowed to sit in the warden's office and call Attorney Smith. She sat staring at the life-sized painting of Warden Thomas hanging behind her double-wide mahogany desk. The dark wood paneling in the hundred year old building matched Belinda's gloomy mood. Her bruised body was tired, sore, and aching in places she didn't even know existed. But nothing, not even the horror she'd recently experienced, could keep her from finding out how Desmond could have possibly divorced her while she was confined.

Attorney Smith answered the telephone and asked

Belinda how she was doing. Belinda explained that she'd been attacked while performing her kitchen duties and was dealing with the pain from that as well as the pain from receiving the divorce papers.

"What happened? How is this even possible?" Both questions flew out her mouth in rapid succession.

The attorney cleared her throat, trying to think of the easiest way to explain this to her client while meandering through traffic.

"I'm not sure what happened. I can only assume that he filed a petition for divorce and since you were unable to contest it, the judge granted his request."

"How could I contest something that I didn't know about?"

"That's exactly the point. He probably claimed abandonment and denied knowing your whereabouts. If I had my computer in front of me, I could tell you more, but I'm in the car, and it's my best theory."

"You've got to be kidding me. How did he get away with that?" Belinda was bent over the desk, rubbing her head with one hand, trying to keep the throbbing from getting worse.

"The courts don't have the money to track people down. So, they run a public notice in the local newspapers, and if you don't respond after two weeks, they set a court date. And then, if you don't show up to contest the divorce proceedings, it's granted to the petitioning party. It's that simple."

"There has to be some type of recourse behind this. I mean there has to be something that I can do." Belinda pounded the desk with her fist, making the headache come on full force.

"I'm sorry, Mrs. Taylor, I wish I'd known about this. There's just nothing I can do at this point. It sounds like the divorce is already final."

"That bastard! What about my kids? Can my parents get the kids?" Her heart was beginning to pump faster with each second she waited for the attorney to respond.

"Honestly, if he was granted a divorce, he was probably granted sole custody of the children, too."

"Nooo!" Belinda dropped the telephone receiver. Her screams could be heard all the way down the corridor from the warden's office. She slid out the leather armchair onto the hardwood floor and cried harder than she did after receiving a beat down from her fellow inmates. Nothing could compare to the pain of losing both your children at once.

11

(Belinda's Counselor)

Belinda didn't appreciate being escorted by two female guards to the mandatory counseling session Dr. Carter had set up for this afternoon. Although she'd been on pain medication and bed rest for the last couple of days, it still hurt some when she walked. Most of the swelling in Belinda's face had gone down, but she still lacked enthusiasm about sitting across from some old, gray-haired prison psychiatrist trying to pick her brains about the most intimate details of her personal life. Belinda shivered at the thought of sitting in some stale, white-walled room for an hour with a pointed-nosed doctor who she didn't have any desire to know. All Belinda wanted to do was get past this horrendous episode and get out of this dreadful place as quickly as the law would allow. She didn't want anyone else to bother her, and Belinda didn't have any plans to bother anyone for the remainder of her prison stay. Belinda confirmed, "I'm going to keep my mouth shut so I can ease on out of here when the time comes. I hate those bastards, but I'm not dumb enough to get caught up in prison revenge games."

Belinda had taken two Psychology classes while in college. She was familiar with the tedious process of mental therapy awaiting her. "The doctor will start with probing questions about my family history, and then try to get me to talk about my problems so she can diagnose me with some strange-sounding illness. But that's okay. After two days of being in that sun-deprived cell, I can play this game with the best they have," she deduced.

The second Belinda entered the psychiatrist's office, her widened eyes scanned the room faster than a laser beam. It was definitely the opposite of everything she'd expected to see. Somehow, it felt like she'd been magically transported to New York and entered a suite at the plushest hotel in the city. For one thing, the wall to wall beige carpeting was three inches thick and felt like it had extra foam padding beneath it. The walls were painted a warm, neutral color, making the room feel larger than it was and twice as inviting. There was a row of windows on the opposite side of the room covered with satiny copper and burgundy-colored, floor length drapes blocking out most of the bright afternoon sun. Inhaling the fresh scent in the air, Belinda wondered where the doctor had stashed the can of Febreze she'd just used.

The young female doctor met them at the door wearing a tailored blue suit more befitting of the corporate business world than a prison employee. Belinda thought they'd made a mistake, this child couldn't possibly be a doctor.

"Thank you, guards," the woman said, holding the door open. "I'll take it from here. We'll be fine," she declared, closing the door. The two officers spoke kindly to the doctor and exited the room peacefully.

Touching Belinda's elbow, the doctor guided her newest patient to the chair in front of her espresso wood, L-shaped desk. Taking a seat in her high-back, microfiber chair, seemingly designed for comfort, she picked up a silver pen.

"My name is Dr. Gabrielle Michaels, and I've been assigned to counsel with you today, Mrs. Taylor," she stated, extending a French manicured hand.

Giving Dr. Michaels a firm handshake, Belinda envied the woman's stupendous personal appearance. Still, she responded with a warm greeting as she observed the doctor's perfectly relaxed hair with a short bang and blunt cut at the shoulders. Her slanted shaped eyes made the

African-American woman look more like a porcelain china doll than a state certified psychiatrist.

Dr. Michaels continued. "It's a pleasure to meet you, Mrs. Taylor. Do you mind if I call you Belinda?"

"No, I don't mind at all," Belinda replied, leaning back into the comfort of her fabric-covered chair. Glancing past the seated doctor, her eyes focused on the floor-to-ceiling bookcase filled with medical books.

"Since this is our first meeting, I have to explain a few things to you before we get started with our session for today. I've reviewed your records, and I want you to know that everything you share with me from this point forward will be held in the strictest confidence. Do you understand?"

"Yes," Belinda replied with a nod.

Dr. Michaels smiled at her as she pulled a microcassette recorder from her desk. "And I have to record all of our conversations for my records," she said, pushing the red record button.

Again, Belinda nodded in agreement.

"Are you comfortable where you are, or would you be more comfortable relaxing on the sofa over there?" Dr. Michaels asked, motioning towards the sofa across the room.

"Well, this chair is very nice, but I believe I'd be more comfortable if I was in a reclining position," Belinda answered, eyeing the buttery, soft-looking, retro-styled, leather sofa across the room.

"No problem," the doctor said, rising. Holding her pen and pad, she walked around her desk, assisted Belinda to the sofa, and sat in the brown, oversized, leather pillow-top chair next to her patient. Placing the microcassette recorder on the glass coffee table in front of her, she said, "All right, now that we're both settled in, I'd like to know how you're feeling today."

Resting her head against the pillow with her hands crossing her midsection, Belinda cautiously replied, "Well, my stomach is still a little sore and my leg is bothering me some, but other than that, I'm physically fine since my face looks almost normal again." She smoothed a hand down her right cheek and felt some tenderness on that side, but Belinda was eighty percent better than she'd been on the previous day, thanks to the multiple ice packs she'd used.

The doctor made a note on her pad before continuing. "That's good news. And how are you feeling mentally?"

"Well, let's just say that I've had better days. But overall, I feel kind of numb emotionally after everything that's happened to me. You know, at first I was in so much pain it felt like my insides were going to burst, and now, there's just this strange sense of numbness like I couldn't cry even if I wanted to."

"The meds that you're taking could be contributing to that, so I'll have to reevaluate your prescriptions." Dr. Michaels took a second to write that on her pad. "Have you had any trouble sleeping, concentrating, or any other problems you could tell me about?"

"Yes, I've had a couple of nightmares since being admitted here, but they weren't related to my attack."

"What were they related to?" Dr. Michaels asked, clicking her fountain pen.

"They had more to do with my fear of losing my family than anything else. I was blacked out during most of my assault and since Dr. Carter assured me that I wasn't violated in any way, I've put that incident behind me as a prison learning experience."

Dr. Michaels leaned forward and remained calm. "I can tell you that some people rebound quickly from tragic events, while others are devastated by those same experiences for life. So I can understand how you think you're past that, but that's the reason for you being here today, and I'd like to hear everything you can recall about that event before we go any further."

After releasing a deep breath, Belinda easily relayed the sequence of events to Dr. Michaels, beginning with the morning of her parole hearing and ending with the morning that she woke up in the infirmary connected to an IV unit. Belinda spoke as if she was watching a movie unfold on television, and she acted out each character in their voice as they appeared on the screen. Dr. Michaels made several notes and asked few questions as Belinda shared the traumatic experiences with her. The doctor's main goal was to keep the patient talking with little interruption.

Approximately thirty minutes later, Belinda seemed drained from reenacting that one eventful day, along with a few other highlights from her drama filled life. She'd expressed her anger, irritability, fears, and sadness to the easy listening doctor. In fact, Belinda had shared more regarding her sordid past than she'd planned on sharing. But after months of being withdrawn from the general population and only semi-communicating with Yvette at night, it was relieving to be able to vent her frustrations to another female, even if she believed the woman was too young to understand her plight.

"How old are you, Doc?" Belinda asked. She eyed Dr. Michaels suspiciously, wondering if the psychiatrist would tell the truth regarding her age or try to pretend like she was older than Belinda believed. *I know she's got to be in her twenties.*

"I'm twenty-eight years old. Why do you ask?" Dr. Michaels responded with a bold smile, like maybe she was used to hearing this question.

Belinda was impressed with the doctor's response. Still, she had to share her opinion. "You don't look old enough to be working in a prison or to be a psychiatrist, so I know it's impossible for you to understand how I ended up here."

Leaning in towards Belinda, Dr. Michaels placed her notepad and pen on the coffee table. Clasping her hands together, she spoke with the maturity of someone way beyond her years.

"It's not just my responsibility to figure out how you got here. It's my duty to help you deal with the emotions that you're feeling now as a result of your assault. I've been a doctor here for over a year and prior to that time, I interned here for almost three years, so I'm experienced in treating emotional and psychological trauma patients."

Belinda wasn't fazed by the seriousness in the doctor's voice. "Yeah, that may be true," Belinda began, holding up one finger at a time as she continued. "But if you've never been married or divorced or incarcerated or attacked, there's no way for you to diagnose the type of pain that I've had to internalize."

"That may be true, but I'd like an opportunity to try."

Pressing her lips together, Belinda sat up, and stared at Dr. Michaels. "No, thanks, I'm not interested in being psychoanalyzed by a child."

Returning her stare, Dr. Michaels politely said, "Have you got something better to do with your time besides meet with me once a week for the next month or are you afraid that you might actually learn something about yourself?"

"Oh, I'm not afraid of anything," Belinda retorted.

"It sounds like you're getting upset. Are you angry with me?"

Belinda sighed. "I'm not angry. I just don't want to be here anymore."

"Okay, I just need to ask you a few questions regarding your childhood, and we'll be done for today." Dr. Michaels leaned back in her seat and crossed her long legs. "Are you an only child?"

"Yes, I am, but what does that have to do with anything?"

"Many psychiatrists believe that being an only child shapes one's personality in a different way than it would if they had siblings. For example, an only child may tend to be more self-centered or demanding than one with siblings. Would you agree with that?"

Belinda thought for a second before replying. "I guess that could be true to some extent."

"Are you self-centered or demanding?"

Belinda shrugged. The doctor continued. "When you were a child, how did you react when things didn't go your way?"

"I would normally throw a temper tantrum, and if that didn't work, I'd start crying until my parents gave in."

"How would you describe your relationship with your parents?"

Seeing where this was headed, Belinda decided to head off the good doctor.

"I have a great relationship with my parents. They provided me with nothing but the best of everything."

"I see," Dr. Michaels replied, glancing at her watch as she stood. "Our time is almost up for today. I'll set an appointment to meet with you again this time next week." Dr. Michaels stepped behind her desk, pushed the intercom button, and spoke into it. "Mrs. Taylor is ready to be escorted back to her room now."

Belinda walked out between the two guards knowing that she wouldn't be seeing Dr. Michaels again. This was her first and last counseling session. Yes, she was self-centered, demanding, and had some anger issues, but Belinda didn't need a psychiatrist to tell her that.

12

(Belinda's Parole)

Over the next six months, Belinda spent most of her free time in the library reading paperback novels, a few nonfiction titles, exercising whenever allowed, and writing daily in a journal that her mom had sent shortly after the attack. At first, Belinda didn't see the point of documenting a paltry existence that she was planning to forget the second she was released. But after reading a book published by Triple Crown Publications and written by its founder, Vickie Stringer, a former convict, Belinda thought maybe she'd get a book deal based on her past, too. After all, she was an Ivy League graduate serving time for a felony. From what she'd read, Vickie had turned her publishing company into a multimillion dollar business. Belinda wasn't up on the urban street life, but she'd learned enough about the prison life to fill a couple of books.

Fortunately, Belinda wasn't returned to kitchen duty after her incident. And after one counseling session with Dr. Michaels, she never returned to the young doctor's office for a follow-up visit. Yes, they were both African-American women, but that's where their similarities ended. As much as Belinda admired the well-spoken doctor, she didn't see how talking with her anymore was going to make doing her time any easier, especially after learning that their sessions wouldn't have any bearing upon her parole hearings. Belinda never tried to identify the three women who'd attacked her, but they never bothered her again, and she was smart enough to let it go. Instead of retaliation, she continued going to church on Wednesday nights and claiming to be a born again Christian.

Belinda was planning to turn her tragedy into victory when the time came to meet with the parole board members again. She didn't need counseling on how to do that. Belinda would play the good, God-fearing Christian role to the hilt to secure her release.

Yvette had been released last month, and her new roommate, Shannon, and she didn't get along. Shannon was even younger than Yvette, and arrogant to top it all off. She was serving time on a drug charge and acted like the whole world owed her something. Belinda didn't know what the world intended for Shannon, but she didn't have any intentions of being friends with her. As long as she stayed on her side of the room, they'd both be fine.

Belinda refused to admit that she missed Yvette Riley's smiling face and positive vibe. Her friendship had almost made this a bearable place to live. Yvette had written Belinda several times and sent her telephone number, inviting Belinda to call her once she was freed. In every letter, Yvette expressed how happy she was to be back home with her family and how good God was being to them.

Belinda responded to the first letter from Yvette, but after that she didn't want to hear any more good news. So Yvette's letters were resting in a drawer unopened along with the many opened ones she'd received from her mother. Yes, Julia Hines was still writing her daughter at least once a week and was confident that Belinda would be home with them soon. She told Belinda about the new young pastor at the church and how the whole congregation was praying for her safe return. As much as Mrs. Hines wrote to Belinda, she rarely ever mentioned her husband unless it was to complain about how much time he spent on the golf course. She also expressed her disappointment with Desmond and the fact that he was keeping the grandchildren away from them.

It was difficult for Belinda to accept the fact that Dr. Desmond Taylor was now her ex-husband, and she no longer had the status that came with being the wife of a renowned dermatologist. Somehow, she would live without the heartless bastard as long as she had her children living with her. And that's exactly how she planned for it to happen once she was released from prison. Her love for Desmond that was once so strong had eventually turned into intense hatred. Every day that Belinda opened her eyes in that steel cell, she cursed the first day that she'd met the prince of darkness disguised as a prince of peace and thought, "I still don't understand how he was able to divorce me without my consent. I guess if you have enough money, you can do anything you want. But he's not going to keep me from my children. Nobody on this earth can do that."

With a parole board hearing coming up at ten o'clock in the morning, Belinda channeled her thoughts to the future. She would have to cry and act even more remorseful than she did the last time if she wanted to get out of this dungeon. Surely the tragedy she'd suffered at the hands of the inmates would help the committee members sympathize with Belinda, especially since she didn't try retaliating against her attackers. She'd already played the Christian card with the prison staff and claimed to have forgiven those who had harmed her. Now she would play the sympathy card for all it was worth to help her get back home. *This could be my last night in this place. Oh, please, let it be true.*

For the first time since being incarcerated, she got down on her knees and prayed for the parole board members to rule in her favor. Belinda couldn't remember the exact prayer Yvette had prayed for her many months ago. She just asked Him to let it come to pass, "If You let me out of here, Jesus, I promise to repair my life. And I'll never bother You for any reason again. Please, Jesus, let me go home to see my children, and we'll be even."

Closing her eyes, Belinda breathed in a stream of fresh air. It had been over a year since she felt like this. Stretching out her arms, Belinda savored the scent of pine trees and the sound of birds whistling in the wind. She even enjoyed the light breeze blowing against her chocolate skin as she walked down the driveway of the prison yard. Yes, the freedom she'd longed for had been granted. The parole board had unanimously ruled in her favor after they'd heard the emotional pleas of a remorseful convict. Remembering her Academy Award winning performance, Belinda strutted in a pair of Fergie pumps down the driveway like it was a red carpet event.

Appreciating the opportunity to wear designer clothes again, Belinda glanced down at the brand new outfit her mother sent last week. Even though she'd lost a few pounds, the black, Donna Karan, jean jumpsuit clung to her breasts and hips as if it was tailor-made for her. With her kinky hair pulled up into a bun, Belinda couldn't wait to see her hairdresser's chair.

Belinda looked up and saw her mother standing outside the prison gates leaning against the hood of a brand new car. She had a floral scarf wrapped around her head to match the pale yellow suit she sported on this windy October day.

"Oh, thank you, Lord, I'm so happy to see my child! This is the day that I have been hoping and praying for," Belinda's mother cried out in joy.

Belinda hugged her mother with all of her strength. She was the only person who had visited her in prison over the last year. And she was the only person who had written to her while she was incarcerated. Not even her own children had bothered to write one letter to their mother. Anyway, she knew that had to be Desmond's doing, wherever the hell he was. She was going to make him pay for keeping the kids from her all of this time. Nothing gave him the right to keep her daughter and son away from their natural mother.

"Hi, Momma. Thank you for coming to get me. Where is Daddy?" Belinda asked, peeking over her shoulder for a sign of her father.

"Ah, he wasn't able to make it today, baby. He'll be home waiting on us by the time we get there. Don't you worry about that, okay?"

Trying to hide her disappointment, Belinda lowered her head, wiped the small tear from the corner of her right eye, and responded softly, "Sure, that's all right. I'm just ready to get away from here."

"Let's go, sweetheart," Julia responded, walking towards the parked car.

"I see you finally bought yourself a new ride," Belinda stated, admiring the plush interior of her mother's Jaguar XJ Sport. "You've never had a Jag before, have you?"

"No, but it's what I've always wanted. I finally bought the car that I wanted and not the one your father wanted me to have," Julia replied, smiling at her daughter.

"Mom, do you know if Daddy had any luck finding Desmond and the kids?" Belinda regretted that Max Collins wasn't alive to take on this case. He was an excellent investigator who would have found her children by now.

"Don't you worry about that right now. We have plenty of time to talk about that once you're home safe."

"I haven't seen my children in a whole year, and you're telling me not to worry about them? All I've done is think about them. Now, if you know anything, please tell me."

"Oh, God!" Julia screamed, slamming on the brakes. The car came to a screeching halt, jerking both of them forward and then throwing them back against the soft leather seats. Looking up at the glaring red light, Julia tried to calm her rapidly beating heart. "Are you all right?" she asked, staring at Belinda.

"I just got out of prison today, and you're trying to kill me before I can even get home," Belinda snarled, bracing herself with one hand leaning against the dashboard.

"I'm sorry. They just put this light up a few months ago. I'm not used to having to stop here. Let's just try and relax the rest of the way home." Julia gripped the steering wheel with both hands, staring at the traffic light, willing it to change. This piece of news would have to wait until they got home. She couldn't risk her daughter getting upset in this heavy traffic.

"Sure, Mom, whatever you say," Belinda replied, leaning back against the headrest, rubbing her temples. She thought, "There's something that she's not ready for me to find out about my family. But I'm going to get to the bottom of this one way or another before the day is over. No one is going to keep me from my children. And I mean no one. I may belong to the state of Texas for the next five years, but I'm going to have my family."

"Look, Mom, can you drive me by my house? I'd like to see if anyone is living there. They might know something about where Desmond and the kids are living."

"Baby, I promise you that your father has someone working on this. Besides, you live in a gated community, remember. How do you think we'll get in? Now, let me take you home with me and everything will be all right."

"No, it won't. Just let me see the area that I used to call home. It's all that I've been dreaming about for the last year. The least you can do is drive me by the community."

Julia's face softened at her daughter's words. She couldn't imagine the pain she'd endured during the past twelve months.

"Okay, I'll drive you by there, but promise me that you'll go home with me after that."

"I promise," Belinda gently replied.

Thirty minutes later, Julia pulled into the community to find that there wasn't a security guard on duty and the gates were wide open. Belinda couldn't mask the joy on her face as they sped through the opening.

Julia pulled into the circular driveway that once belonged to her daughter and son-in-law. The huge red and white "For Sale" sign in the yard was the first thing they both noticed.

"What's going on here? Why is my house for sale?"

"I don't know, baby. Let's write down the number to the realtor so we can call them to find out."

The second Julia stopped the car and placed the gear in park, Belinda bolted from the car. "What are you doing, Belinda? You promised me that you wouldn't get out," Julia sighed, looking up at her daughter through the open car door.

"I'm just going to buzz the intercom to see if anyone's home. I'll be right back, don't worry," Belinda replied, closing the car door.

Her heart pounded harder with each step she took towards the front door. Belinda couldn't believe how much the landscaping had changed. Some of the huge palm trees that she loved so much had been removed and replaced with shrubbery. Even the front door had been repainted a hideous green. After pressing the button twice, Belinda waited to see if anyone would answer.

"Yes, may I help you?" a woman asked over the intercom system.

"Ms. Rodriquez, is that you?" Belinda immediately recognized the Spanish accent. "It's me, Belinda Taylor, Dr. Taylor's wife. Please open the door."

Pulling the door open just enough to peep over the loosely hanging chain, Ms. Rodriquez peered at her former employer.

"Yes, may I help you?" she asked again. "Dr. Taylor no

longer lives here."

"I know. I was just wondering if you know where he's moved to."

"I'm sorry, but I can't give you that information. I no longer work for you."

"Yes, that's true. I just thought that you'd be willing to help me find my family. I've been away from them for over a year."

"I can't help you. Now leave me alone," she replied, closing the door in Belinda's shocked face.

"I know this crazy woman didn't just slam the door in my face. I'll drag her out of this house and beat her down in the front yard."

Belinda pressed the buzzer several more times to no avail. She looked to the front window and saw Ms. Rodriquez peering out at her. Storming over to the window, Belinda started yelling obscenities at the woman. Ms. Rodriquez glared at Belinda, made a fist at her, and then raised her middle finger in protest as she released the curtain. Searching the grounds for a brick or rock to throw through the glass pane, Belinda suddenly felt someone tugging on the sleeve of her jumpsuit.

"Belinda, have you lost your mind? We're on private property. She can call the police and have you sent right back to jail today. Come on, let's get in the car," Julia begged.

Swelling with anger, Belinda glared at her mother, then began stomping back and forth across the grass.

"Let's go, right now, or I'm leaving you here alone. You know she's probably going to call the police. Are you ready to go back to jail?"

Finally, her mother's words seemed to seep through Belinda's blinding anger. She followed Julia down the walkway, got into the car, and slammed the door shut.

Pulling away from the curb, Julia screamed, "How could

you be so foolish? I never should have brought you here! You promised me that you were going to stay in the car!"

Belinda screamed back at her mother, "I know! I know what I promised! But I just couldn't sit here and not ask any questions! She knows something!"

"Yeah, well, she's not going to tell you whatever she knows after the way you cursed at her today, now is she?" Julia asked, keeping her eyes on the road. "The best thing you can do is to relax and let you father handle this situation. He's going to hire someone to find Desmond and your kids. We'll know something soon."

"It won't be soon enough. I miss my babies," Belinda whined, slumping down into the seat. She did something that she'd promised herself she'd never do again. She cried.

Julia's heart ached to see Belinda crying. She didn't know what all her precious daughter had been through, but she knew prison life wasn't a picnic. Pulling the car over to the side of the road, Julia shifted the gear to park, and took a deep breath before addressing Belinda.

"It's okay, baby. I understand what you're feeling. It's been a long time since you've seen your babies. I've missed you almost as much as you've missed them," Julia said, taking Belinda's hand.

"Momma, you can't possibly understand how I feel," Belinda retorted, crying harder. "I feel like a vampire has his fangs buried in my neck, and he's slowly draining all of the blood from my body. Nothing has ever hurt me like this. I just want to see my children."

Julia searched her purse for a tissue. She pulled out several from the small pack she normally carried in her bag and handed them to Belinda. Wiping away the tears, Belinda stared at her mother through red eyes.

"I've got to find my babies, Mom. Please help me find them."

"We will, baby. Don't worry, we're going to find your

children and bring them home. You'll see. No weapon formed against us shall prosper."

13

(Belinda's Home)

One month later, all of Belinda's high-class, married girlfriends had turned their backs on her. Not one of the housewives she'd shopped and dined with in the past answered her phone calls or even bothered to return a single message. She should have known that if none of them had mailed a letter while she was incarcerated, that not one of them would welcome her home. They were too busy trying to keep up with their husbands to ensure that their lavish lifestyles remained intact. And Belinda couldn't blame them for that. If the situation was reversed, she'd probably do the same thing. But accepting the facts didn't make Belinda feel any better about herself or her current living conditions.

Belinda was still cohabitating with her parents in a five-thousand square foot Tudor-style home. It wasn't as grand as the three-story mansion she'd shared with Desmond and the children, but it was the best she could do for now. The depression from being without her kids was wearing Belinda's body down. She'd lost an additional five pounds since her release, making her look like Robin Given's twin sister. With the holiday right around the corner, Belinda felt desperate to find Justine and Jesse. Justine had to be a budding fifteen-year-old in need of her motherly advice. And Jesse should be an eighteen-year-old senior preparing for college. She was missing out on the most exciting times of their young lives.

"Yes," Belinda answered. Someone was knocking at the door.

Julia turned the doorknob to Belinda's well-decorated room and stepped in. The blue painted walls were a match for Belinda's gloomy mood. Mrs. Hines found her daughter awake, lying on her back, and staring up at the ceiling. "Good morning."

"Hi, Mom. How're you?" Belinda asked, raising her head.

"I'm great. Your father just called, and he wants us to meet him at the club house right away." Julia was smiling like she might have some good news.

"Really? I was just thinking about him. What else did he say?" she asked, stumbling out of bed.

"That's all he had to say. He'll tell us the rest when we get there," Julia replied, closing the bedroom door on her way out.

Belinda pulled a designer-inspired, beige suit from her closet, laid it across the bed, and rushed to the shower. Hoping that this was the day she'd been dreaming of, she sent up a quick prayer.

"Oh, Jesus, I know that I've never been the praying kind, but I'll do anything to find my children. Just let me know if they're okay, and I'll try to become a better person."

Both of Belinda's parents were church-going people. They made it clear that if she was planning on living with them, she'd have to attend First Jerusalem A.M.E. Church every Sunday morning just like they did. She didn't have to be there for Sunday school, but they expected her there in time for the regular service, which started at ten-forty-five a.m. It was humiliating being an over forty woman living with her parents, but what choice did she have? It was either their way or no way. All she had in her name was the silver Mercedes Benz which had been paid off before she went to prison. So, she didn't have to feel like a child riding with her parents to church every Sunday morning in the backseat.

At first, Belinda was a very begrudging churchgoer who

would sit in the last row half listening, occasionally nodding off to sleep like she did as a teenager. Then, as the Sundays passed, she found herself drifting closer and closer to the front row to get a closer look at the finest pastor in the county. Alonzo Mitchum was at least six-feet tall with an athletic build and golden brown skin. Belinda might have been attracted to the handsome man if so much about him didn't remind her of Desmond. If he had green eyes, yellow skin, and curly hair, he'd pass for Desmond's twin brother.

This past Sunday, Belinda had marched down the aisle wearing a gold dress and taken a seat on the third row from the front, next to her mother. Julia was proud to have her daughter sitting beside her in church for once. She kept eyeing Belinda as if she was expecting her to jump up and run out of the building at any second. However, Belinda had become drawn to the pastor like a moth to a flame, and she yearned to be closer to the man.

As they prepared to close out morning service, the pastor did an altar call for prayer. Julia slipped her hand into Belinda's and led her down the aisle to the altar. She obediently followed her mother. Bending on their knees in prayer, they both prayed for Belinda to be reunited with her family in the near future. By the time they finished praying, Belinda's face was covered with colossal tears. Julia had both arms wrapped around her daughter, rocking her back in forth against her bosom. Wiping the tears from Belinda's face with a white handkerchief, Julia strained to help her into a standing position.

"Jesus loves you," Alonzo Mitchum whispered in Belinda's right ear. He reached down, caressing her right arm to help Julia pull her up.

Feeling like a wet noodle, Belinda managed to gather enough bearings to make it back to her seat. Standing beside Belinda with a church fan in her left hand, Sister Hattie touched Belinda's shoulder with her right hand.

"It's going to be all right," she whispered. "Just let it all out."

And that's exactly what Belinda decided to do.

After service, Belinda stood in the long line to shake the pastor's hand.

"Thank you for helping me today," she cooed, holding the pastor's hand, thinking that they were as soft as Desmond's.

"You're welcome. It's my duty to assist all who come to the altar. Hopefully, you'll be back next Sunday," he stated. Giving Belinda a broad smile, his white teeth looked like cotton against brown satin lips. The sparkle in his eyes captured Belinda's attention for just a second before he looked away to greet the next person in line. She wanted to say more to the handsome dignified reverend, but decided to keep the line moving, especially when Belinda heard the impatient sisters behind her clearing their throats.

Watching the other women in the church make fools of themselves trying to get the pastor's attention was sickening to Belinda. Even the older women giggled as they extended a hand to the pastor. And the young ladies lining the front row with their short dresses on looking like hoochie mommas were ridiculous. However, he was smart enough to greet each one with a quick handshake and a warm greeting. He did a great job of pretending not to be interested in the panties. Still, Belinda wondered about the story behind those glistening eyes of his. He seemed to be too happy for a single man in a church filled with almost three-hundred lonely, single women.

Belinda had learned from her mother that the charismatic Pastor Mitchum was originally from Austin. He was only thirty-five years old, had never been married, and didn't have any children. He had been in charge of First Jerusalem A.M.E. Church for the past year, and apparently he'd helped increase the female membership by at least fifty percent in the last eleven months. Belinda could see why, but the last thing she needed on earth was a preacher man regardless of his fineness.

"Belinda, are you ready?" Julia yelled.

Snapping back to her senses, Belinda replied, "I'm on my way!"

She had to get the pastor's smiling face out of her mind and move on to the matter at hand. Alonzo Mitchum would have to wait until a better time to flood her consciousness.

This would be Belinda's first time setting foot in the extravagant clubhouse of the subdivision in which her parents lived. Since it was a beautiful day out, Julia talked her daughter into walking the short distance down the street. After changing into a pair of comfortable athletic shoes, Belinda met her mother at the front door.

"Hi, Daddy," Belinda said, greeting her father with a warm hug, proving that she'd always been and would always be a daddy's girl. George returned her embrace with a strong grip. Dressed in gray pants and a plaid shirt, he smelled like the fatherly figure Belinda had always loved.

"Hello, sweetheart. Won't you and your mother have a seat right over here," he said, pulling out two leather chairs from the conference table.

"Oh, this is nice," Julia said, glancing around the room.

"Ah, yeah, this is one of the smaller meeting rooms they let us borrow for a few minutes," Mr. Hines stated, checking the time on his watch. "Our guest should be here any second."

"What's this all about, Daddy?"

"I was hoping to have some good news for you. But… here he is right now," Mr. Hines said, looking at the gentleman entering the room carrying a brown leather briefcase. The well-dressed man walked directly to Mr. Hines, extended his hand as well as an apology.

"I'm sorry for being late, Mr. Hines."

"No problem. No problem, at all," Mr. Hines replied, rising to shake the man's hand. Pointing to his family, he said, "This is my wife, Julia, and my daughter, Belinda."

Then, turning back to the gentleman, he said, "This is Mr. Paul Williams, the detective that I hired to help us find Desmond and my grandchildren."

Taking a seat beside his wife at the conference table, Mr. Hines crossed his legs, and stared straight at Belinda. "Hopefully, he has some information for us."

First, Paul shook Mrs. Hines' hand and then reached out to Belinda.

"It's nice to meet you, Ms. Taylor," he said, flashing a gentle smile.

"Have you found my children yet?" Belinda blurted out. The suspense was killing her. She was impressed by the presence of the slim, semi-dark-skinned man with thick eyebrows and a magnetic smile, but she wasn't here to flirt.

"Yes, as a matter of fact I have," Paul stated, getting straight to the point. Though he was eager to share the information with them, Paul was the ultimate picture of calmness. In his profession, it paid to keep your cool.

"Okay, can you tell me where they are?" Belinda asked, trying to match his calmness. Her heart was beating like it was ready to jump out of her chest as she struggled to maintain herself.

Placing his briefcase on the table, Paul snapped it open and pulled out a manila folder.

"Ms. Taylor, this is everything I know," he replied, passing the folder to Belinda. "Your family is living in Madison, Wisconsin."

"Wisconsin! What is Desmond doing with my family in Wisconsin?" Belinda asked, sliding to the edge of her seat. She picked up the folder and starting reading the first page.

"It seems that he married a young woman who was born and raised there. She had been living in Dallas and working in his office for over a year. Several months before your release from prison, he closed his practice, and put the house up for sale. They got married and moved to Madison where he became employed at the University of Wisconsin in the dermatology department. Apparently, they received a huge medical grant this year and hired Dr. Taylor as the Director. Since this was a new grant position, he wasn't listed in the regular directory which made it a little difficult to find him. His new wife, Kaira, also works as a registered nurse at Madison Memorial Hospital. They have your children enrolled in private school a couple of blocks from where she works. Both of them look like they're doing well. I've seen them for myself."

Belinda gasped for breath. It was getting hard for her to breathe in this small room.

"Did you say that you've actually seen my children?" Belinda asked, searching his face for an honest response.

"Yes, I have. I have pictures of them in the folder that you're holding."

"What?" Belinda asked. Her hands were shaking uncontrollably now. She wouldn't believe he had pictures of her kids until she saw them for herself.

Paul took both of Belinda's hands into his and said, "Take a deep breath, and let it out." Belinda did as she was instructed.

Picking up the folder, Paul pulled out several large photographs and spread them out on the table. Both her parents rushed to stand behind Belinda so they could look over her shoulders at the pictures. They couldn't wait for her to pass them around.

Jesse and Justine's melancholy faces stared back at their mother from the glossy photographs. Paul had snapped them leaving their school wearing plaid uniform pants with white shirts. Blinking back the tears welling in her eyes, Belinda turned to Paul and asked, "How soon can you get me on a plane to Wisconsin?"

Looking away, Paul released a deep sigh like he was expecting her to ask that question.

"What's wrong?" Belinda asked. "I want to see my children right away."

Paul looked up at Belinda's parents and shook his head. Both of them returned to their seats across the table from Belinda.

"Well, I believe we have a problem, Ms. Taylor," he began. "You're on probation and as such, you can't leave the state without written permission from your parole officer."

"Okay, let's call him and go pick it up today," Belinda stated bluntly. "I don't understand what the problem is."

"It's not that simple. He'll have to get a judge to sign it, and with today being Friday, that probably won't happen until Monday or Tuesday."

"Oh, great. I have to suffer through another weekend without my children," Belinda whined, placing her hands flat on the table.

"At least we know where they are, sweetheart," Mrs. Hines said, reaching out to touch Belinda's hand.

Sighing heavily, Belinda picked the folder up again, and pulled out a couple more pictures. This time she saw a profile picture of Desmond walking into the main entrance of the University of Wisconsin building. She couldn't see his face that well, but Belinda would know Desmond's svelte body from any angle. The next picture she roamed to didn't surprise Belinda at all.

"Is this his wife?" she asked. Paul nodded.

"She looks like a foreigner," Belinda commented, staring at the oval-shaped face of a dark-haired woman.

"Well, her family is from the middle east. But her parents and siblings all live in the Madison area."

Belinda chuckled. "I figured he would never marry another black woman. And I'm not surprised at how young she is either. All I can say is that she doesn't know what she's gotten herself into." Closing the folder, Belinda handed it over to Paul. She'd seen enough for one day.

Paul tossed the folder back into his briefcase, snapped it shut, and said, "I'm going to pay your parole officer a personal visit. Maybe he can help things move a little faster. I just need you to hold on a little longer, Ms. Taylor. I'll call you Monday with something."

Belinda noticed his straight aligned teeth as he smiled at her. Then, she watched him swagger out the door with the confidence of President Barack Obama. Belinda hoped he would be as successful as the President at finding her kids.

14

(Belinda's Pastor)

"Why don't you come with me to prayer meeting tonight, Belinda?" Mrs. Hines asked, standing in front of the mirror adjusting her brown felt hat. She glanced at Belinda sitting on the textured leather sofa flipping through an Ebony magazine. "It'll do you some good to get out for awhile after the day you've had. Besides, you've done all you can do. You're going to make yourself sick worrying about those children."

"Momma, they're my kids!" Belinda snapped, tossing the magazine on the coffee table. "I haven't seen them in over a year! What do you expect me to do?"

"You can calm down for one thing," Mrs. Hines replied, taking a seat beside her daughter. "I know you're worried, but what you need to do now is pray for those children. You walk around here all day every day like you're in a daze or locked up in your room watching those stupid reality shows," Mrs. Hines said, elevating her voice. "Now I'm tired of it, Belinda. That's not how I raised you!"

"What's going on in here?" Mr. Hines asked from the doorway. "I could hear you two yelling all the way from the garage."

Mrs. Hines stood to face her husband. "I'm headed to prayer service; I was trying to get Belinda to go with me only she doesn't seem to be interested." Mrs. Hines picked up her purse with one hand and the car keys with the other. "I'll see you all when I get back."

George Hines turned to stare at Belinda. He gave her that

look of disappointment that she'd seen on his face so often lately. The look that usually came with a long lecture disguised as a father-daughter chat. On second thought, Belinda decided prayer meeting might not be a bad idea.

"Hold up, Momma. Let me have a minute to get changed, and I'll ride with you," Belinda said, rushing from the room. Her heels tapped with every step she took across the polished Brazilian, cherry, hardwood floors.

Julia couldn't keep the smile from her face as she said, "Okay, baby. I'll go pour me a Coke while I'm waiting on you."

In a matter of minutes, Belinda had changed into a gray, knit dress covered by a matching sweater the same length. She'd pulled her long relaxed hair up into a high ponytail and reapplied her Fashion Fair make-up. Belinda wasn't trying to impress anyone; at least that's what she told herself, but she wanted to look good just in case the attractive pastor looked her way.

The church was as full on Friday night for prayer as it was for Sunday morning services. And just like on Sunday mornings, the participants were ninety percent female, young and mature alike, giving their testimonies. Belinda remained in her seat, shaking her head, while the majority of the church members, including her mother, walked up front to the altar. She listened to the pastor's soothing voice urging his parishioners onward.

"Won't you come?" he asked, rotating his hand. He glanced over the crowd, but his eyes landed on Belinda's face more than once. Whenever he looked at her, as if he was searching for something inside her soul each time their stares connected, Belinda simply smiled.

It pained Belinda to look at his handsome face resembling Desmond Taylor. Although Pastor Mitchum was younger than her ex, he seemed to be more mature judging from the way he carried himself with confidence instead of arrogance. Belinda could hear the caring in the way he delivered his sermons and the special prayer requests he honored tonight. While the pastor's voice was powerful, it was mesmerizing at the same time. In her mind, he was a true man of God and the total opposite of her devilish ex-husband, regardless of how much they favored one another.

Standing in the vestibule after prayer meeting, Belinda looked at Julia, and said, "Thanks for bringing me, Momma. I really did need to get out of the house tonight. I hate to admit it, but I enjoyed everything."

Mrs. Hines took her daughter by the hands. "I'm glad you came, too. I knew you needed to be here tonight. Now, I hope you don't get mad at me, but I arranged for you to meet with the pastor for a few minutes. He's waiting for you in his office."

"Why would you do that?" Belinda asked, releasing her mother's hands like she'd been burnt. She could feel her temperature starting to rise. Only she couldn't tell if the heat was from her sudden anger or excitement.

"Because I love you, baby, and you need to talk to somebody besides me and your father. The pastor is a wonderful counselor. He can help you through whatever's bothering you. Now, please, do this for me. It won't take but a few minutes of your time, and I'll wait right here for you."

"I don't need his help. I'm tired. Let's just go home so I can relax," Belinda whined, swinging her shoulder bag.

Julia sighed, placing an arm around Belinda's free shoulder. "Please, talk to him for just a few minutes. I promise not to ask you again if you do this tonight."

Belinda knew how relentless her mother could be. She could give in to her mother's request or listen to her mouth for the entire weekend.

"Okay, I'll do it. But I promise you, I'll be out in ten minutes or less."

"That's fine," Julia said, stroking Belinda's cheek. "I'm

sure you won't regret it."

Dragging her feet like a spoiled two-year-old, Belinda found herself knocking at the pastor's office door a few minutes later.

"Come in."

Holding the doorknob, Belinda cracked the door just enough to poke her head inside and say, "Hi, Pastor."

Pastor Mitchum was sitting behind his desk in a high-back, leather chair with both elbows on his desktop, looking directly at Belinda.

"Come on in. I've been expecting you."

Creeping into the room, Belinda smiled at the man as she took a seat across from him. Her first thoughts were of how warm and inviting his office felt. It wasn't at all what she'd expected. Only she couldn't decide whether it was the earthy office colors or the humble-appearing man making her feel comfortable.

The pastor cocked his head to one side, and said, "How can I help you this evening, Sister Belinda?"

Leaning back in her seat, Belinda crossed her legs. She'd become accustomed to being called sister by the good church folk. Although she wasn't feeling very sisterly at the moment, Belinda was feeling relaxed in his presence. Maybe it would help her to talk about her tragedies with a neutral party.

"My Mom asked me to come speak to you this evening. I'm sure she's told you about my past," Belinda began, eyeing the pastor, not sure how much to expose about her criminal indiscretions.

"Ah, yes, she did tell me that you were incarcerated until recently. That's when you started attending church, right?" he asked, turning his chair to the side. His voice was strong, yet gentle to Belinda's ears.

"Yes, I've been coming here since my release from prison last month." Belinda placed her shoulder bag in her lap and folded her hands across the top of it.

"And, ah, how have you been enjoying our services?" he asked, flashing a slight smile in her direction.

Nodding her head, Belinda replied, "I'm finding your messages to be quite interesting."

The pastor threw his head back, releasing a short laugh. "That sounds like a diplomatic answer if I've ever heard one."

Matching his tone, Belinda said, "Well, that's exactly what I was aiming for."

The pastor straightened his face, cleared his throat, and seemed to be pondering what to say next. Belinda thought that was odd because she would've never guessed that he'd be at a loss for words in any situation. She'd never been sold on attending church services during her marriage, but Belinda knew a charismatic speaker when she heard one.

"You know, people come to church for different reasons. And I'm not here to judge anyone, but I hope you'll find whatever it is you're seeking here at New Jerusalem," he said, staring at Belinda. Then, in a lower voice, he asked, "Do you know what you're searching for?"

Now, it was Belinda's turn to be at a loss for words. Fidgeting in her seat, she unfolded her hands, and uncrossed her long legs. *What am I doing here? Why am I even talking to him?*

The pastor noticed Belinda's hesitation and decided to let her off the hook.

"It's all right if you're not prepared to answer right now. That's why I'm here, to help you find whatever you're searching for through the teachings of Jesus Christ."

Belinda leaned forward in her seat, focusing on the pastor's words. She might not have been able to speak, but she understood the words coming across his smooth lips.

"Do you pray?" he asked.

"Yes, I pray." What she wanted to say was, "I pray but

not every day."

"Good, because as a pastor, one of the things I'm charged with is teaching people to pray. Sometimes people have the wrong idea about prayer. They tend to think that prayer is what good people do when they are doing their best, but it's not. Prayer is simply a way of getting everything in our lives out in the open before God and then allowing Him to help us."

"Okay, pastor, thank you for explaining that to me. I know that's something I need to work on." *But not today.*

"Hopefully, with time, you'll truly understand what I mean," he said, opening his desk drawer. Pastor pulled out a small-sized book with a blue cover on it, and handed it to Belinda.

"What's this?" she asked, reading the title. "Is this some type of Bible?"

The pastor looked at Belinda, chuckling at the confused look on her pretty face. "Yes, it's called *The Message*. It's the Bible written in contemporary language."

"Okay, and you're giving it to me because..."

"I'm giving it to you because I want this book to become your close personal friend. Just take it and start reading the book of Psalms and really listening to what you read. There will be plenty of time for studying later on. But right now, it's important to read, leisurely, and thoughtfully."

Belinda stood up, thanked the pastor for his time, and casually tossed the book in her bag. It was way past the time for her to leave.

"Please, let me walk you to the door." Pastor rose from his seat and rushed to Belinda's side. "I'd like to speak with you again soon if that's all right. I really didn't give you a chance to talk much about yourself."

"That's all right, pastor. I didn't really want to talk about myself. It was just a pleasure listening to you."

"Well, thanks for your ears. Now that we know each

other a little better, I'm hoping that I can depend on you to do some volunteering around the church. I could certainly use some help in the young people's ministry with our campaign against violence and all. I know you'll be able to deliver a positive word to them."

Belinda smiled up at the pastor. She wasn't sure how positive her words would be to the youth considering what she'd experienced in prison, but from the staccato of her heart, she had some positive words for him.

"I won't let you down."

"Good, good," the pastor said, grasping Belinda's hands. His eyes stared into hers like he was expecting her to say more. "You know, I'm planning to turn our congregation into a megachurch within the next five years. So I need all the help I can get around here."

"That would be something," Belinda said, releasing his hands. "My parents are certainly devoted members, and I look forward to doing my part as well." Belinda exited the minister's office and walked down the hallway with her head held high enough to be a runway model.

"How did it go, baby?" Mrs. Hines asked the second Belinda reached her. She was still standing in the vestibule chatting with one of the church mothers. Noticing the extra bounce in her daughter's step, she couldn't hide a smile.

"It went well. Thanks for setting that up," Belinda replied, holding open one side of the double door.

"I told you he was a wonderful counselor. Are you going to meet with him again?"

"I sure hope so," Belinda responded grinning, hoping her mother didn't notice the double meaning of her reply. "He even gave me a Bible to study."

"That's nice. I think you're going to get to know our pastor real well."

Belinda smiled inwardly and outwardly. That was definitely her plan. The young hussies would have anything on a seasoned woman of the world. She'd seen more than simple concern for her soul in that man's eyes. The minister needed a worldly woman to help him run things.

Her initial reluctance regarding the pastor was fading fast. If she could get past his Desmond-like, good looks, they'd make a magnificent couple. She'd fooled the parole board with her Christian-like behavior, how difficult could it be to continue the charade? Not that she wanted to be a preacher's wife, but Belinda reasoned that it wouldn't hurt to spend some quality time with the ambitious man. Besides, volunteering at the church would give her something to do instead of moping around the house all day watching her mother drink Coca-Cola and read *Ebony* magazine.

15

(Belinda's Flight)

Tuesday didn't come quickly enough for Belinda. She was finally boarding a plane at Delta Airlines this morning to be reunited with her family. The anticipation of seeing how much Justine and Jesse had grown had kept her up most of the night. By the time Belinda drifted off to sleep, Mrs. Hines was waking her up, and telling her to get changed.

Paul Williams, the detective, had called their house after five yesterday informing them that he had obtained legal permission for Belinda to travel with him to Wisconsin and had purchased first-class plane tickets as well. Within an hour, she had packed enough clothes to change every day for at least two weeks.

Belinda brushed a speck of lint from her stretch, suede pants suit, buttoned down her black leather coat, and pulled on a pair of soft suede gloves. Now she was ready for the cold winter storm Paul had warned her about. Nothing was going to keep her from making this flight. Belinda didn't care anything about the weather conditions as long as the plane landed in Wisconsin safe and on time.

"Mr. Williams, I haven't had a chance to thank you for everything you've done," Belinda uttered, settling into her window seat.

"You don't have to thank me for doing my job," Paul replied, fastening his seatbelt. "And since we're going to be together a lot over the next few days, you can call me by my first name."

"No problem, and you can call me Belinda."

They both stopped what they were doing as the voice on the intercom intruded.

"Passengers, this is your captain speaking. We're preparing to take off in a few minutes for a direct flight to Madison, Wisconsin. Our expected travel time is two hours and fifty-five minutes. So, sit back, relax, and enjoy your flight."

"Oh, goodness, that's a long time. Can't this plane fly any faster than that?" Belinda asked, frowning at Paul.

Paul couldn't help but laugh at Belinda's agitation. "It's all right, the time will go by really fast. You'll see."

Releasing a sigh, Belinda asked, "Well, now that we're in the air, what's the game plan?"

Adjusting his seat, Paul replied, "The plan is to call Desmond after we check into the hotel and set up a time to meet with him and the kids this afternoon. Hopefully, he'll be amenable to that."

"What do you mean by hopefully? I'm their mother. He can't stop me from seeing my children," Belinda hissed, pointing to her chest.

"I'm sorry to say this, but yes, he can. He has sole custody, remember?" Paul whispered. "So you need his permission to see them."

Belinda opened her mouth to respond, only the words wouldn't come out. This fine looking joker was about to make her act a fool in the first-class section. She snapped her mouth shut and spoke through clinched teeth.

"I don't give a damn about that. I wish he would try to stop me from seeing my own children."

"You might not care, okay, but I'm responsible for you. I don't need you getting arrested on my watch. So let's try playing the game by the rules and see what happens," he said, placing a hand on Belinda's arm.

At the mention of the word arrest, Belinda glanced down at his warm hand, and decided to mellow out. The last thing in the world she needed to do was violate her probation. Prison was the one place she never wanted to see again.

"All right," she relented. "I'll try playing it your way."

"Thank you," Paul said, sliding down in his seat. He put his hands together like he was about to pray. "Let's enjoy the rest of our flight and see if we can get to know one another better. How does that sound?"

"Fine, what would you like to know about me?

"Have you been to Wisconsin before?"

"No, I've never had any reason to visit before. What about you?"

"Yes, my work has brought me here several times. I know that Madison is the capitol of Wisconsin, and the dome shaped structure is based on the dome of the U.S. Capitol. And it's the second largest city in Wisconsin next to Milwaukee."

"Thanks for the history lesson, Mr. Williams."

He laughed. "You're welcome, anytime. I'm sort of a history buff."

"So, what else do you do with your time when you're not playing detective or historian?"

"I bowl a lot, just about every Friday night. My bowling team has won our district championship two years in a row," he said, proudly. "What about you? What are some of the things you like to do?" He leaned in closer to Belinda.

"I don't really have any hobbies if that's what you mean, unless shopping counts as a sport."

Paul laughed, and said, "Nah, I don't think so. If it did, you'd have a lot of competition, including my ex-wife."

"I'm ready to get off of this plane so I can get comfortable." Belinda fidgeted in her seat. "What's the name of the hotel we'll be staying in?"

"It's called the Madison Concourse Hotel. It's only five

miles from the airport in the heart of downtown. You'll love it. It's a magnificent place located across the street from the capitol."

"Well, I'm not here to see the capitol so it doesn't matter to me," Belinda snapped.

"I was just trying to answer your question. Most people like to know when they're visiting a capitol city. You don't have to be so short with me."

"I'm sorry, Paul." Belinda noticed the hurt in his eyes and realized that she wasn't being congenial with someone who'd been doing his best to help her. "I didn't mean to be snappy. I'm just tired and frustrated. I've been up most of the night."

"I understand. Listen, I know what you've been through. And I'm here for you. I don't know how I'd feel in your position," he said, giving Belinda a sympathetic smile, which she returned. *I wonder if he knows everything that I've been through.*

"Thanks, Paul, you're a really nice man. I was just wondering. How did you get into this line of work?"

"It's a long story. How about I just give you the short version since we won't be aboard the plane all day?"

"I'm listening," Belinda responded, relaxing against the back of her seat. She was eager to hear the story of how this appealing man became a detective.

He was about to begin when the airline stewardess interrupted long enough to offer them soft drinks or coffee. Both of them passed, and Paul began.

"Well, I actually worked in construction for about fifteen years. I was married to a lovely woman during that time. We never had any children, but I loved her just the same. About five years ago, I started noticing a change in my wife."

"Really, what type of change?" Belinda thought the story was interesting so far. She tilted her head so she could hear him well.

"You know, she started coming home late, disappearing on the weekends, not returning my phone calls, and things like that. Then, I started seeing changes in her personality. You know, she didn't ever want to talk or be intimate with me anymore. So my curiosity just finally got the best of me. I decided to rent a car for a couple of days and followed her around. Needless to say, I found out that she was having an affair with more than one man, and we ended up getting a divorce. When I told my friends what happened, some of them complained their wives and girlfriends were treating them the same way, so several of them hired me to do a little surveillance. Eventually, I was making more money from the side gig than my regular gig. Anyway, I thought it was time for a career change, so I applied for my license and the rest is history."

"Has it been personally rewarding or just a job?"

He took a few seconds to think before responding. "It's been different. And that's exactly what I needed. But I'd have to say—I'd have to say that it's been personally rewarding to some extent."

"How so?" Belinda asked, using a curious expression.

"Well, I look at it like I'm helping these men and women. I mean, if you're living with a liar, you deserve to know about it. Now, if you chose to stay with that person, then that's on you."

"Have all of the men and women you investigated been cheaters? I mean did you ever have a case where you found out that the spouse or whatever was being faithful?"

"Oh, yeah, it's happened before, but only a couple of times. Ninety eight percent of the people who suspect their mates of cheating are correct. Let's be real about it. Most intelligent people can feel when something is wrong in their relationship. They just need that solid proof to help them make an informed decision."

"Let me ask you one more question, Paul. Have you ever had anyone to find out their mate was cheating, but they decided to stay with him or her anyway?"

Paul lowered, and then raised his head. "Yes, that happens, too. It surprises the hell out of me, but I've seen it occur."

Belinda's ego was soothed by knowing that she wasn't the only coward who'd ever decided to remain with a Casanova.

"Well, it sounds like you enjoy your job. It's certainly an interesting line of work. I've played detective with my ex-husband a few times myself."

"It started out as a hobby. I didn't think much about it at first. Then, I realized that these men were actually paying me well to do something I didn't mind doing for free. Now I get to travel everywhere, stay in five star hotels, and eat the finest foods at someone else's expense. What could be better than that?" Paul looked at Belinda, waiting for her to agree.

"You're right. I never thought about it like that," Belinda replied, staring into his eyes. She found herself getting lost in his funny stories and the cadence of his voice as he recalled one case after the other, being careful not to disclose any names. Still, the more he talked, the more Belinda realized he was a strong but sensitive man who'd been hurt by love the same way she had, only he knew how to use humor to deal with his problems. He had Belinda laughing like she was in the audience at the taping of a BET comedy show. She would have laughed even harder if she hadn't seen a trace of herself in some of the wives he described. Belinda wondered, "Was I really that bad? No, I was worse."

They communicated like former classmates at a twentieth year, high school reunion trying to catch up on one another's lives until they were interrupted for the final time. Holding in her laughter, Belinda tried listening to the intercom.

"Ladies and gentlemen, this is your captain speaking again. We're preparing for landing in the beautiful city of Madison, Wisconsin. The temperature right now is thirteen degrees under cloudy skies with an eighty percent chance of snow later today. I hope you'll enjoy your stay here. Please remain seated until the "unfasten your seatbelt" sign comes on. Thank you for flying Delta."

"Well, looks like we made it," Paul beamed.

"Yes, we did." Belinda glanced at the passengers rushing off the airplane. She wanted to push everyone out the way and run through the airport, but Belinda placed a hand over her heart like she was about to recite the pledge of allegiance. Sighing, she eyed Paul's calm demeanor and willed herself to be patient because her wait was over. Believing that she'd be reunited with her children before the end of the day, Belinda asked herself, "What could be better than that?"

16

(Belinda's Desire)

It was snowing around noontime as they stepped out of the yellow taxi in front of the Madison Concourse Hotel and newly renovated Governor's Club. Holding her head back, the snow drops tickled Belinda's face. Even though the captain had said the temperature was in the mid-teens, it didn't feel that cold. Growing up in Michigan, she'd loved playing in the snow with her childhood friends, but since Belinda had been living in Dallas, snow this heavy was a thing of the past. Turning her head, Belinda had a clear view of the State's capitol and had to admit that it did look like a replica of the White House, and wondered how sparkly it would look at night.

"Now that we're all checked into the hotel, would you like to get a bite to eat before we head up to our rooms?" Paul asked, returning his business credit card to his wallet. They were standing in the main lobby surrounded by the complete luxury of the premier facility. Belinda felt comfortable in the midst of well-dressed patrons entering and exiting through the rotating doors. Even the air smelled wealthy.

"No, I'm not hungry. I'm just ready to talk to Desmond."

"Ah, you're not going to talk to him, I am."

"I thought you said…"

"Listen to me for a second, please. Let me talk to him alone first. If you talk to him right now, he's going to get all defensive and blow us off. Just give me an opportunity to pave the way for you. That's all I'm asking."

Belinda couldn't focus. Her mind was on one thing and one thing only, and that was getting to her children. She hadn't come all this way to pussyfoot around with Desmond or Paul.

"Let me walk you up to your room. You can relax for a minute while I call Dr. Taylor and work out a time for us to meet."

Belinda wasn't happy with his strategy. However, her more reasonable side won the debate. She had to be careful or risk losing everything.

"Fine," Belinda stated, strutting across the hotel lobby.

Entering her Jacuzzi suite located on the executive level, Belinda instantly fell in love with the contemporary design of the inviting space. She surmised that the millions they'd spent on renovations would be a profitable investment for the owners of the hotel. As she passed through the living room that showcased a forty-two-inch plasma television, her eyes were drawn to the expensive framed artwork placed around the spacious area. In the bedroom, the walls and satin window treatments offered a rich contrasting color palette to the look of the luxurious quilted bedding and plush carpeting. Pulling the comforter back, Belinda ran her hands across the crisp, three-thread count linens and awed at the triple sheeting.

Walking across the bedroom, she was pleased with the twenty-inch flat screen television by the bed, granite top furniture, and the large work desk offering high speed wireless connections, and an ergonomically designed chair. Belinda entered the spacious bathroom, admiring the marble floor tile, the glass walk-in shower, granite countertops with under-mounted sinks, and a private oversized Jacuzzi with a twenty-inch flat screen completed the grand package.

Belinda walked back to the bedroom, kicked off her Sergio Rossi pumps, and sprawled across the king-sized bed. She was dog tired, but a nap was the furthest thing from her active mind. Only minutes had passed before Paul was knocking at her door.

"Did you talk to Desmond already?"

Paul nodded his head as he entered the room carrying his computer bag. "Yes, I did. He said it's not possible to see them today. He's going to meet us at nine-thirty in the morning in the private lounge here at the hotel."

"Why can't we meet with him this afternoon? I tell you that devil is up to something, Paul. He's trying to play me," Belinda stated, pacing the room.

"Well, he wasn't too thrilled to know that you were here in Madison, but I managed to talk him into meeting with us so we have to take that for now."

Belinda stopped and stared at Paul. "This is driving me crazy. I don't trust Desmond."

Paul swaggered over to Belinda. Placing his arms around her shoulders, he said, "I know what you mean. But he's not going to do anything outrageous. He has a job and home here; you're not a threat to him. Now, I have an idea."

Belinda watched as Paul sat down at the wooden desk and pulled out his Toshiba laptop computer. "I'm going to sign onto the Internet and log onto this site called Facebook. Are you familiar with it?"

"I've heard something about that and MySpace, but I don't spend a lot of time on the Internet. It's a waste of time for me."

"Well, I'm not into a lot of the new technology and all the social networking websites that are privately owned like Twitter and Facebook. Somehow Facebook has really become popular with teenagers. Anyone over the age of thirteen with a valid e-mail address can become a user, so I was thinking we might be able to locate your kids on here," he said, logging into the site.

Now Belinda was suddenly interested in technology, too. Maybe this Facebook thing would be worth a try. "How does this work?" she asked, pulling a chair next to Paul. She leaned closer to him, staring at the computer screen.

"It's real simple. Once you set up a free account, you complete a profile, and then you can post messages on your wall and interact with other members. All I have to do is type a name in the search line at the top of the page and see what happens."

Belinda watched Paul type in Jesse's name first. A list of eight-hundred and sixty-six results came up. "That's a lot of people with my son's name. Try a search including his middle name, Lamont."

Paul typed in Jesse's full name and came up with zero results. Then, he tried Justine's full name which yielded the same results. Next, he just put in her first and last names and there were two-hundred and eighty-six members registered under that name.

"Okay," Belinda began, turning the computer towards her. "Show me how this works, and I'll go through every one of these profiles until I find my children."

Hours later, Paul returned to the room and asked if Belinda had any luck on Facebook.

"No, I got tired of sitting at the desk and came over here to relax. I can't believe I fell asleep in the bed with my fingers on the keyboard," she said, rubbing her eyes. "But I'm going to keep going if I have to stay up all night again tonight."

"Well, if that's the plan, we might as well order room service and make ourselves comfortable," Paul said, sliding a menu between his fingers. "Let's see, I think I'll have the chef's special, filet mignon with braised oxtails and purple potato puree."

"Mmm, that sounds exquisite."

Paul continued reading the meal description. "The filet mignon is tender but discreet in flavor, while the oxtail is incredibly flavorful." He paused to glance at Belinda. "That sounds like a winner to me."

Belinda agreed with his suggestion, adding the mascarpone torte with illy espresso sauce for dessert to their order. Gripping the laptop with both hands, she scooted over to the desk, and continued her Facebook friends search.

Paul picked up the remote, turned on the plasma television, and asked, "You don't mind if I stretch out on your bed, do you?"

"No, of course, not" she replied, with a wave of her hand. "I appreciate the company because I don't want to fall asleep again. Besides, I need you to tell me what to do when I find one of my kids."

After enjoying a three course meal together, Paul fell asleep lying across Belinda's bed while watching a rerun episode of CSI: Miami. It had become one of her favorite shows, too, only you wouldn't know it from the way she ignored it tonight. Belinda was all caught up in another program that ranked higher on her priority list than any television show she'd ever watched. Thinking that this new technology and social networking was amazing, her attention remained fixed on the computer screen. While strolling down another search results page, Belinda cocked her head at the faint sound of snoring coming from the man in her bed.

Switching her attention to Paul, lying with his back against a pillow, she scanned every inch of his toned body with admiring eyes. Belinda licked her slick lips. She could still taste the steak they'd devoured earlier, but she was developing a taste for another type of meat right about now. One she hadn't had the pleasure of sampling in quite some time. And this meat was well done on the outside just like the other one she'd savored.

He wasn't physically the type that she was normally attracted to, but he was attractive nonetheless. Belinda preferred taller men with lighter skin and longer money. In the short time they'd known each other though, she felt a sense of trust with him that she'd never felt with any other man. He had a gentleness about him that was difficult to resist, especially since she hadn't been intimate with anyone since before her divorce. And Belinda couldn't even remember the last time she'd had an orgasm from Desmond's limpy lovemaking. He was all about getting his and leaving his wife to fend for herself. If it hadn't been for those sex toys she'd purchased at one of those Party Gals functions, Belinda would have gone insane years ago. Fortunately, something from her collection of uniquely shaped vibrators was sometimes better than the real thing.

But now that Belinda was drooling at the site of Paul's warm body stretched out on her bed, she was feeling an urge to merge with him. Belinda was reaching out to touch some part of his anatomy, but decided to take another look at the computer screen.

At the top of the search page, a young lady's blurry face caught her attention. Belinda asked herself, "Could that be Justine?"

"Paul, wake up! I just found my daughter!"

Paul sprang to life, scuffling to sit up on the side of the bed. Belinda turned the laptop towards him and pointed at her daughter's face. "It's her. What do I do now?"

"You click on the 'add as friend' icon and wait to see if she responds," he replied, rubbing his sleepy eyes. His voice was deeper than usual.

Belinda did as she was instructed, then read down Justine's profile page. She clicked on the button to see Justine's hundreds of friends and saw Jesse's name. Belinda went to his wall, and sent Jesse a friend request as well. She wasn't alarmed by the thousands of female friends on Jesse's page. Belinda had figured out a long time ago that her son had a fondness for the opposite sex that was only surpassed by his Casanova father. Her only hope was that someday he'd treat his family better than Desmond had ever treated them. Belinda pondered what lies Desmond could be telling the children about her.

"How long do you think it'll take them to get back to me?" Her heart was speeding like a runaway train about to jump off the track.

"I have no idea. It just depends on whether or not they're online right now. Every time someone receives a friend request, they send an e-mail notification to them."

"Oh, that's how it works. I hope at least one of them responds tonight." Belinda couldn't sit still any longer. She stood up, glided over to the window, and pulled back the satin curtains. The view was just as beautiful as she'd imagined it would be when they'd arrived earlier today.

"Didn't I tell you that you'd love this place? The night view from here is incredible. It's very romantic, isn't it?" Paul asked, strolling towards her. His mind was fully awake now and so was his body.

"Yes, it is. It's just too bad we're not romantically involved," she replied, smiling to herself.

"Well, we could be," Paul whispered, wrapping his arms around Belinda from behind. She shimmered like the cold winds from outside had touched her body. "It's all right."

Stroking her arms with his heated hands, Paul pulled Belinda even closer to his firmness. His tender lips found Belinda's earlobe. He nibbled on it for a second, and said, "I can take care of you."

Placing her hands over his, Belinda wanted to believe that. Maybe she could for just one night. Maybe she could pretend they were more than friends. Maybe they could do all the things that lovers do, and she'd worry about the consequences tomorrow. Belinda told herself that her body deserved some manly attention. She'd completely forgotten how wonderful it felt to be in the presence of man who wanted her.

Belinda maneuvered around to face Paul. Stroking his bushy eyebrows with her thumbs, she studied his darkening eyes. Placing her thick lips on his, she licked the top one with her scorching tongue. He did the same to her only with more fervor. Their bodies collided like two magnets unable to pull away from one another without extreme force. Their moans could be heard outside the bedroom door, but that didn't stop them from moaning even louder.

Neither one wanted to loosen their grip on the other so they slid down onto the carpet while maintaining their passionate lip lock. They kissed each other with such intensity that the building could have tumbled down around them, and they would have been oblivious to it. A fire could have blazed out of control through the room, and they would have been too heated to notice.

Finally, Paul found the inner strength to release Belinda. He raised his head gasping for air, and cooed, "You're trying to kill me."

Belinda giggled, reminding Paul of an infatuated teenager as he struggled to rise. Reaching out his hand, he gently pulled her up. She followed him to the bed as he lowered his back onto the silky comforter, motioning for her to get on top of him.

"Come here," he said, grinning.

Belinda straddled his body, leaned over, and reclaimed his juicy lips. She was ready to release all her years of sexual frustration on a willing partner, someone who could give her the super sexing she craved. *This is going to be so good.*

"Are you ready for me?" she asked, peering into his anxious eyes.

"What do you think?" he asked, licking his lips.

Overcome with desire, Belinda was raising her hands to unbutton his shirt when she heard the computer's animated voice say, "You've got mail."

Belinda scrambled over Paul's excited body rushing to

the computer. She read the message out loud saying, "Justine Taylor added you as a friend on Facebook."

17

(Belinda's Confrontation)

Belinda was the first one to enter the private lounge on the twelfth floor at nine o'clock Wednesday morning. Her nerves were bad, and she needed time to get them settled down before meeting with her ex-husband. That's why she was wearing her favorite designer-styled, burgundy power suit. It had taken three clothes changes to get to this outfit, but it gave her the extra confidence she needed to face someone who had made her feel so worthless in the past. Belinda wanted to show Desmond that he hadn't broken her spirits and that he never would. Over and over again, she'd replayed the scene in her mind. Desmond would walk through the door, be taken in by her ageless beauty, and beg for another chance. Only she would laugh in his face, demand custody of her kids, and leave him on his knees crying like the wimp that he was.

She'd already called Paul, informing him that she was heading out early. Walking past a waiter who was standing behind the food bar wearing a crisp white shirt with a black vest, Belinda found an available table in the sitting area next to the business corner. She partook of the complimentary continental breakfast which included fruit, various pastries, and pancakes. Since she only drank fresh coffee, Belinda asked the available waiter to bring a pot of brew to her table. After the close call she'd had last night with Paul Williams, she needed a strong cup of brew loaded with cream and sugar to help clear her head and remember why she was here in the first place.

Belinda couldn't think of anything worse than becoming sexually involved with someone working for her father. "It's easy to get distracted by a handsome man when you haven't had any in a long time. I hardly know the man, yet I was about to give up the goods. He seems nice and everything, but I need to be on my A-game to deal with Desmond this morning," she thought.

The excitement from reconnecting with her daughter last night online had Belinda floating on a natural high. Justine shared that she'd been on Facebook for months hoping that her mother would eventually find her there. Desmond had forbidden them to call their grandparents or any of their friends in Dallas, but he couldn't keep them from the Internet even if he'd tried. He'd changed their cell phone numbers and threatened to cut off all their activities and allowances if they contacted anyone from the past. Justine didn't even know that her mother had been released from prison.

What really melted Belinda's heart was the fact that Justine had posted a picture of them together in her Facebook photo album. In the photograph, Justine was about nine-years-old wearing a pair of pink pajamas. They were sitting side-by-side on the living room sofa with their heads tilted towards one another flashing huge smiles. It reminded Belinda of one of the happiest times in her life because the bond of a mother and daughter could never be broken, regardless of time or space. Desmond had taken her daughter away physically, but he'd never separate them spiritually. "That bastard tried to take away everything that I loved. He tried to destroy me, but he's going to be the one destroyed. After I get the kids back, he's going to pay for what he's done to me. Somehow, someway, I'm going to hire an attorney to kick his ass in court," she thought.

"Good morning," Paul said, pulling out a chair. He sat down, reached for the aluminum pot, and poured himself a full cup of coffee.

Belinda greeted him, glancing towards the doorway. It was nine-twenty-nine, and she was hoping against hope that Desmond wouldn't be late this morning. The nervousness she felt in the pit of her stomach was making Belinda feel like a prisoner again. So much for arriving early to calm herself. She couldn't figure out why this man was still causing her more grief. Hadn't he already done enough to hurt her?

Belinda was thinking about Desmond but kept her eyes on Paul while he did his best to avoid hers. Words couldn't describe how fast she'd dropped him last night after hearing the computer say, "You've got mail." Then, when Belinda saw that Justine had confirmed her as a Facebook friend, it was all over until almost midnight. They used the Instant Messenger function to chat back and forth in real time. Once she realized that Paul wasn't trying to go anywhere, she politely asked him to give her some privacy.

"Are you sure that's what you want?"

"Yes, I'm sure," Belinda responded, heading towards the door. "Things got pretty heated, but we need to focus on why we're here."

"I agree," he said, placing one hand on the door handle. "Call me in the morning when you're ready to go."

Belinda ogled Paul sitting beside her now; wondering what was going through his mind. As much as she liked him, Belinda knew he'd never be able to give her the rich lifestyle she'd grown accustomed to living. Staying with her parents was already a huge step down. They had money, but it wasn't as long as Desmond's doctorial salary. If she ever got her kids back, she could work on finding a new man, like the pastor, who could at least meet some of her expensive expectations.

Taking a sip of coffee, Paul lowered his cup, and asked, "Are we going to talk about last night?"

Belinda wasn't trying to avoid the subject; she just didn't want to be the one to bring it up. And she really wasn't ready to discuss it at that particular moment. She wasn't ready to tell him that she'd almost made the second biggest mistake of her life last night.

"I think we should…" Belinda stopped in midsentence at the sight of Desmond, looking like his usual smug self, walking towards her wearing a navy suit with a heavy coat draped over one arm. Except for the short beard and a few gray hairs at the temple, he'd hardly changed.

Belinda couldn't help it. Her stomach did three somersaults at the very sight of him. It seemed she'd sucked all the air out of the room into her lungs and didn't have the strength to blow it out—even if it meant that she would never breathe again.

"Well, well, if it isn't my ex-wife," he said, halting at the table. He extended a hand towards Paul and said, "You must be Mr. Williams. I'm Dr. Desmond Taylor."

Paul rose halfway up from the table, shook Desmond's hand, and said, "Yes, I am. Thanks for meeting us this morning. Please, pull out a chair and join us."

Belinda didn't speak; she just glared at Desmond as if she was trying to send him a telepathic message. Willing herself to be cool, Belinda finally exhaled and politely offered her ex a cup of coffee.

"Thank you, Belinda," Desmond responded, faking a surprised expression. "I didn't know you had it in you to still be nice to me."

"Why wouldn't I be nice to you, Desmond?" she asked sarcastically, filling his cup. "I mean, you are the father of my children."

He eyed Belinda for a few seconds, studying her body language before he spoke. "Okay, let's cut through the chase.

Tell me why you're here," Desmond demanded, adding artificial sweetener to his black coffee.

"Don't play games with me, Dez. You know the only reason I tracked you down is to see my children," she said, folding her arms across her chest. Belinda leaned her elbows on the table, raised her voice an octave, and continued. "What did you think I'd do? Drop out of their lives forever?"

"You know, it's funny you would mention that because that's exactly what I was hoping you'd do. You know, you don't deserve those kids. I'm trying to protect them from living a life of shame. Who wants a convicted criminal for a mother?" he asked, staring down his narrow nose at Belinda.

"You've got some nerve," Belinda began. "You're a..."

"Stop!" Paul interrupted. He placed both hands on Belinda's shoulder blades and both eyes on Desmond. "Let's not get into a name calling brawl. Dr. Taylor, I know you did what you thought was best for your kids, but Ms. Taylor has suffered a great deal and lost a lot in the last year. I don't think it's asking too much for you to at least allow her an opportunity to visit with Justine and Jesse while she's here," Paul stated, trying to be a peaceful negotiator.

Shrugging off Paul's comments, Desmond reared back in his seat, turned to Belinda, and said, "That's not going to happen. In fact, it's never going to happen."

"What do you mean by it's never going to happen?" she asked, leaning towards Desmond. "You can't be serious."

"I didn't stutter. You are never going to see my kids again. Now get your jailbait ass back on the airplane with your two-dollar detective," he said, cutting his eyes at Paul. "And stay the hell out of my life."

Belinda stood up so fast, her chair fell backwards, making a loud thump. The other patrons turned to stare at the black woman gone wild in the middle of a premiere establishment. Placing both hands on her hips, Belinda proceeded to lash out at Desmond. This was the last time he was going to disrespect her. Not even Paul could stop her now.

"What the hell are you talking about? You're nothing but a low-life, self-absorbed, two-timing bastard!"

"You know what, Belinda, you're not the classy woman that I married, either. Somewhere during our marriage you turned into a common hood rat."

"Oh, yeah, I wonder why that is, Desmond. Running behind you and your whores made me almost lose my mind."

"Well, it looks like you did lose it if you ask me. I'm out of here," Desmond retorted, standing. He grabbed his coat, threw it across his arms, and pointed an index finger in Belinda's face. "If you come near me again, I'll call the police, and have you arrested. The only way you'll ever see those kids again is over my dead body."

"Well, that doesn't sound like a bad idea to me. In fact, I wish you'd drop dead right now so I could walk all over you!" Belinda raised a hand to slap Desmond, but he caught her wrist in midair and held it there.

"You're crazy, woman! I should have left you a long time ago!"

Snatching her wrist from his forceful grip, Belinda said, "I was crazy for staying with your cheating ass!"

Desmond wanted to spit in her face, but instead he turned his back on Belinda and moved towards the exit door. He passed the waiter standing behind the counter holding a black telephone receiver.

"Would you like me to call security, Sir?"

Shaking his head, Desmond kept speed walking towards the exit. He didn't want any more of this madness. If Belinda wanted to look like a fool, she'd have to do it by herself.

Still spitting fiery words, Belinda started to follow him, but Paul wrapped his arms around her waist, holding on to her with all his manly strength. Belinda struggled, beating him with her fists and kicking with her sharp-heeled boots.

"Let me go! Let me go! He's not going to get away with this!"

As soon as the elevator doors closed behind Desmond, Paul relaxed his grip on Belinda. She slumped down to the floor in tears. It seemed every time she promised herself she wouldn't cry again, Belinda cried even harder when she did.

The lounge remained quiet in the aftermath of Belinda's blow-out with Desmond. Not one of the city dwellers moved a muscle as they looked from one to the other trying to figure out what was going on. Suddenly, Paul felt someone tapping him on the shoulder. He swerved around to find the waiter standing beside him looking scared. The young man wiped the sweat from his brow and said, "Sir, I'm sorry, but I have to ask you and your friend to leave the lounge area now. Security officers are on the way."

Paul knelt beside Belinda and pulled her into his thick arms. She buried her wet face in his shirt, clinching the fabric with her hands as he lifted her up. Leaning against his solid frame, Belinda crept with Paul into the hallway. Balancing her weight against him with one arm, he pressed the down elevator button.

Minutes later, Belinda had regained her composure. Bursting through the door of her hotel room, she transferred her anger from Desmond to Paul.

"How could you let him talk to me like that? Why didn't you punch him in the face or do something besides hold me back, damn it?" Belinda was pacing the floor and massaging her arms like a heroine junkie feening for a fix.

"Because I didn't come all the way to Wisconsin to get in trouble with your ex behind your foolishness! You might be ready to go back to prison, but I'm not even trying to go there. Now, what you need to do is find yourself a good attorney and start working on getting your kids back.

Obviously, he's not trying to play nice."

"That's what I was trying to tell you from the beginning. I should have gone straight to see my children and said to hell with Desmond Taylor. Now, he'll never let me near them. But I'll tell you what," she continued, pumping a fist in the air. "I'm going to see them tomorrow, come hell or high water. It'll be worth going back to lock up for life if I can see Justine and Jesse one more time," Belinda said, slumping down on the bed. She was talking a good game, even though her body was saying something different. The constant mental stress in her life was starting to weigh heavily on her physical appearance. Belinda had such a scowl on her face that Paul wondered if it would have to be surgically removed.

Propping her head up with both palms, Belinda could feel the pain of a migraine coming on. The center of her forehead felt like she was receiving a Botox injection with an elongated needle. She didn't want to see the sunlight or hear the sound of anything, especially not the cell phone buzzing in her purse.

Snapping the cell phone open, she piped, "Hello, Momma. I'm really pissed right now because Desmond wouldn't…"

"Belinda, I'm in the ambulance with your father!" she cried. "He's had a heart attack! I don't think he's going to make it!"

18

(Belinda's Return)

"Thank you for flying Delta Airlines again. I'm sorry your trip was cut short," the perky ticket agent said, handing Paul his ticket. "Your flight will be boarding shortly." Luckily, he'd been able to secure a direct flight back to Dallas shortly past noon.

Belinda was trying her best to hold it together. She was trying to sit still, but from the way her legs were shaking, they hadn't received that message. Belinda was worried because she hadn't been able to reach her mother back on her cell phone, and the nurses weren't giving her any information except to say that a Mr. George Hines had been admitted to the Intensive Care Unit. She knew her mother probably had to turn off her cell phone at the hospital. Still, Belinda wished that she'd call back with more information.

Since this was a standby flight only, they had to take the last two available seats in the coach section. For once, Belinda didn't mind traveling with the commoners. She was just anxious to return to Dallas by any means necessary. No one could have told her yesterday that'd she'd be heading back to Dallas this fast without seeing her kids.

Leaning against Paul's buffed upper arms, Belinda gazed out the window at the gray clouds circling the wings of the airplane. She felt a bit uncomfortable, tugging at her navy turtleneck sweater. Belinda was too warm, her life was a mess, and it seemed like misery had decided to become her best friend forever. Just when she thought the day couldn't get any worse after being denied the right to see her own children, Belinda found herself trying to comfort her hysterical mother over the telephone. The way Julia Hines was sobbing into the telephone this morning, Belinda wouldn't be astonished to learn that she had been admitted to the hospital along with her father. She wondered if she'd be able to handle having two parents in the hospital at the same time. That would beat all she'd ever known.

"Are you all right?" Paul asked. His voice was low, filled with genuine concern.

"I've been better," Belinda replied.

Paul moved his hand on top of hers, squeezing it gently. He said, "I know what you mean. But I promise you this, Belinda, and you can mark my words on it. You are going to get those kids back."

Belinda sighed. For someone who had been so full of hope a couple of days ago, she was starting to feel defeated.

"Come on now, we've only just begun to fight. I'm going to do everything in my power to help you," he added.

"Thank you, Paul. You're wonderful. You know, we never did get to talk about what happened, or almost happened last night."

At that moment, the airplane dipped and gasping could be heard throughout the cabin. They heard a beep; looking up they saw the "fasten your seat belts" sign come on. Next, they heard the captain say, "Ladies and gentlemen, we're about thirty minutes outside of the Dallas/Fort Worth International Airport, and we're experiencing some turbulence right now due to the heavy rainfall. We're asking that you fasten your seatbelts and please remain seated for the duration of the flight. Thanks for your cooperation."

Belinda rested her head on Paul's shoulder, wondering when or if her troubles would ever end.

"Don't worry, it's going to be okay," Paul said, squeezing her hand a little harder.

The airplane dipped and shook a couple more times.

Each time it did, Belinda's heart skipped a beat, and her hands got sweatier. She inched as close to Paul's body as she could possibly get without melting into his skin. Belinda didn't know which cologne he was wearing, but it smelled like a euphoric blend of lemons, leather, cedar, and amber. It reminded her of a fragrance that Desmond used to wear, only this one was more intense. She wondered why every man reminded her of Dez and if she'd ever get over him.

Feeling her tension, Paul reached over, and said, "Come on, let me have your other hand, and let's pray." Closing his eyes, Paul bowed his head, and starting praying like a deacon on his knees in Sunday school for their safe landing. When he was finished, he opened his eyes, and raised his head to find Belinda staring at him as if he was a haunt. "What's wrong? You've never seen a grown man pray before."

"I just didn't take you for the praying kind," Belinda said, reclaiming her hands. She rubbed them together, helping them to dry.

"What do you mean? You don't think I know Jesus?" he asked, tilting his head.

"I didn't say all that," Belinda replied, looking away. She didn't want to get into a Jesus discussion with Paul.

"Well, I know the man. I may not be an A-One Christian," he added, raising one finger, "But I do know the man."

Belinda frowned. "What's an A-One Christian?" She reached into her bag, pulling out her journal, which she hadn't written in very much since being released from prison.

"What's that for?"

"It's my journal. I write down stuff about my life in it and interesting things that I learn from day-to-day. Now you were about to explain to me the definition on an A-One Christian, and I want to write it down."

"Okay, I got you. That's someone who's perfect. You know, someone who thinks that he can't make any mistakes and always talking about his good deeds. I'm not all that. I just believe in treating people right and praying every day. What about you? Don't you pray?"

Belinda stopped writing and started stuttering. "I—I haven't prayed in a long time." Straightening her back against the seat, she glanced out the window, avoiding his probing stare. "The last time I really prayed was the night before my parole board hearing. I promised God that if he allowed the board members to grant my parole, I wouldn't bother him again."

Paul chuckled and said, "You're kidding me. What kind of promise is that to make to the Lord? There's no such thing as bothering him. That's why we have prayer in the first place."

Feeling embarrassed about her confession, Belinda raised a hand to her mouth and coughed into it. She gazed out over the Dallas skyline, elated to see several buildings over seven-hundred feet in height coming into view. Relieved at the sound of the intercom, she reached for her handbag.

"Ladies and gentlemen, we've been cleared, and we're preparing to land under cloudy skies. The current temperature is thirty-three degrees. If this is your final destination, welcome to Dallas, if not, enjoy your stay here."

Directing Belinda to his late modeled Nissan Armada, Paul clicked the remote control and heard the door lock pop up. It had stopped raining for a minute, and they were able to get inside the vehicle without getting soaked. "Which hospital did they take your father to?"

"He's at Parkland Memorial."

"Okay, I'll jump on the interstate, and we'll be there before you know it. That's a good hospital. Their cardiac care unit is ranked among the best in the nation."

"And how would you know that?" Belinda asked, staring

at the driver.

"I know that's the hospital that treated President Kennedy after his assassination. Plus my uncle had a heart transplant done there almost three years ago, and he's still kicking. He received top quality care in my opinion," Paul replied, turning on the windshield wipers. It was beginning to sprinkle.

"There you go surprising me again," Belinda said, managing to smile at Paul.

"What are you trying to say? You thought I was just a dumb detective who didn't know how to pray or know about the local health care facilities?"

Belinda really didn't know how to answer that question because that's really what she'd thought about him. Now slowly but surely, he was proving her preconceptions wrong. Playing the diplomatic card, she said, "I think you're a very intelligent man. And I'm glad my father hired you."

Paul simply smiled at her response. Reaching for the radio, he tuned to a smooth jazz station with a mellow-sounding saxophone, and said, "Now, that's real music right there."

"Who is that?" Belinda asked, feeling the vibes.

"That's my man, Kirk Whalum. He does a combination of gospel and jazz. You like it?"

Belinda shrugged. "It sounds relaxing," she replied, leaning her head against the leather covered headrest. She'd never cared much for either category of music, but this soothing beat was hard not to appreciate after the day she'd had so far. "What am I going to do?" she asked herself, "I came so close to seeing my children again. Now I'm back in Dallas, and I don't know if my father is going to live or die. And I certainly don't know how my mother would survive without him in her life."

Once they arrived at the hospital, Paul handed the keys to the valet and escorted Belinda through the lobby doors.

The elderly receptionist stationed at the front desk informed them that inpatient George Hines was in the Intensive Care Unit located on the sixth floor of the facility. Jetting to the nearest elevator, they pressed the up button and waited for the doors to open. It seemed like it was taking an eternity for one of the three elevators to return to the first level. Belinda glanced around the space searching for the stairways and remembered they were heading to the sixth floor. Tapping her foot, the steel doors finally parted, and they rushed in.

Belinda stopped in her tracks at the site of her mother and Pastor Mitchum huddled together in the small waiting area. Pastor had his arm around Julia Hines, who was sobbing on his shoulder as he patted her back. Seeing them like that frightened Belinda, and she feared that the worst had happened. Swallowing the bitterness rising in her throat, she asked, "Is Daddy all right?" Belinda trembled at the thought of the answer.

Julia snapped her head up, wiping her eyes with a white handkerchief.

"Oh, thank God, you made it. I was so worried about you all flying in this weather," she said, glancing at Paul. He nodded at her and spoke to them. Paul shook hands with the pastor as Belinda bent down and hugged her mother. "Your father is resting well," she whispered.

Releasing a sigh of relief, Belinda glanced over at Alonzo's smiling face. "Thank you for staying with my mother, Pastor."

"No need to thank me. It's an honor to be with a member's family in time of need," Alonzo replied, lifting his chin proudly.

"The Pastor has been here with me since I called him this morning, right after I spoke to you. I don't know what I would have done if he hadn't gotten here as fast as he did. I thought they were going to have to admit me to the hospital, but Pastor helped me calm down," Julia said, touching the

Pastor's hand.

"When can I see Daddy?"

"He's still in the recovery room. We won't be able to see him for at least another hour."

"What did the doctor say?"

"Well, you can ask her right now," Julia replied, looking past Belinda at the young doctor who'd just entered the room wearing a stethoscope around her neck. "Dr. Chan, this is my daughter, Belinda."

Extending a hand to Belinda, she said, "I'm glad to see you here with your mother."

"It's nice to meet you, Dr. Chan," Belinda said, shaking the doctor's cold hand. She was about four-feet tall and looked like she should have been in the fourth grade instead of performing heart surgeries. Her jet black hair was pulled back into a long hanging ponytail at the top of her head, emphasizing her Asian features. Getting straight to the point, Belinda asked, "What can you tell me about my father's condition?"

"He's resting peacefully, and we expect him to make a full recovery from the triple bypass surgery. They should be transferring him back to ICU shortly. We'd like to keep him here awhile so we can monitor his heart, blood pressure, breathing, and other vital signs. If there aren't any complications, he'll more than likely be released within a week. But it should take about six to twelve weeks for him to fully recover," she said, placing both hands in her white coat pockets.

Belinda and her mother were so happy; they both breathed a sigh of relief and hugged one another as the doctor continued. "He has a long road to recovery. You want to make sure he stays with the lifestyle changes that he needs to make once he's back home. He'll still be at risk for more blocked arteries in the future, but if he takes care of himself, and follows his regular doctor's orders, the risks are minimized."

"Oh, praise the Lord!" Julia cried, squeezing Belinda's hand.

"He'll need to watch his diet and get more exercise because he needs to maintain a healthy weight and reduce his cholesterol levels. Overall, he's in good condition for a sixty-five-year-old man. Do you have any more questions?"

"Ah, no, that's about it. Thank you for the good news," Belinda replied, looking at her mother. Julia nodded her head in agreement.

"You're welcome. Now, if you'll excuse me, I have several other families I need to meet with," she said, scurrying down the hallway.

"Okay, that is good news," Pastor Alonzo said. "Now, if you all don't mind, I need to get back to the church." He shook hands with Paul, and then hugged Belinda and Mrs. Hines before leaving.

19

(Belinda's Date)

"I'd like to take you out to dinner tomorrow night." Paul was holding Belinda's hand at the front door to her parents' home, grinning as he spoke.

"That's awfully nice of you, but I plan to be at the hospital sitting up with Momma. I would have stayed tonight if I wasn't so tired. I've got to get some sleep." Belinda covered her mouth and yawned. "Excuse me."

"I understand what you're saying. Why don't we do this? Let's have an early dinner together at Spaggio's, and then I'll take you to the hospital before it gets late. How does that sound?" He leaned a shoulder against the opened doorframe.

Belinda had planned to pass on his dinner invitation until he mentioned Spaggio's, an elegant Italian restaurant and one of her favorite places to eat in the downtown area. They could take traditional recipes to unparalleled culinary heights. Many celebrities had actually been known to dine there.

"It sounds like that might work."

"Okay, how about six o'clock then?" He straightened his body.

"I'll be ready."

Paul leaned in, planting a kiss on Belinda's cheek. "I'll see you then. And wear something short and sexy," he said, in a playful tone.

"You're crazy." She laughed. He seemed to make her do that a lot.

"I'm crazy about you," he said, dancing on the way to his car.

Closing the door behind Paul, Belinda wondered what she'd gotten herself into with this "happy-go-lucky" man and how she was going to get out of it. But she was way too tired to figure it out tonight. And the way Belinda was barely moving, she'd be lucky just to make it to her bed without collapsing on the living room floor.

"Thank you for bringing me here tonight." Belinda gazed across the round table at Paul. He was super sharp in his chocolate suit, striped shirt with a silky tie, and a gold chain around his neck. His hair was wavy and brushed backwards like it had just been processed.

"It's my pleasure. Thank you for joining me." Paul stared back at Belinda. She hadn't followed his request to wear something short, but she was wearing a sexy low-cut black dress. In his eyes, she was the picture of feminine elegance.

"May I offer you all something to drink besides water?" the petite waitress asked. She recited the list of available wines and took Paul's order for a bottle of Cabernet from their private selection.

"I see you have a taste for expensive wines. Or are you just trying to impress me?"

"A little bit of both. I allow myself a few pleasures every now and then when I'm dining out." Paul gave Belinda his signature smile showing bleached white teeth and added a wink.

This was the ideal date spot. The romantically set tables with fresh, white, floral arrangements as centerpieces were a vision to behold and emitted a sweet aroma. Combined with the dimmed lighting surrounding the dining room and the gentle music playing in the background, this setting provided the perfect atmosphere for a sophisticated couple to admire one another.

They continued making light conversation until the waitress returned with two glasses of water and a bottle of their best wine covered with ice in a sterling bucket. For the main course, Belinda ordered poached Mediterranean Sea bass with braised fennel, and Paul selected the grilled lamb chops and braised lamb shoulder with potato puree.

Preparing for their salads, they removed their utensils and placed the cloth napkins across their laps. Belinda was enjoying the sweet taste of wine on her palette when she suddenly felt someone staring at them from her peripheral view. Turning slightly to her left, she saw another table with three fashionably dressed young women, and one of them had an unwavering eye on her date. She waited several minutes before mentioning her discovery to Paul.

"Don't look now, Romeo, but someone is scoping you out."

"What are you talking about?" Paul lackadaisically scanned the room and shrugged his shoulders.

"Look to my left about two tables over, and you'll see a table with three black ladies. The one in the middle can't seem to take her eyes off you."

Paul chuckled. "Oh, don't tell me you're trying to play jealous."

"Please, I just thought you might want to know in case she was a stalker or something."

Paul decided to take another look in the direction Belinda mentioned. This time, he came eye-to-eye with the striking beauty. Squinting, a feeling of uneasiness came over him. He twisted in his seated, returning his full attention to Belinda.

"I have to admit, she looks familiar, but I can't say that I know her for sure. Anyway, you're the only woman I have eyes for tonight. She can look, but she can't touch."

Raising his glass, Paul said, "I'd like to make a toast to your beautifulness."

Creating a deliberate smile, Belinda bent over the table, raised her glass towards Paul's, and heard a voice say, "Oh, you gone act like you don't know me now after you ruined my life!"

Paul looked up into the darkening eyes he'd made contact with across the room just moments ago. She was staring down at him like a lioness ready to attack her prey. If it wasn't for the negative vibrations emanating from her pores, she'd be a quite attractive woman.

Being an expert negotiator, he wanted to handle this without consequences.

"Excuse me, lady, but I don't believe that I know you."

"Like hell you don't know me! My husband paid you big bucks to follow behind me last year!" She had both hands on her full hips and a long curly weave bobbing from side to side. Shaped like a model who'd just stepped out of a fashion magazine, the young lady continued staring down at her adversary like it was about to be his last day on earth.

Paul removed the napkin from his lap, tossed it on the table, and stood up. He still didn't recognize the irate woman, but it didn't take a genius to figure out what happened in their past. Unless he wanted this to turn into a boxing match like the Thriller in Manila, he'd have to act quickly.

"Ma'am, I'm sorry for whatever pain I might have caused you. But my friend and I would like to get back to our meal," he said calmly, motioning towards Belinda.

When he turned back, the woman had her left hand raised in the air with a fork in it coming at him.

"I'll show you what pain feels like!"

Paul instantly threw up his right arm to block her assault and fired off an upper cut to her chin with his left fist. He didn't mean to knock the woman out, but he was trained to have quick reflexes in situations such as this.

It all happened so fast, Belinda couldn't believe what had

transpired right before her eyes. In all the years she'd been dining at this upscale restaurant, she'd never seen anything like this. Now Paul was bent over the woman, tapping her cheeks, trying his best to revive her. The two friends were rushing towards him like they wanted to finish what the other woman had started. That's when the two brawny security guards appeared seemingly out of thin air, holding them back from Paul.

Doing some quick thinking herself, Belinda snatched a tall glass of cold water from the table and splashed it in the woman's face. She immediately came back to life screaming, kicking, and cursing on the floor. Paul stepped away from her insults as another security guard arrived on the scene. Touching Belinda's arm, he said, "I'm sorry about this. Are you all right?"

"Yes, I'm fine."

The entire restaurant was in pandemonium. People were walking back and forth, pushing one another, trying to see what was happening. Only a few customers had sense enough to head towards the exit doors without glancing in their direction. One of the security officers was calling on the radio for back-up.

"I've got to get you out of here," Paul whispered in Belinda's ear. He stopped one of the waiters, handed him a bill, and asked him to escort Belinda outside. "Make sure she gets in a cab for me."

Belinda didn't hesitate on following the tall barkeeper outside. In the midst of confusion was the last place she wanted to be. Belinda gave the taxi driver her home address, relaxed in the back seat, and wondered how Paul was going to handle the mess at the restaurant. Belinda thought, "I could see the evil in her eyes, but I still can't believe a decent-looking woman actually acted that terrible in public. I wonder who she is. Well, whoever she is, she must have been married to a rich man to hate Paul that much for breaking up her relationship."

Belinda sympathized with the crazed female on some level. She reminded Belinda of how far a woman would go to keep a married man, especially her husband.

20

(Belinda's Invitation)

"All black women are crazy! I don't know why, but you all are plain insane!" Paul exclaimed. He was calling Belinda the next morning to make sure she'd made it home okay last night. Wiping the toothpaste from his mouth with the end of a white towel draped around his neck, he asked, "What's wrong with y'all?"

"Don't blame all of us for your drama. Some men just attract crazy women," Belinda responded, rummaging through her double closet with the cordless phone to her ear. She also thought the situation would be amusing if it didn't remind her so much of herself. Belinda knew she'd done her share of crazy stuff. She was beginning to see just how stupid she'd made herself look in the past by running behind Desmond's women and always trying to hurt somebody. But at least she'd never acted a fool in public like that.

"Seriously, though, I'm calling to apologize. It's not in my nature to hit a woman, but when I saw that fork coming at me, I had to defend myself. I didn't have any control of those reflexes."

"How is she doing? Did they lock her up?"

"Nah, they let her go on home with a busted lip since I refused to press any charges against her. Anyway, I felt really bad for the lady once I remembered her case."

"You did? What happened?" Belinda took a purple suit off of a hanger, and tossed it on the bed. Maybe some of her questions regarding the mystery woman would be answered after all.

"Well, I don't want to talk about that one. Just suffice it to say he left her pretty bad off, and some people don't realize what they've got until it's gone."

"For what it's worth, you're still a gentleman in my book. I don't know how I would have responded if I'd been in your shoes."

"Thank you very much. Does that mean I get another chance to take you out?" he asked, sounding hopeful.

"I don't know. You might have another mad woman stalking you or something worse. Maybe we shouldn't see each other again." Belinda saw this as a golden opportunity to cancel her budding relationship with Paul. Although she'd felt some attraction to him at the hotel in Madison and again on the airplane, Belinda was more interested in a fish of a different species.

"Look, I have to head out to California this afternoon for a few days to work on a case out there. Why don't you think about it while I'm gone, and I'll call you when I'm back?"

Belinda hesitated. She wanted to end it with Paul. Let him know that while she found him appealing, he wasn't what she really wanted, but he'd vowed to help her get her children back. Belinda felt it would be wise to keep him around for a minute. At least until her Daddy was well enough to hire an attorney.

"Okay, I'll do that," she cooed.

Paul was elated, and it showed in his voice. "Okay, then, I'll talk to you soon. And if you want to call me for any reason at any time, you have my cell number, right?"

"Yes, I do," she replied, hanging up the phone. She needed to get dressed and get to the hospital to relieve her mother.

Belinda had called the hospital once she made it home last night to check on her parents. Mrs. Hines sounded tired, but decided to stay another night. She'd insisted that Belinda remain at home, get a good night's sleep, and come pick her up early the next morning. Considering she was still upset from that spectacle of a date with Paul, Belinda agreed. Only she was too mentally stimulated to sleep after changing into her silk pajamas and crawling into bed.

Pulling out her journal, she'd spent some time writing out all the events that had occurred since her last entry. It felt good to express her thoughts on paper. She thought, "When Momma sent me that first journal while I was incarcerated, I thought she was loony. Now, I can see that this is the best possible form of therapy. I may not ever write a book like Vickie Stringer, but I'm beginning to see some things in myself that I don't like. Maybe one day, I'll figure out how to change them. It's amazing how seeing yourself in others can make you want to be different."

As soon as the last journal entry was completed, Belinda placed the binder in her nightstand and pulled out the Dell Netbook she'd borrowed from her Mom's room. Belinda opened it, pressed the on button, and waited for the screen to light up. It didn't process as fast as Paul's Toshiba laptop, but it was all she needed to get online.

Belinda didn't even know Julia had the small computer until she mentioned at the hospital that she'd found Justine and Jesse on the Internet. That's when her Mom's face lit up. "That's wonderful, baby. You can use my new computer when you get home to communicate with them. I've barely used that thing."

Belinda could have fallen to the ground like a feather. She didn't know what had possessed her Mom to buy it, but she was planning to use it frequently. Belinda had said it before, but she felt it now more than ever that Julia Hines would never cease to amaze her. Belinda signed into Facebook with a smile on her face. It was time to see what her kids were up to. She just wished that she didn't miss them so much.

They communicated using IM, Belinda's favorite Facebook feature. Sending messages back in forth took too long to post and respond. Anyway, it had gotten late by the time she logged in, so Belinda only chatted for a few minutes with Justine since it was a school night. It usually took Jesse awhile to respond to a message, but Justine always responded immediately as if she was sitting on top the computer just waiting to hear from Belinda.

The memory of their mother/daughter exchange was still fresh in Belinda's mind this morning as she changed into the Dolce & Gabbana, purple suit with matching pumps. Spritzing on a touch of Light Blue fragrance, she checked her hair and make-up before exiting her bedroom.

Humming to herself, Belinda strolled out into the warm sunlight. She felt happy to be alive and a free woman again. All those months of being deprived of the sunshine made Belinda appreciate nature more than she'd ever imagined that she would. This was a day she planned to enjoy to its fullest. Friday's were always good.

Belinda stepped off the elevator of the sixth floor, heading for the ICU unit. She pressed the intercom button, informing the nurses that she was there to visit her father, George Hines. They buzzed her right in without question. When she stepped into the room, Mr. Hines was sitting up in bed looking salubrious for a man who was supposedly near death a couple of days ago. If it wasn't for the IV needle in his arm, he probably would have walked out of there on his own. His wife was by his side, holding his hand like they were teenagers falling in love again. Her mother spoke first.

"He's going to be moved to a regular room later today. And the doctor said he should be able to come home on Monday." Julia beamed.

"That's great news," Belinda said, bending to hug both of them.

"It sure is." Belinda spun around to see Pastor Mitchum

standing in the entranceway holding a potted green plant and smiling broader than all of them put together.

Taking in the whole picture, Belinda admired the Pastor's presence, from his freshly cut hair to his spit-shined, leather shoes. She didn't part her lips, but her insides were smiling with pleasure at the vision dressed in a blue, Calvin Klein, multi-striped suit.

"Hello, Pastor." Julia and George greeted him at the same time.

Stepping further into the small room, Pastor swaggered to the opposite side of Mr. Hines' bed and placed the pot on the nightstand.

"Thanks, Pastor. I was just about to tell Belinda and my husband how I was looking forward to prayer service tonight. We have so much to be thankful for, there's no way I'd miss it after the way we've been blessed this week."

"Well, I'm real happy to hear that, especially since I was hoping your daughter would be the speaker for the youth ministry's anti-violence meeting right after service." He turned his attention to Belinda. "I've been trying to reach you at home, but there seems to be something wrong with the answering machine or the telephone."

"It's the answering machine. I was getting ready to go out and buy a new one the morning George came into the hospital." Julia glanced at the Pastor and then turned to Belinda, expecting an affirmative response.

"I—I'm not exactly prepared to speak tonight, Pastor. I was hoping to have a little time to at least write a speech or something." Belinda nervously rubbed her hands together.

"I know it's short notice, but I'm sure you'll be fine. There's no need to prepare anything. Just come and speak from your heart. That's all I ask."

"You can't go wrong when you speak from the heart," Mrs. Hines mumbled.

"I don't know. I'm not used to speaking in front of

people. And teenagers can be a tough crowd. What would I talk about?"

"Ah, you can talk about ten minutes and that should be enough," Pastor replied, glancing down at his wristwatch.

Everyone laughed, including Mr. Hines.

Placing an arm around her daughter, Julia whispered in Belinda's ear, and said, "You can do this. I know you can."

Belinda thought she should have been the last person in human existence to be asked to speak at a church function. What could she possibly say to a group of young adults when she didn't even have custody of her children?

Taking a deep breath, Belinda peered into her mother's eyes and knew how she'd respond. She slowly exhaled, turned to the Pastor, and said, "Okay, I'll be there."

"Good!" Pastor clapped his hands one time. "We're going to have a short prayer session starting at six. And the youth meeting can start promptly at seven o'clock. Now, I've got to run. But thank you, Ms. Taylor," he said, shaking Belinda's hand.

Standing there looking stunned, Belinda didn't know what she had agreed to or what she planned to say. "Momma, I've got to go home and try to write up something before tonight."

"Well, you're a Harvard graduate. It shouldn't be too hard to put that degree of yours to good use." Julia chuckled.

"Thanks for the vote of confidence."

"Yeah, I need to go home, take a quick shower, and change into some fresh clothes. I was scared to get too close to the Pastor the way I smell." Julia fanned her underarms, turned to George, and said, "I'll be back shortly."

Mr. Hines motioned for his wife to come to his side. Julia walked over to him, leaned an ear toward his lips, and smiled. Looking up at Belinda, she said, "Your father wants to speak with you for a second. I'll wait outside."

Belinda waited for her mother to exit the room before she took small steps towards Mr. Hines. They'd been close in the past, and Belinda still considered herself a Daddy's girl. His opinion had always mattered to her even though she didn't always take his advice. With an aching heart, she moved as if she was walking on eggshells. The spirited man she'd loved all her life was still fighting for full recovery.

Smiling at her father, Belinda asked, "What is it, Daddy? Are you feeling okay?"

Mr. Hines was growing weak, but he was determined to speak to Belinda. Gradually lifting one hand, he reached out to his daughter. With his hand in hers, Belinda felt the warmth of her father as she leaned over. Mr. Hines whispered, "Please, take care of your mother."

Staring into her father's teary eyes, Belinda responded. "Of course, I will. I'll do my best."

"Promise me that you won't leave her again."

"I promise, Daddy. Now you get some rest while we're gone."

Taking her free hand, Belinda wiped the tear falling from the corner of her father's eye. She could tell he was hurting from more than a heart attack.

"You're going to be fine, and you'll be home soon."

"I should have been a better husband. I'll always regret cheating on your mother."

For a second, Belinda was stunned by his words. Gracefully accepting her father's tearful confession, Belinda squeezed his hand a little tighter. She knew he had some regrets, but wondered if Desmond has ever regretting cheating on her. She seriously doubted it.

"Daddy, what finally made you stop?" Belinda's eyes pleaded with her father. She knew this wasn't a good time to question him, only the temptation was too strong to resist. Belinda was dying to know the secret to making a cheater convert to being a faithful mate.

Mr. Hines closed his eyes for a couple of seconds, and then opened them again. He turned away from Belinda as he spoke softly.

"The woman I was seeing behind your mother's back for years, the married woman I thought I loved, died in a car accident fifteen years ago. I was really sad at her funeral. I mean I cried and carried on something awful. Then, I asked myself how I would feel if that was Julia lying in a cold casket. And it was that moment, that very moment that I realized I wouldn't want to continue living at all without my wife. So I made a decision to be a faithful husband from that day on."

It had taken all of Mr. Hines energy to complete his last sentence. Relaxing his head against the pillow, he closed his eyes and his mouth. He released Belinda's hand as she slowly pulled away from him. As Belinda stared down at her father, she cherished the peacefulness surrounding his face, and whispered, "I guess confession really is good for the soul."

"How's our patient doing?"

Belinda balked at the sound of the woman's voice. She turned around to see a rotund-shaped nurse entering the room carrying a medicine tray.

"Oh, he's doing well," Belinda replied.

"All right, then, that's what I like to hear," the nurse said, handing Mr. Hines a cup of pills to swallow followed by a cup of water. Once he'd taken the medicine, the nurse said, "That should knock you out for awhile, and I'll be back to check on you in an hour."

"Thank you, nurse..." Belinda said, straining to read the nurse's name tag. "Nurse Heidi, I'm going to be leaving shortly, but my mother will return soon."

"Okay, don't you worry. We'll take good care of him while you're away," the nurse said, pulling the cover around Mr. Hines shoulders as he began to drift away to dreamland.

She smiled at Belinda, grabbed the medicine tray, and headed out the room.

Belinda leaned over, kissed her father on the cheek, and thought she heard him say, "I'm sorry about losing the money."

Since she didn't quite understand what her father had mumbled, Belinda narrowed her eyes, and asked, "What was that, Daddy?" She waited patiently for several seconds, but her father never responded. Apparently, he'd fallen asleep that fast. Belinda just shrugged her shoulders, thinking that maybe she'd misunderstood his last statement or maybe it was the drugs kicking in.

Stopping at the doorway, Belinda looked over her shoulder at her sleeping daddy, and thought, "I'll never know why some men cheat. But it feels good to know that some of them eventually regret it."

21

(Belinda's Speech)

"God is good! Yes, he is!" the congregation sang with uplifted voices until the Pastor directed them to be seated.

"I want to thank you all for coming out tonight. I promised our youth that we wouldn't be here too long this evening. But we have several members on the sick and shut-in list who need prayer. And our own Brother George Hines is still in the hospital recovering from a heart attack. His wife has asked us to say a special prayer for him tonight. So, I'd like to ask Sister Julia and her daughter, Sister Belinda, to meet me at the altar."

Belinda followed her mother's steps down the aisle, placed her knees on the cushion, and listened to Pastor pray. It wasn't a long prayer. Still, it stirred something in Belinda. She could feel the spirit moving through her body, touching her very soul, but for some reason she wasn't ready to make that commitment to Christ. Her attitude was getting better as she began to question her old ways of thinking and acting. Belinda just felt like she needed more time to become a better person—that Christ would never accept her the way that she was right now. She wanted to clean up some more of her mess.

Returning to her seat, Belinda held onto her mother's trembling hand. She fought back the tears trying to burst from her eyes. As soon as they took their seats, Julia hunched over and released a guttural cry from deep within. Belinda held her mother in her arms, rocking her like Julia had done Belinda so many times before when she needed comforting. One of the elders was on his knees praying now, and the shouts of "Amen" could be heard from every corner in the sanctuary.

At six-fifty-five that evening, Pastor closed out prayer service. He asked the mature members to support the youth ministry by staying for their anti-violence meeting.

"You know, violence is prevalent in our neighborhoods today. We need to show our young people that there's another way. There's a positive way to handle themselves; a Godly way to take care of business. Too many of our black boys and girls are filling up the prisons today. They need to be reminded that they come from kings and queens, and we serve a powerful God who can protect and provide for all our needs."

The Pastor was pleased at the congregation's response, as many of them started clapping and standing up.

"I'm not going to preach right now. I just want to encourage you all to support the young members of this church who are taking a stand against violence. Our very own Sister Belinda will be their speaker this evening."

He waved at Belinda, flashing white teeth her way.

"As most of you know, she was recently released from the judicial system and has been here to worship with us every Sunday since then. I'm hoping that she'll share some of her experiences with our young people so they'll know how to think twice before committing an act of violence."

Belinda wasn't pleased about being pointed out like that, but she had agreed to speak. She was sure that everyone in the congregation knew about her past troubles, so it shouldn't have been an issue for her. Still, she flinched at the mention of her being in the judicial system. Although she'd felt uncomfortable returning to the fold at first, most of the members had actually been nice to her, which was more than Belinda had expected. Raising her head like a brave soldier after returning home from war, Belinda stood and waved a hand at the congregation. The proud look beaming on her mother's face made Belinda feel even more encouraged about speaking to the waiting teenagers.

Standing before a packed room in the church's brightly-lit basement, Belinda clutched a sheet of paper in her hand. At the pastor's request, many of the adult members had remained for the youth meeting and were seated at the surrounding tables, while many of the youngsters stood in the rear of the elongated space.

China Jackson, the sixteen-year-old president of the youth ministry, spoke properly as she gave their speaker a glowing introduction. She cited Belinda's educational background, as well as some of the community organizations she'd been a part of a in her former life as a prestigious doctor's wife and a dedicated mother.

Shifting from one foot to the other, Belinda tugged on her turquoise suit jacket and tried to settle the nerves in her rumbling stomach. She'd written down a few ideas, only Belinda wasn't sure which topic was the best one to speak on. After spending an hour surfing the Internet this afternoon, she'd found some startling statistics to share with the group.

Belinda stepped to the podium, anxiously adjusted the microphone to her level, and began to speak.

"Thank you, China, for that beautiful introduction, and thanks to the youth ministry for inviting me to speak. I'd like to begin by sharing a few statistics with you all this evening." Belinda placed the sheet on the podium, and looked out at the attentive audience which had grown deathly silent. Clearing her throat, Belinda swallowed her last drop of nervousness as she began sharing with the group.

Adhering to the Pastor's advice, she was wrapping up her speech in less than ten minutes on the consequences of violence. Belinda closed by saying, "It was a whole year of my life that I'll never get back. So, if you don't remember anything else I've said tonight, just remember that all acts of violence have serious consequences and then ask yourself, am I willing to accept the consequences of my actions?"

The room exploded with clapping and cheers. Everyone in the facility, from the youngest to the oldest member, was on their feet. Belinda felt like she'd just scored the winning shot at a high school basketball game the way those young adults applauded her closing.

Pastor was at Belinda's side, leading her through the crowd of people who were saying their congratulations on a job well done. Belinda didn't think she'd said anything spectacular, but she was appreciating the praise.

"I'd like to see you in my office if you have a minute." Pastor was holding the door open for her.

"Sure," Belinda replied, entering his private space. She felt more at ease being alone with him this time than she'd felt last Friday. Fitting snuggly into the black leather armchair, Belinda crossed her legs.

Instead of taking a seat behind his desk, Pastor leaned against the desk in front of Belinda.

"I like the way you handled yourself out there. You told them exactly what they needed to hear."

"Thank you, Pastor. I felt shaky when I started. But by the end, I felt pretty calm."

"Good. I think you're going to make a fine speaker someday."

"Oh, no," Belinda said, raising both hands. "That's my first and last time speaking in church, period. I never want to do that again."

"Well, you know what they say. Never say never." He smiled down at Belinda's shaking head. Tilting his head to the side, Pastor scratched his neatly trimmed sideburns.

"I know what they say, and I know what I say. So, let's drop that for now." Belinda watched Pastor scratch his sideburns again and frown like he was struggling with a way to say something to her. "What's wrong, Pastor?"

"I, ah, I need to ask you for a favor." He sat down in the chair next to Belinda, placed an elbow on the armchair, and slanted sideways. "I'd like to invite you to ride down to Austin with me tomorrow."

"What?" Belinda was astonished. "Why would I do that?"

This time he scratched his head as he responded. "My sister and some of my cousins down there got together and organized what they're calling a Cousin's Ball. It's kind of like a family reunion, but it's just the younger cousins uniting for an evening of fun. They rented out a ballroom at the Wyatt Hotel downtown. I think it's going to be real nice."

Belinda listened, but furrowed her eyebrows. She was attracted to the pastor, yet still taken aback.

"And you're asking me because..."

"I'm asking you because my sister is expecting me to bring a female guest to the ball. And, ah, I've been so busy as the pastor here I haven't had any time to date. And, ah, I thought you might want to get away with me for a day so we could get to know one another better."

Belinda patted her chest, leaned over, and laughed lightly. She was amused at the pastor's feeble attempt at asking her out. Apparently, he wasn't too experienced at this type of thing. And she wasn't exactly interested in going anywhere with him. Returning to a serious tone, she said, "As you know, my father is still in the hospital. He won't get out until Monday. I don't want to leave my mother alone this weekend. She really needs me right now."

"Yes, yes, I understand that. But I've got it all worked out. I've arranged for some of our mothers in the church to sit with Mrs. Hines all day tomorrow. We'll only be gone for a few hours. Austin is less than three hours away. We can leave after three and have plenty of time to get there before the ball starts a six. And then, we can leave around eight or nine and be back in Dallas by midnight. I just need to make an appearance. We don't even have to stay that long if you don't want to." He held out his hands to Belinda. She reached out to him.

Belinda thought for a second, "He's trying to make a compelling case. I know there are some women in this church who would strangle me to take my place right here. I knew he liked me, but I wasn't expecting him to move this fast. Still, I'm not about to be an easy mark. I want to see what his true motives are."

Shifting in her seat, Belinda stared into his eyes.

"Pastor, you have a large female congregation. I'm sure that any number of them would jump at the chance to make this trip with you."

"True, but I'm not interested in any of them. None of them have moved me the way that you have in the short time you've been here. Look at you, you're an amazing woman. I can't help it if I'm attracted to you."

Lowering her eyes, Belinda smiled.

"And I'm attracted to you, too. I mean you're a very handsome man, but..." Releasing his hands, she turned away.

"But what?" He looked confused.

Belinda stood up, wrapping her arms around herself, protecting her heart. She decided to let him know what was really bothering her.

"It's just that you remind me so much of Desmond, my ex-husband. I mean physically you remind me of him, and I might not be able to handle being with you."

Alonzo stood, moving towards Belinda.

"Come on, now. I've never met your ex, but I'd like you to get to know me and decide for yourself. This experience would give us an opportunity to communicate away from the prying eyes of the congregation. We can be loose with each other. No worrying about anyone whispering behind our backs."

"Except for your family. What are they going to say?"

"Well, ah, one thing they'll say is that I'm a lucky fellow to have such a beautiful woman on my arm," he said, deepening his voice. "You know, your mother would be excited about you going with me to Austin. She's been talking you up to me ever since she found out your release date."

"Speaking of my past, how do you think the congregation will feel about you dating an ex-convict?" Belinda leaned against his desk, raising her head to stare into his eyes.

"It's none of their business, and besides, everyone deserves a second chance in life. The way you spoke to those kids tonight let me know that you're on the right path. You just need more direction."

"And you'd like to be the director?"

"Yes, if you'll let me."

Belinda lowered her head for a second, and then lifted it again. She wanted to scream an affirmative response, but decided on using a more demure attitude, and said, "I'll think about it and call you in the morning, if that's okay."

"Yeah, that would be great!" Pastor said, giving her a warm embrace. "I'm looking forward to the phone call."

Walking around his firmly rooted body, Belinda headed for the door. She was already making plans for the unsuspecting minister and thinking, "I don't know what he wants from me, but he'll certainly make a good character witness for my custody case when I go to court to get my kids back. I just can't wait for Daddy to get out of the hospital so he can hire me a good attorney. But in the meantime, it wouldn't hurt to see what Alonzo has to offer behind that handsome exterior."

Belinda licked her lips and glanced back to see if the pastor was watching her sashay out the door. And yes, he had his eyes glued to her shapely derriere. She thought, "My goodness, a man is a man is a man. I might be able to get my groove back after all."

22

(Belinda's Trip)

"I love the GPS function on this new cell phone." Alonzo had his Apple iPhone charging in the dashboard outlet of his Toyota Sequoia sports utility vehicle. "We're only about thirty minutes from Austin. We have an exit coming up in a minute or two. Would you like to stop for something to eat or to use the restroom?" He glanced at Belinda, returning his eyes to the highway.

Belinda had her seat slightly reclined, listening to the Sounds of Blackness lead singer, Ann Nesby, confirming how she believed in the power and would never ever doubt. Wishing someone could help her believe, Belinda responded, "No, thanks, I'm fine."

"All right, then. We'll keep it moving. I know you'd like to have some time to change out of those jeans and freshen up before the ball in the hotel's dressing room."

"Yes, that will be nice." Belinda gazed out the side window. There wasn't much scenery on the interstate, so she turned back to Alonzo. She'd have to get used to calling him by his first name, now that they were doing whatever they were doing. So far, the ride was going smoothly. The more she got to know Alonzo, the less he reminded her of Desmond. He seemed to be a straightforward man with a good heart for helping people in the community. And he was exceptionally concerned about the youth population and keeping them out of the judicial system.

Alonzo graduated from a historically black college in Texas with a master's degree and joined their ministry at the age of twenty-seven. In the last eight years, he'd been working on building his reputation as an Assistant Pastor and jumped at the invitation to become Head Pastor at New Jerusalem last year. From what she could tell, he was doing an excellent job and was well respected by the elder church members. With the membership steadily rising, his dreams of pastoring at a megachurch were on their way to being fulfilled.

"Have you ever been married?" she asked.

"No, I've never been married, and I don't have any kids. Why do you ask?"

"I guess I was just wondering how a man of your status could still be single. I mean, I've seen the way the young women who wear mini-dresses and sit in the front of the church react to you." Belinda chuckled. "Don't tell me you haven't noticed them?"

"Oh, yeah, I noticed them all right. And sometimes they can be downright distracting. I've fumbled over more than a few words because of it, too," he replied, shaking his head. "But it's not as easy as you might think for a minister to find a wife. I have to be very careful that I don't step on anyone's toes. And the hours that we have to keep counseling with members are not always friendly, and some women can't deal with it."

"Okay, I see what you mean," Belinda said, batting her long eyelashes.

Alonzo looked upward. "It's starting to get cloudy again. I thought the rain was gone after the pretty day we had yesterday, but it might be following us southward."

"I just hope it holds up until we can make it back. There's nothing worse than trying to drive in a rainstorm."

Belinda looked at the dark clouds brewing in the sky as she agreed with Alonzo.

"I know, I know, it's not the ideal situation. Hopefully, we won't have that problem though."

Entering the semi-filled, Texas-sized ballroom decorated with crisp white tablecloths, floral centerpieces, and glowing wall sconces, Alonzo steered Belinda across the empty dance floor. They stopped abruptly at a table occupied by three pleasant-looking females and one familiar-looking male.

"I know the first person I want you to meet."

He had their undivided attention the second he approached the square-shaped table flaunting his platinum-colored tuxedo. All three ladies and the gentleman stood to greet Alonzo and his guest as the D.J. prepared to play the first jam of the evening. The sound of Al Green singing his classic song, *Love and Happiness*, filtered through the air the way a welcomed breeze would on a scorching summer night.

"Belinda, I'd like you to meet my sister, Anna. And Anna, I'd like you to meet my friend, Belinda." Alonzo motioned with his hand from one to the other as they shook hands and exchanged greetings. Anna had a gracious smile, a thin body, and a firm handshake. She reminded Belinda of that actress who used to be on the Young and the Restless, Victoria Rowell. Belinda could tell from the admiring look in Anna's eyes that she worshipped her only sibling.

"And these are my cousins who helped her organize this event," he began, pointing to each individual as he called their name. "This is DeWanda, Cynthia, and her brother, Bernard." They also greeted Belinda warmly. All the ladies modeled designer gowns for the festivities. It was as if a Parisian fashion show had landed in the center of Austin, showcasing the finest clothes and women in the land. And Cousin Bernard, showing a gleaming smile, could have been a reincarnation of the late, great comedian Bernie Mack.

Bernard grabbed Alonzo's hand and started shaking it enthusiastically.

"Man, it's great to see you! I haven't seen you much since we were in college together. Those were some crazy times. I mean some crazy times, weren't they?"

Alonzo hesitated for a second, like he had to think about how to answer properly.

"Well, that's true. How you been doing?"

"Ah, man, I've been doing great! Yeah, I've been doing great. I see you doing pretty well yourself," he responded, admiring Belinda's figure. "I mean you're doing pretty well yourself."

"Bernard, tell me something. How did they get you on the planning committee?" Alonzo asked, ignoring the way his cousin was ogling Belinda.

"They needed a man's opinion on this thang. You know what I'm saying; they needed a man's opinion." Bernard grinned like he'd just won an Oscar for his performance as the best supporting actor. And Belinda wondered why he had to say everything twice.

"I love your dress," Anna said, eyeing Belinda's floor length Collette Dinnigan dress in black with exquisite white trimming around the bust line.

"Thank you. Your dress is gorgeous, too. You look like a goddess in white."

"So, who picked out this place for the ball?" Alonzo asked, interrupting the girly conversation. He did a three-hundred and sixty degree turn to take in the whole room.

"Your sister found this hotel," Cynthia responded, swinging dark-blonde, highlighted bangs from her face. "She wanted to have it somewhere near the water, and she said the night skyline view from downtown would be awesome."

"And it is," Anna responded, looking out over Lady Bird Lake.

"Anyway," Cynthia continued. "You know, she has to have the best of everything. Personally, I thought they wanted way too much money to rent an orange and gold ballroom for one evening."

"Look around you, Cynthia." Anna spread her arms out like a butterfly. "This place is the epitome of luxury. And no price is too high to pay for the perfect location."

"I guess, but everybody don't have it like that."

"Okay, ladies, play nice with one another. How'd you all plan this without chopping off each other's heads anyway?" Alonzo asked, stifling his laughter.

"Believe me, cousin, it was hard being caught in the middle of these two," DeWanda said, crossing her arms, and pointing a finger at each cousin. "I had to be the constant peacemaker."

"I bet you did. But everything turned out great. This place is an eye-catching site for sure. You all did a wonderful job with the decorations."

"Thank you," DeWanda responded, grinning from ear to ear. "The colors were my idea."

As the evening progressed, Belinda found herself seated at the table with Alonzo and Anna. She'd met at least fifty of his closest cousins and wouldn't be able to match a name with a face from a police line-up if she had to. It seemed almost everyone in his family was a doctor, lawyer, teacher, or pastor. And the food tasted divine. Belinda had a plate filled with a sample of every dish they had to offer, from the grilled shrimp, cocktail skewers, to the pasta fruit salad, olive-stuffed, chicken breasts, pork tenderloin with mushroom sauce, baked salmon with seasoned vegetables, and more.

"It's almost time for us to go," Alonzo whispered. "I would like to have at least one dance with you before we leave."

"Okay." Belinda held up her hand, Alonzo took it, and led her out to the tiled dance floor. He pulled her into his arms, holding her gently as their bodies swayed together to the rhythm of Luther Vandross crooning, *So Amazing*.

Lowering his lips to Belinda's ear, Alonzo sung the

sensual lyrics along with the well-loved singer. To her amazement, he actually knew the words and carried the tune almost as sweet as Luther. When the song ended, Belinda excused herself to go to the restroom. She wasn't sure if her stomach was turning flips because of her closeness to Alonzo or the variety of food she'd eaten earlier. Either way, she zoomed past every stall in the humongous facility until she reached the one at the very end.

Belinda had been on the toilet for almost five minutes when she heard two other ladies enter the room talking loud like they were the only ones in there.

"Girl, I just need to check my make-up real quick. But I can't believe your cousin is out there parading around that bourgeois woman from his church like he's straight or something," one voice said.

"I know that's right. And his sister is getting on my nerves introducing him to everybody as Pastor Alonzo Mitchum like he's somebody special. He ain't no T.D. Jakes," the other voice chimed.

"Yeah, but he's still fronting because once you go gay, you stay that a way." She heard them laughing and slapping palms as they exited the room.

If Belinda thought her stomach had been upset before, it was really churning now. She thought, "I knew he was too good to be true. I can't believe I was beginning to fall for another damn liar. No wonder his fine self has never been married and don't have any kids. Well, I should have known better."

By the time Belinda returned to the ballroom, Alonzo was in the D.J.'s corner, holding a microphone to his mouth.

"Family, I want to thank you all for hosting a wonderful event. This has been an exciting evening for me. I'm sorry that I have to leave early, but the weather is starting to change for the worse, and I promised my date I'd have her home by midnight," he said, glancing at Belinda. Some people laughed and looked in Belinda's direction. "Before I go, I'd like to invite all of you up to Dallas next Sunday for my first anniversary celebration at New Jerusalem. I would be honored to see some of you there. Now, enjoy the rest of your evening and good night."

Belinda sighed, put on her best happy face, and started saying her good nights to everybody. She was the master of facial disguise, but it still took all of her energy to get out of the ballroom without blowing a gasket.

23

(Belinda's Night)

"This rain is really starting to come down." Alonzo turned the windshield wipers on high. It was pitched black dark, but the lightning was lighting up the sky better than Fourth of July fireworks. Sitting up straight, he peered over the steering wheel trying to stay on the right side of the road.

"Umm huh," Belinda moaned. She'd been quiet for more reasons than one for almost the whole hour since they'd left Austin.

"If this keeps up we're going to have to stop at the next exit and look for a place to spend the night. Is that all right with you?"

"Ah, yeah, that's fine. It's not safe to keep driving in this."

"Are you feeling okay? I mean you've barely said two words to me since we left the ball."

"Actually, I'm not feeling well. My stomach has been upset for awhile."

"I'm sorry about that. I did notice that you stayed in the restroom a long time at the ball. Maybe when we stop, I can get you some medicine or something."

"Okay." Belinda wanted to explode on Alonzo after what she'd heard in the ladies' room. But once they took off in the pouring rain and rapid lightning, common sense told Belinda to bite her tongue until she was in a secure location. Confronting him about his sexual orientation wasn't worth dying over in a car accident.

Minutes later, Alonzo pulled into a Chevron gas station. He filled the truck with gas, bought Belinda a bottle of seltzer water, and bought a Coke for himself. There was a Best Western Hotel next to the store, so he pulled under the covered driveway and hopped out of the vehicle.

"I'll be right back," Alonzo said, closing the vehicle door.

Belinda remained in the truck, sipping her seltzer water, and listening to the radio. She scanned the parking lot, noticing that it was packed. Belinda could see Alonzo at the front desk handing someone his credit card.

Alonzo returned to the truck and handed Belinda a key card.

"Here's the deal. They only had one room left, and it's a single bed. Now I went ahead and took that because I don't want to keep riding around in this weather, but you can have the bed, and I'll sleep on the floor. It'll be good for my back anyway. Is that all right with you?"

"Whatever."

"Are you sure?"

"I said whatever."

"Okay, okay, you just don't look like you're sure about this," he said, turning the key in the ignition. "Our room is all the way in the back on the second floor."

Alonzo cruised around the building several times before finding a creative place to park. He snatched their garment bags from the back seat and ran to the other side to help Belinda out of the truck. With umbrellas covering their heads, they sprinted through the downpour until they reached the covered area.

Alonzo pushed the room door open, and the smell of stale smoke hit them square in the face. It was freezing cold in there, too. Belinda strutted straight to the thermostat on the opposite side of the room and turned the heat on high. They were both soaking wet in their designer outfits. Grabbing her garment bag, Belinda closed herself in the bathroom and changed back into the DKNY skinny jeans and blouse she'd worn on the way to Austin.

"It's almost eleven, and the rain hasn't let up." Alonzo sauntered out of the bathroom, holding an electric toothbrush in his hand. He looked at Belinda sitting on the side of the bed barefooted, watching television, holding the remote control in her hand. She didn't mumble a word. "Why do I get the feeling that something's wrong with you besides a stomach ache?" he asked, standing between the doorway and the bed.

Placing her face in her hands, Belinda took a deep breath, and decided to let it all out. Inching her head upward, she gave Alonzo a penetrating stare.

"Can I ask you something?"

"Yes, you can ask me anything. Just please tell me what's going on." He placed the toothbrush on the bathroom counter and stepped back into the main room.

"While I was in the restroom at the ball, a couple of your cousins came in running their mouths about you. They were laughing about you being gay and trying to parade me around like you're straight. Is it true, Alonzo? Are you a homosexual?"

He cautiously walked towards Belinda with his hands out, never blinking an eye. "I can explain. Please, just give me a minute to explain."

"Oh, I'm sure you can. And while you're at it, try explaining to me how you were planning to use me to cover up your ..."

"Okay, okay, I was never planning to use you in any way." He moved closer to Belinda, easing down on the bed next to her. "Now take your time, tell me what you heard, and who all said it."

Belinda shrugged. "How would I know? I met over fifty people in that room tonight. I don't have any idea who they were. And why would that matter, anyway? Stop trying to

BS me and answer the damn question, Alonzo!"

He started scratching his face like he'd done yesterday when he was struggling to ask Belinda about coming on this trip with him. Alonzo sighed heavily like he was weighing his options about whether or not to tell the truth or try bluffing. "I'm not gay, and I'm not a homosexual," he answered, straightforwardly.

"Well, then, why would your own family members say something like that if it wasn't true? Huh, answer that question."

"I—I did some things when I was younger, but most of my family knows that I'm not like that anymore."

"Like what?"

"I'm not like gay. Look, I was confused about my sexuality in high school. And then when I went away to college, I got involved in a scene that I deeply regret. But all of that was before I got saved. Unfortunately, some people can't seem to accept the fact that I've been changed."

"What happened to you? Were you molested or something?" she asked, sounding concerned.

"No, it wasn't anything like that. I wasn't molested as a child. I was just different, and it led to confusion in my personal life."

"So how did you change? People don't just change overnight, you know."

"It wasn't overnight," he mumbled. "It wasn't overnight. After graduate school, I started attending church regularly, and studying the Bible. About a year later, I was attending an old-fashioned revival when I decided to give my life to God, and He changed me over. Through Christ, I became a brand new creature and cast my old ways to the side."

Belinda eased further away from him and shook her head. Surely, he didn't think that she was buying that. She wasn't a fool anymore.

"So, you see, I wasn't trying to use you at all," he said,

taking her hand. "I just thought that you, out of all the beautiful women in the congregation, would understand how it's possible to regret your past and want to change. I mean, isn't that why you've been coming to church, because you want to change, you want a second chance in life. Don't you want to be accepted for who you are now and not be judged on your past mistakes? Well, that's all I'm asking," he said easily, with a sincere expression.

All she could do was gaze into his droopy sad eyes, searching for the truth hiding behind them, because she really didn't know how to respond. For once in her life, she was at a loss for making a comment. Belinda pondered why she'd been coming to church recently, aside from the fact that her parents made it a requirement. But she could have defied them if she'd really wanted to. It's not like they would have actually put her out on the street. So why was she going to church. Was she really ready to change? Was it even possible for someone like her to change after all the evil she'd done?

"Belinda," he called, snapping his fingers. "Belinda, are you still with me?"

"Ah, yes, I was just thinking about something," she replied, shaking her head. "I honestly don't know what to say, Alonzo. I want to believe what you're saying, but I don't know how to process this." She stood up, rubbed her covered biceps, and walked over to the television set at the foot of the bed. Belinda turned around and noticed Alonzo scratching his head again, and instantly felt that he hadn't told her everything.

"Is there something else you need to tell me?"

Smoothing his hands down his face, Alonzo sighed again, and peered up at Belinda. His eyes answered for him first. The truth was always in the eyes.

"Yes, there's more. I, ah, I'm being blackmailed." He said it as if he didn't believe his own words. Alonzo rose up,

174   *Barbara Joe Williams*

swaggered over to the desk, and clicked some buttons on his iPhone. "Some sicko sent me this video clip last week. He sent this with a text message telling me that if I didn't step down as the Pastor of New Jerusalem by next Saturday, all my members would receive a copy of this in their email boxes on Sunday morning."

Belinda viewed the clipping for all of five seconds before turning her head in disgust. She covered her mouth, swallowed the bile rising in her throat, and downed the rest of her seltzer water.

"When was this taken?"

"That's from my last semester in grad school over ten years ago."

"What were you thinking? How could you participate in something like that?" she asked, pointing to the phone. Belinda eased down on the foot of the bed, her back to Alonzo.

"It was a frat party in one of the dorm rooms. All the guys were drunk. And all the guys there were bi-sexual, homosexual, or sexually confused like me. Anyway, one of the dudes took his clothes off, and the next thing I know, I'm participating in an orgy. I didn't have a clue or even a hint that it was being taped, but I think it was after that night when I finally realized that wasn't the lifestyle I wanted. It wasn't for me, and I started searching the Bible for answers."

Belinda turned around, facing Alonzo, narrowing her eyes.

"If you really want to find out who's behind this, you need to hire the detective that you met at the hospital. You know, Paul Williams, the one who helped me find my kids. He'll know what to do."

Alonzo curved his lips upward, showing some teeth.

"See, I knew we'd make a great team."

24

(Belinda's Meeting)

"Hi, Paul, I'm glad to hear that you're back in Dallas. How was your trip to sunny California?" Belinda grinned as she spoke into the cell phone. Sitting at a table alone in the hospital's cafeteria on a Monday morning, she sipped from a cup of steaming, hot, French vanilla-flavored cappuccino. Eyeing the burnt toast and soggy eggs on her plate, she hadn't touched either one.

"It was productive. I got the job done and came on back on the first available flight heading out before sunrise. I'm walking out of the airport as we speak. How was your weekend?"

"It was interesting, but it was quite productive, too," she responded, thinking of Alonzo's revelation on Saturday night.

"Okay, that's good to know. What are you doing tonight? Have you had enough time to think about us going out again?"

"Actually," she began, shifting in the seat, "I was just thinking about asking you to meet me at my house this evening. I really need to talk with you about something, if you don't mind. My mother will be at the hospital, and we can talk freely."

"No problem. Is everything okay?"

"Ah, yeah, everything is fine."

"How's your father doing? Any word on when he's being released?"

"Yes, there is. He's being released in the morning."

"Oh, well, that's wonderful. I know he'll be happy to see home."

"Yeah, I'm sure he and my Mom will both be very pleased to see their house again." Belinda laughed.

"What time would you like me to be there?"

"Ah, how does seven o'clock sound?"

"It sounds like a date, and I can't wait to see you again," Paul replied, clicking his cell phone. He smiled to himself, thinking of the possibilities of the romantic evening ahead.

Hours later, Paul arrived at Belinda's place one minute early and pressed the doorbell wearing a broad smile, straight leg jeans, a white cotton shirt and a brown blazer. He had a bouquet of fresh, cut flowers waiting on Belinda when she opened the door.

"These are for you," he said, handing them to Belinda.

"Oh, thank you, Paul. This is really sweet of you." Belinda looked stunned, but she couldn't resist sniffing the lovely flowers. "Come on in," she said, stepping aside.

"Okay, you look lovely this evening," he said, approving the fit of her snake-printed, long-sleeved dress.

Stepping into the foyer, Paul heard the sound of music coming from the living room. He looked backwards at Belinda, massaging his palms, and said, "I see you have a fondness for the old school music like myself."

"I guess you could say that." Paul snapped his head back around at the sound of a man's voice.

Staring Alonzo in the face, Paul's eyes bulged for a millisecond.

"Oh, good evening, Pastor, I didn't know you were here."

"Good evening," Alonzo said, shaking hands with Paul.

"I invited him." Belinda walked past both men, placing the flowers on the coffee table. "Let's all have a seat."

Belinda sat down in the recliner and crossed her legs. Alonzo sat at the end of the leather sofa closest to her while

Paul relaxed at the opposite end. Holding her hands across her lap, Belinda began.

"Paul, thank you for coming over this evening. It seems that Alonzo has a situation which requires your professional expertise. And I'm hoping that you'll be able to help him."

Paul was taken aback by Belinda referring to the pastor by his first name. He glanced at Alonzo, and then returned his eyes to Belinda, casually observing their body languages. They both had their legs crossed and appeared to be more comfortable with one another than they were the day he'd met Alonzo at the hospital.

"What type of situation are we talking about here?" Paul asked, raising and lowering his hands. He glanced from Belinda to Alonzo this time. "Reverend, would you like to tell me what's going on?"

Uncrossing his legs, Alonzo straightened his back, and faced Paul. He explained how he was being blackmailed by someone from his past and gave Paul all the details regarding how the video clip was delivered to him. When he finished, Alonzo looked drained, as well as embarrassed. His face had turned a shade darker than it was just minutes earlier.

"Wow, that's some story," Paul said, leaning on one elbow. "Do you have any idea why someone would want to blackmail you?"

"No, I don't. But I'm assuming that it's someone who knew me from college and just wants to get revenge on me for some reason or another. I really don't know."

"And they didn't ask you for any money?"

"No, they didn't request any type of financial payment. They just want me to step down as head pastor of my church."

"So, ah, who would benefit from you doing that?"

"Well, my assistant pastor would more than likely take over my position. But it can't be him. He just moved here a

Barbara Joe Williams

couple of months ago from Oklahoma. There's no way he'd know something like this about my past." Alonzo shook his head and scratched his chin.

"What about other members of your congregation? Do you have a history with any of them?"

"No, I don't. I moved here from Austin almost two years ago. And I didn't know any of the members when I started attending here."

"You know, most blackmailers are people who are the closest to you. So if you're ruling out your assistant pastor and members of the congregation, then I have to ask you this question. Could someone from your family be doing this?"

"What? No way. Nobody in my family would have anything to gain from blackmailing me. Besides, my whole family is proud of me. Right, Belinda? You saw how close we all were in Austin this weekend," he bragged, gesturing towards Belinda.

Paul turned to Belinda for confirmation of Alonzo's statement, but she lowered her eyes, smoothing both hands down her dress. He asked, "Really? What happened in Austin this weekend, Belinda?"

Belinda felt a frog in her throat. She turned her head and coughed, hoping it would leap out. Raising her eyes to meet Paul's, she replied, "They had a Cousin's Ball on Saturday night, and I rode down with Alonzo to participate in the event."

"Look, I know it's not one of my family members so let's just move on. What else you got?" Alonzo asked, slightly raising his voice.

Paul kept his eyes on Belinda as he answered Alonzo's question.

"Well, that would just leave your former lovers." Turning to Alonzo, he asked, "How many do you think that number might include, Pastor?"

Alonzo sprang from his seat like a rabbit jumping out of

a magician's hat.

"I tell you what, why don't you just look at some of my former college classmates and try to find out which one of them made the video? And that'll be your answer right there."

"Thank you for telling me how to do my job, Pastor. I just thought there might be a secret, scorned lover from your past looking to exact 'his' revenge. I mean, that's usually how these things work out. But, ah, if you let me hold your cell phone, I should be able to get to the bottom of this by the end of the week."

Alonzo pulled the phone out of his pants pocket and handed it to Paul.

"Do you think you'll be able to trace someone from that?"

"Probably not," Paul responded, eyeing the phone in his hand. "But it's worth a try. If they were halfway smart, they used a disposable cell phone, but I'll still try."

"Well, I'm praying that they weren't smart, not smart at all."

"Most blackmailers aren't. They usually find a way to slip up," Paul said, placing the phone in his jacket pocket. "And when they do, I'm there to catch them."

"No problem. I appreciate you helping me out, Mr. Williams. About how much do you think this is going to cost me?" Alonzo rubbed his palms together.

Paul stood up before he answered. "I'm sure it won't be more than you can afford. But we can discuss that when I return your phone. Now if you don't mind, I'd like to speak with Ms. Taylor in private regarding our other business," he said, gazing at Belinda.

"Sure, no problem. I need to get going anyway." Alonzo checked his wristwatch, tapping the dial face with his index finger. "I'm late for a meeting at the church. Belinda, I'll call you later," he said, speeding towards the exit.

The moment the door closed on Alonzo's coattail, Paul faced Belinda.

"This isn't exactly what I was expecting for a second date. I guess you spent the weekend with him down in Austin, huh?" Paul asked, placing both hands in his pants pockets.

"Ah, it was supposed to be a one day trip," she began, waving a finger in the air. "We'd planned to leave Saturday afternoon and return by midnight, but we got caught in a thunderstorm and had to spend the night at a Best Western. He slept on the floor, if that's what you're wondering."

"What I'm wondering is how you could spend the night with him at a hotel when we almost slept together in Wisconsin?"

Belinda crossed her arms, lowering her voice. "Almost doesn't count."

Paul shook his head in disbelief, smacking his lips. "Okay, okay, I see what's going on here. I just hope you know what you're getting into with this so-called preacher man claiming to be a redeemed homosexual," he commented, staring her down. "And you're supposed to be an educated woman."

That little dig hurt Belinda to the core of her self-esteem. But she'd be damned if she'd let it show. "Thank you for your concern. I know all I need to know about Alonzo's past. He told me everything at the hotel," she responded calmly.

"All right, then. I guess the only thing left for me to say is good night." Holding both hands out, Paul took a few steps back, and then turned around.

"Good night," Belinda replied, watching him walk past the foyer, and out the front door. She jumped at the sound of the door slamming and wondered, "What am I going to do about these two men?"

25

(Belinda's Notice)

"Okay, the discharge papers for your husband will be ready in a few minutes." Dr. Chan glanced over the top of her clipboard at Mrs. Hines radiating face.

"Finally, some good news in this place," Belinda beamed, glowing brighter than her mom.

"I need you to remember Mr. Hines' diet restrictions and make sure he gets plenty of daily exercise. He needs to follow up with his regular physician one week from today. If he should have any shortness of breath or any unfamiliar pain, you need to get him back to the emergency room as soon as possible. And make sure you get all the prescriptions filled on the way home," she said, making one final mark on the check-out form. "Do you have any questions for me before I send the nurse in to escort him out?"

"No, Dr. Chan," Julia began. "I think we got it. And I just want to say thank you, thank you for all that you've done for my husband. You have truly been a blessing to us."

"You're welcome, Mrs. Hines. Thank you for those kind words." She bent down to Mr. Hines, sitting quietly in a wheelchair. He was casually dressed in a pair of gray slacks with a white shirt, and ready to go home. "Take care of yourself, Mr. Hines. I don't want to see you back in here anytime soon, okay?" She patted his hands.

"That's fine with me because I don't plan on coming back to this place," he joked. They all laughed at his response.

"Well, you all have a great day. The nurse will get him

out of here in just a second," Dr. Chan said, scurrying out of the room.

Nurse Heidi came in right behind the doctor and wheeled Mr. Hines to the elevator. When the elevator doors opened on the first level, Belinda ran ahead of them to get the Mercedes. By the time she made it back to the front entrance, several nurses had come downstairs to help them load the overwhelming amount of cards and flowers from their family, friends, and church members. Belinda waited patiently for both of her parents to get settled inside the luxury vehicle before driving away. This was one of the happiest days of her life, and she'd never known her parents to be this happy about being together. Belinda thought, "Maybe Momma did the right thing by leaving the other woman alone. It seemed to have worked out for her. Sometimes I regret going after Desmond's women, but I didn't see any other way at the time."

Belinda pulled up to the front of their brick house, parked the car, and hopped out. She rushed around to the passenger's side to help Mr. Hines out of the vehicle. Belinda reached for his hand, but he pulled it back.

"I know how to get out of a car," he snapped.

"I'm just trying to help, Daddy. You need to take it easy for awhile. Didn't you listen to anything the doctor said?"

"Yes, I did, but I can get out of this car and walk in my house by myself," he replied, straightening up his back.

"I guess being in the hospital a whole week made you cranky," Belinda retorted.

Sighing quietly, she left him alone. Belinda hurried to the mailbox, pulled out the latest issues of *Ebony* and *Jet* magazines and marched up the driveway with her parents trailing behind. Belinda opened the door for them as they entered the foyer and headed directly to their bedroom.

"I'm going to get your father settled in and see if he'll take a nap. Could you pour me a Coke in a glass of ice, baby? I'm really thirsty."

"Sure, Momma, I can do that," Belinda responded, tossing the magazines on the granite countertop as the doorbell rang throughout the house.

"And could you get the door? That's probably the pastor or somebody from the church coming to visit with George!" she yelled, continuing down the hallway.

"Yes, Ma'am!"

Belinda swung the door open and looked into the face of an unknown man. He was approximately her height, with long reddish hair, wearing a lightweight khaki coat.

"Is this the George Hines residence?"

"Yes, it is. Why?"

He handed Belinda a white envelope, and said, "You've just been served with a foreclosure notice." He turned around and started whisking down the driveway.

Belinda took the envelope, and ran behind him. "Wait a minute. What is this about?"

The man stopped in his tracks, turned around, and replied, "Miss, that's a foreclosure notice. You all have thirty days to move out of this house. That's all I can tell you."

Standing in the middle of the driveway, Belinda's heart dropped to her stomach at the same time her mouth dropped to her chest. She was sure that this had to be a gross mistake. There wasn't any way that her parent's house could possibly be in foreclosure.

Belinda stomped back into the house. Her mother was standing in the foyer, squinting down the driveway at the young man leaving their house.

"Who was that peculiar looking fellow?" Julia asked.

"Mom, he gave me this." Belinda handed Mrs. Hines the envelope. "He said it's a foreclosure notice, and we have thirty days to get out of this house. What is he talking about, Mom?" she asked, searching Mrs. Hines' face for understanding.

"It's nothing for you to be concerned about, dear," she said, taking the envelope from Belinda. Mrs. Hines crept to the living room and melted down into the recliner like the exhausted woman she was. "Did you fix my Coke yet?"

Belinda stared at her Mom, wondering if she really was suffering from Alzheimer's and was totally oblivious to the reality of their situation.

"Mom, we're about to lose the house, and you're asking me about a soda? Have you taken leave of your senses!"

"No, but you're going to take leave of something if you don't lower your voice. Your father is trying to sleep, for goodness sakes."

"They can't just take our house in thirty days. They have to give us more than one months' notice. Don't they?" Belinda paced the floor, fumbling with her hair. "Mom, I'm freaking out over here. Will you just tell me what's going on?" Her body and voice were trembling. "How can we possibly be losing this house?"

"Come sit down," she said, waving Belinda to the sofa. Mrs. Hines waited patiently for Belinda to take a seat along with a couple of deep breaths. "If you really must know, we're over a year behind in the mortgage payments."

Belinda gasped loud enough to scare the hearing impaired. She placed one hand over her opened mouth and fanned herself with the free one. Mrs. Hines continued, dropping her head.

"I'm sorry to have to tell you this, but it's the truth. And you're old enough to handle the truth, Belinda."

"But—but what happened to Daddy's retirement money?" she asked, looking bewildered.

"Well, that's simple. It's all gone."

"But how, Momma?" Belinda asked, wringing her hands. "This isn't making any sense. I thought you two were set for life when you moved to Dallas. What happened to all the retirement accounts and the investment funds?"

"I don't have all the details," she began, placing both hands across her midsection. "You know, your father hardly tells me anything about his business dealings. But about eighteen months ago, he came home all excited about meeting this man on the golf course who was going to help him make a lot of money."

"Why would he need to do that if he already had enough money for you guys to live on? Why take that risk?"

"You know your Daddy. He's always been about making more and having more. That's why he was so excited about you marrying a doctor. He wanted you to have more than we ever had, but he never stopped wanting bigger things for us. Like this house," she said, waving both hands in the air. "We didn't need a five-bedroom house with an indoor pool resting on a fancy golf course resort for two people. Anyway, what I'm trying to say is that if we had kept living the way we were, the money was going to run out soon. So when George saw an opportunity to become richer than he'd ever dreamed, he leapt at it. He thought it was safe because several other distinguished businessmen in this community were involved in the plan, which turned out to be nothing but a Ponzi scheme."

Belinda's face sagged. "I can't believe Daddy fell for a fraudulent investment operation. What happened to the man behind the scheme? What's his name? Has he even been arrested?"

"His name was Benjamin somebody," she responded, rubbing her chin. "Ah, why can't I remember that man's name? Anyway, I know he was an older, white head man claiming to be a billionaire. I've got some of the news clipping in my bedroom. They had pictures of his arrest all over the front page of the local newspapers. But what good is that going to do anybody? The money is gone. Most of the people who live out here that were involved in the scheme have already sold their homes and moved on. George was stressing over how to catch up on the mortgage when he had that heart attack."

"Oh, Momma, I didn't know. I've been so concerned about finding Desmond and getting the kids back. I didn't think anything about how this could be financially draining you and Daddy. I'm so sorry, Momma. What are you going to do if they foreclose on this house?" Belinda asked, inching to the sofa's edge.

"They can have this big house. We can move into my mother's old house we've been renting out for years. It's still in decent living condition. It's only got two bedrooms, but we can make it fine without having a mortgage."

"Are you serious?" Belinda asked, grimacing. "Grandma's house is way on the outskirts of town like you're going into the country. Who wants to live way out there with the animals? Anyway, I would never be able to look at myself in the mirror again if I have to move there."

"I know where it is, Belinda. I was raised there. It's not the poorest neighborhood in Dallas. It's better than living on the south side in Cedars. Sometimes, you know, we have to do things we really don't want to do. I know you're used to living the high life. Moving from that mansion of yours to this place is bothering you like a sickness," Julia faced her child. Belinda frowned as if she didn't comprehend what her Mom was saying.

"Yes, I see it all in your face, but sometimes you have to be thankful for what you got and who you got. I kept Mama's house because I didn't ever want to forget where I came from. One thing about it, the Lord will always provide for his children. Now you just remember that," she added, shifting in the chair. "We might have to stay in that house until we can find something better. It'll be all right somehow."

"We've got to do something," Belinda said, massaging her temples, trying to think of a plan. "You're talking about how the Lord is going to provide for us, but we have to move out of this house next month. And excuse me, but grandma's old house is not my idea of being provided for."

"Well, I don't know what to tell you, baby. It looks like we're all out of options. Anyway, there's nothing else we can do," Julia added, waving her hand.

Belinda stared at her mom like she was a total stranger. She didn't understand this change in Julia's attitude. "What happened to that speech you used to give me about how important it is to maintain one's appearance of wealth?" Belinda asked, standing up, walking back and forth in front of Julia.

"I did used to feel that way, Belinda. I know that's what I taught you to believe, but I was wrong," she began, looking up at her daughter. "I listened to my mother when she told me that, and I tried my best to want the material things that George wanted, but I know better now that I have God in my life."

Puffing at Julia's last words, Belinda held her tongue. She didn't want to disrespect her mother. But she thought Julia's change of attitude was a direct result of the Alzheimer's disease instead of her conversion to Christianity later in life. Wasn't that one of the ten signs described in the article I read? The mood and personalities of people with Alzheimer's can sometimes change.

Julia slanted over in her recliner, speaking barely above a whisper.

"What I'm really concerned about is seeing my grandchildren again. When you get my age, family is the most important thing in your life. Sometimes I feel like I'm losing my mind because I miss those children so bad. I just don't know what I'm going to do without them."

"I miss them, too, Momma. Being without my children is the worse pain I could have ever imagined. Not to mention the fact, that I may never see them again now that we can't afford to hire an attorney. Desmond is going to keep them away from me forever."

Belinda sat down again, fighting back the tears that were struggling to break through her tear ducts. Her mother was wrong for once in her life, Belinda couldn't handle the truth, and she lost the fight with the tears. They broke through like the dams in New Orleans during Hurricane Katrina, not to be contained for the remainder of the night. She asked herself, "Where is Jesus when I need him? Why does he keep forsaking me when I'm trying to be a better person? It's just no use."

Just when Belinda thought her life was about to change for the better, it had just gotten five times worse. Mrs. Hines made it to Belinda's side, cradling her daughter in her arms, being the nurturing mother she'd always vowed to be. And Belinda remembered the little two-year-old girl residing within her body who needed her Mommy to rock her to sleep at night while she sucked her thumb. Mrs. Hines tried shushing Belinda to no avail, so she did what any good mother would do. She continued rocking and praying for her child with all her might.

"I'm sorry about losing the money." Belinda remembered what her father had mumbled on his hospital bed last week. Now she knew what those words really meant. At the time, Belinda thought she'd misunderstood him or maybe it was the medicine that had made him say those words. But he'd been trying to apologize for creating this situation, which made Belinda sob even harder and wonder, "What have you done to us, Daddy?"

26

(Belinda's Mother)

Belinda woke up Wednesday morning with a crook in her neck and a slight headache from all the crying she'd done last night. Lifting her head for a second, she dropped it back down, and turned over in bed. The blazing sunlight coming through her bedroom window wouldn't allow her to continue resting. Belinda opened her eyes again, realizing that she was lying on top of her comforter with a sheet over her fully dressed body. She asked herself, "How did I get in here? I don't remember coming into my room last night. Oh, goodness, I must be losing it."

Crawling out of her warm bed, Belinda went to her private bathroom searching for some Tylenol pain reliever. The cabinets were empty, so she tumbled down the hallway until she reached her parents room and tapped on the door.

"Come in," her Mom yelled.

Belinda cracked the door, popped her head inside, and exchanged morning greetings with Julia.

"Mom, I have a slight headache. Do you have some Tylenol or aspirin?"

"Yes, come on in while I finish dressing."

"Where's Daddy?" Belinda asked, entering the master bedroom. She noticed that her parents king-sized bed was already made up. The mountain of silky pillows almost completely hid the entire fruitwood sculpted headboard. They had the radio on, listening to the Tom Joyner Morning Show.

"He's in the shower," Julia responded, pulling a red top

over her head. "Look in my purse on that chair over there by the door. I think I have some Advil or something in there."

Rummaging at the bottom of Julia's Coach Signature purse, Belinda pulled out a bottle of aspirin along with a doctor's appointment card.

"What's this?" Belinda asked, holding the business-sized card up to the light. "Did you remember that you have a doctor's appointment scheduled for this afternoon at two o'clock?"

"Oh, Lord, I forgot all about that physical exam for today. Let me have that," Julia said, reaching for the card. "I need to call and reschedule this for another day."

"No, Mom, it's too late to call now." Belinda hid the card behind her back. "You can't reschedule on the day of the appointment unless you want to pay the cancellation fee. Anyway, it's not until this afternoon. Why would you need to reschedule?"

"I just don't feel up to them probing and sticking my body today. I had a good night's sleep for the first time in a week. And I'm not up to driving way across town."

"You don't have to drive. I can take you, Mom." Belinda sat down on the bed. She'd been concerned about her Mom's mental and physical health for the last month, especially after reading that article about Alzheimer's in Prevention magazine. Her mother didn't match all ten signs, but Julia matched enough of them to cause Belinda's concern.

Belinda thought, "She doesn't need to miss this appointment today because I should have done this sooner. The article said that early detection is the key to living a long life with the disease. But I was so caught up trying to find the kids that I forgot about Mom and Dad's failing health."

"With all you've been through with me, the kids, and Dad in the past few months, we need to make sure you're okay."

"Oh, you're worried about me, aren't you? I can hear it in

your voice, but I'm fine, baby," Julia said, pausing. "If it'll make you feel any better though, you can drive me to the doctor's office. Now stop worrying and go take that aspirin."

Belinda sat in the waiting room at Dr. Gross's office with her arms crossed, shaking her legs like she was about to suffer a nervous breakdown.

"Ms. Taylor, are you okay?" the receptionist asked, looking over the counter. She placed a caller on hold and peered over her wire-rimmed glasses at Belinda.

"Ah, yes, I'm fine. It's just so cold in here." Even with long sleeves on, Belinda was freezing and worried. "I'm just waiting to speak with the doctor regarding the outcome of my mother's physical exam."

"He's finishing up with her right now. He'll be able to speak with you in a minute. If you come on back, you can wait for him in his office."

Following the receptionist's instruction, Belinda found her way back to the doctor's private office at the front of the complex while her mother remained in the examining room. She eased into the black leather chair stationed in front of his old-fashioned, oak wood desk. He had an entire wall covered with degrees and plaques that he had accumulated over twenty-five years in the medical profession.

Belinda had requested to speak with the doctor in private before her mother's examination began. Considering she was the Hines' only child, Julia and George had given their doctor full consent to discuss their medical conditions with Belinda at any time.

After explaining her concerns regarding Julia's health, Belinda was met with absolute kindness from the slim doctor with a receding hairline. Although Dr. Gross still had a slight accent hailing from the Republic of India, she comprehended every word the mild-spoken man had to say.

"I'm going to perform several diagnostic tests on Julia today, including a mini-mental state exam. This test will give me insight into whether there were damages to different areas of Julia's brain since her last visit." He finished with a smile.

However, Dr. Gross also made it clear that depression or stress could be causing his patient to experience symptoms similar to Alzheimer's. Belinda knew her Momma had been stressed because of their family issues and hoped that was all it was. She couldn't face the thought of both parents being ill at the same time.

Shifting on the padded leather cushion, Belinda wanted something to read to occupy her mind while waiting on the doctor. After scanning the room, all she saw besides thick medical books were thin medical journals neatly stacked on his desk. Knowing that she couldn't comprehend any of those, she remembered a book she'd tucked in her purse before taking off to Wisconsin.

Belinda pulled out the small blue Bible, holding it in her hands. Feeling the textured cover of *The Message*, she recalled the first time she'd ever visited Alonzo's office. Belinda could still hear his words ringing in her ears now.

"I want this book to be your close personal friend. Just take it and start reading the book of Psalms and really listening to what you read." That's what he said.

Opening to the Book of Psalms, she read over the introduction explaining how most Christians have learned to pray by praying the Psalms. Belinda thought, "Maybe I need to learn how to pray. Nothing else seems to be working for me."

Belinda was reading the end of the third chapter about how real help comes from God, when she was startled by the sound of Dr. Gross entering the office. Being engrossed in the Word for the first time, she almost dropped the light book.

"Oh, I'm sorry for startling you. I apologize for taking so long, but we were waiting for the blood and urinalysis results. I can meet with you for a few minutes while your mother is getting dressed." Dr. Gross' slender body lingered over Belinda for a moment. Then, he dashed behind his desk and opened his laptop computer. He had a handsome poker face, making it difficult to discern whether he would be sharing good or bad news.

"That's okay." Belinda closed the book, and placed it back in her bag. She made a promise to read more of it later.

"Before we go any further, I want you to know that I appreciate the concerns you brought up regarding your mother's health. She's been my patient for a couple of years, so I want to make sure she remains with me for a long time," Dr. Gross said, touching the computer screen with the stylus pen. Belinda heard the computer clicking as he moved around the screen and wondered what he was interpreting from Julia's records.

"Thank you, Dr. Gross. What did you find out? Does my mother have Alzheimer's?"

"We did several tests, Ms. Taylor, and at this time, we don't have any conclusive reasons to believe that Mrs. Hines is suffering from the disease."

Belinda released a huge sigh of relief.

"Oh, thank you. I was so worried about my mother." Placing a hand over her chest, Belinda closed her eyes and took several deep breaths before opening them again.

Dr. Gross faced Belinda. "As I said, the symptoms may be from the family stress that she's been dealing with over the past year. Believe me, stress has a way of catching up with a person over time. But the mini-mental state test, physical exam, chest x-ray, and laboratory tests all came back showing negative results." Belinda nodded as Dr. Gross continued, feeling a small amount of tension leaving her body with each breath she took.

"However, if her symptoms, such as memory loss or confusion with time and people should persist or worsen over the next six months, please call for an appointment to bring her back in for more extensive testing. In the meantime, I've added some Stress-Tab vitamins to go along with her high blood pressure medication, and that's it for now." He turned back to the computer and clicked the screen with the stylus again, closing out the file.

Standing on shaky legs, Belinda thanked the doctor again. She couldn't wait to get out of his office and go meet her mother at the front desk. She made a vow to take better care of her mother and father because she didn't want to lose either one of them.

27

(Belinda's Men)

"Hey, lady, how are you doing? I didn't hear from you yesterday." Alonzo spoke eloquently while sitting at his desk, looking over the minutes from the board meeting last night.

"I was kind of busy with my parents. Plus, I had to take Mom to get her annual physical exam," Belinda replied, standing at the kitchen counter, trying to make sandwiches for lunch. She'd promised her mom yesterday that she'd start doing more to help them out. Tuna sandwiches with Lay's potato chips weren't much, but it was a start and quite an accomplishment for Belinda.

"Well, I'm calling because I heard from your detective friend this morning. He's coming by in about an hour, and I was hoping that you'd come join us. I'd appreciate your support." He paused for a millisecond. "That's if you have time."

"Ah, yes, I should be able to make that. I'll see you shortly."

"Belinda, are you okay?"

"Yeah, why?"

"You just sound... Oh, never mind. See you soon."

It didn't take long for Belinda to change into a charcoal gray, St. John's, knit pants suit with a long jacket. She slipped on a pair of matching pumps, checked her face out in the mirror, and said good-bye to her parents. Belinda was beginning to value their presence in her life more and more. There wasn't anything like the possibility of losing both parents to help Belinda realize how lucky she was to have them in her life. Although she didn't have her children yet, she still had her parents. It was time to start being thankful for them.

"Thanks for coming," Alonzo said, greeting Belinda with a light hug at the door to his office. While enjoying the feel of his warm sweater, the pine scent of Alonzo's Polo cologne tingled Belinda's nose for a second.

She'd entered the room with a plastered smile on her face, trying to convince Alonzo and herself that everything was okay, when in reality, she felt like crawling back into her bed, having a hard cry, and never coming out again. But Belinda promised that she'd cried her last tear yesterday. It was time to face reality, a reality that might include never seeing her children again, moving into a two-bedroom house with her aging parents, and finding herself a job. At least, that's the conclusion she'd come to last night while writing in her journal, that it was time for her to go back to work. After all, a Harvard business degree had to be worth something even if it was twenty years old.

"How are you doing? Is everything all right? You sounded a little strange on the phone." Alonzo pulled away from Belinda, keeping his narrowed eyes on her face.

"Ah, yeah, I told you. I'm good. Is Paul on his way?" she asked, taking a seat in her usual place.

"Yes, he is. And he should be here any minute now," Alonzo replied, clapping one time, returning to the seat behind his desk. He rifled through some papers on his desktop while Belinda tried to make herself comfortable.

Snapping her neck around at the knock on the door, Belinda watched Paul saunter into the room carrying Alonzo's iPhone in his right hand. He was casually dressed in khaki slacks, a striped shirt, and nubuck lace up shoes. They all exchanged pleasant enough greetings as Paul sat down beside Belinda. Leaning across the desk, he slid

Alonzo his cell phone.

"There you go, Rev."

Alonzo snatched the phone up, checked for missed messages, and looked up at Paul. "So what did you find out?"

"Well, I found out exactly what we expected. Whoever called you last week used a disposable phone. If you check your missed messages, you'll see that someone texted you again this morning from a different number."

Staring at the incoming message on his phone, Alonzo said, "Yeah, you're right. He's warning me that time is running out, and I need to resign or be shamed in front of the entire congregation." Alonzo erased the message, threw the phone on his desk, and stood up. "You know, today is Thursday and my anniversary celebration is Sunday. What are you doing about this blackmailer?"

"I'm doing all I can do right now. I have one of my best employees working on tracking it down. It's going to take a minute, but we should meet the deadline."

"Well, it sounds like you're trying to push it to the eleventh hour if you ask me. I thought you were supposed to be an ace detective." Alonzo peered down at Paul, wondering how much the man really wanted to help him. He wasn't blind; Alonzo had noticed how disappointed Paul was to see him at Belinda's house Tuesday night.

Paul rose from his seat, coming eye to eye with Alonzo. He was normally slow to anger, but this hypocrite was making his blood pressure rise.

"Like I said, I'm on it."

"Can you two just calm down for a minute?" Belinda asked, feeling the tension rise several degrees in the room.

"I've got to go," Paul said, maintaining eye contact with his nemesis. "You two enjoy the rest of your day."

"Wait, Paul," she said. Belinda was too late; he was already heading for the door.

"I'll have a bill for you when we close out the case," Paul said, standing in the doorway with his hand on the doorknob.

Belinda looked at Alonzo, watching him shrug his shoulders.

"Let him go, I've got work to do anyway," he snapped, sitting back down.

"Well, I guess I'll see you later." Belinda reached for her purse. She didn't want to be the mediator between two grown men.

Stepping outside the church, Belinda saw Paul waiting at the exit door.

"You're still here?"

"Yeah, I was about to take off. Then I decided to wait around a few minutes to see if you'd come out. I'm trying to tell you, something about that man is strange."

"So you're trying to say that you don't believe people can change." Belinda kept walking to her car.

"Are you trying to tell me that you believe he's changed?"

Detecting the sarcasm in Paul's voice, she replied, "I'm not trying to tell you anything but good-bye, Paul." She pulled the car door open. Paul grabbed it.

"Hold up, hold up just a second."

Releasing a heavy sigh, Belinda felt like she was carrying the weight of the world on her shoulders and neither Paul nor Alonzo was helping her out.

"Let me buy you a cup of coffee. I know a great coffee shop just around the corner," he said, smiling with a quick nod. "Come on, it'll be my treat."

Belinda paused, and thought, "I don't have anything better to do. Why not?"

"Okay, but only because you're buying," she teased. Paul laughed, closing her car door.

Lucy's Coffee House provided an inviting atmosphere. It

was a small, privately owned family business, tucked in the corner of a busy street. Belinda had probably passed by it a hundred times and never noticed it before.

"It's better than Starbucks and cheaper, too," Paul said, holding the door open.

"Thank you." Belinda passed him, inhaling the fragrant scent of fresh coffee beans. She walked to an empty, round table at the back of the shop. "So how'd you find this place?"

"It's my job to know every place of business in this city. And as you know, I take pride in my work."

The smiling waitress appeared, took their orders for two tall mocha lattes, and quickly disappeared behind the counter.

Paul stared at Belinda, sensing something was wrong.

"You want to tell me what's bothering you?"

"Ah, what makes you think something is bothering me?"

"I can see those long stress lines all over your pretty face for one," Paul said, running an index finger down his cheek. "Look, I know you're worried about your children. But as soon as you hire an attorney, I'm going to keep my promise and do whatever I can to help you get them back."

Flinching at the mention of her kids, Belinda lowered her eyes, remembering her promise not to shed anymore tears.

"I'm sorry to tell you this, but ..." Belinda went on to explain everything she was facing with her family and their financial crisis to Paul. She didn't mean to tell him everything. Once she started talking, it just all poured out, and it provided an incredible sensation. Belinda felt like she'd been released from prison for the second time this year.

Loosening her shoulders, Belinda tilted her head from side to side, cracking her neck.

"So, that's the story of my life up to now. I have to find a job, take care of my parents, and save money for an attorney to get my kids back. I don't know how long all of that is going to take, but it's what I have to do."

Paul had been a diligent listener, taking mental notes as Belinda laid out her life before him. The waiter had refilled their tall mocha café cups twice by the time she finished.

"I heard everything you just said, and I appreciate you sharing it with me." Paul reached across the table, placing his hand on Belinda's arm. "And I'm here to tell you it's going to be all right. It really is. But if you need a shoulder to cry on or something like that, you can still call me."

"Thanks, Paul. You're so sweet, and I appreciate you listening to my sob story," Belinda said, dabbing a tear from one eye.

"But, you know, Belinda, there's nothing wrong with working for a living." Paul sat up straight in his chair. "Now, if you want to have a prosperous life, I know the secret to that. I can tell you how to live long and prosper," he said, rubbing his palms together.

Smiling at Paul, Belinda thought that he was simply trying to humor her. So, she decided to indulge him. "Okay and what would that secret be?"

"You want to know? You really want to know?" Paul sounded excited to share his secret. He leaned over the table, staring Belinda in the face. "All right, I'm going to tell you this. The secret to living a prosperous life is in the Bible in the book of Proverbs."

Belinda sighed, and thought, "Here we go with the Bible again. First, Alonzo tells me to read the book of Psalms, and now Paul is telling me about Proverbs."

"Okay, okay, you don't believe me. Listen to this: the book of Proverbs is called wisdom. And wisdom is the art of living skillfully in whatever actual conditions you might find yourself facing. It doesn't have anything to do with a college degree or none of that. It's all about having good ole common sense, but honestly, common sense is not very common anymore."

"All right, I hear you," Belinda said, trying to smile and look interested.

"You talking all slow like you don't believe me. Well, let me tell you this, and I'll leave you alone. An older man shared this with me about three years ago. He broke it down to me. He said, son, the book of Proverbs has thirty-one chapters. If you read one chapter a day for a month, and then repeat that cycle every month, I promise that you'll prosper. So, I tried it, and three years later, my business activity has tripled and so has my revenue. And that's why I read the Bible daily, not just Proverbs either."

Pressing her lips together, Belinda gave Paul a daring look, like she was wondering if his story was truth or fiction. Either way, she reached in her purse, pulled out that little blue book called *The Message*, and turned to the book of Proverbs.

"I'm desperate enough to try anything," Belinda said.

Paul responded in song, "I tried Jesus, and He's all right."

They both laughed. When times are hard, laughter is usually the best medicine. She thought, "Paul is funnier than Cedric the Entertainer."

28

(Belinda's Project)

"Hi, Belinda. Thanks for coming to help me out with my first anniversary project," Alonzo said, sitting at the computer desk in his office with his back to Belinda. He was sifting through pictures of the congregation on the computer screen.

"No, problem. What did you have in mind?" she asked, removing her sateen jacket, revealing a black sweater worn over black pants. "And how can I help?" She glanced over his shoulder.

"That's a good question. I need you to help me select enough pictures to do about a five-minute video presentation of different events we've had this year. These are all my personal photographs. I've got about three different folders of them on my desktop, but I can't decide which ones to use," he said, scooting back in the swivel chair. Alonzo pushed himself up, touched Belinda's arm, and said, "You can have a seat and take a look, if you don't mind, while I run to the men's room."

"Sure, I can handle that," she replied, occupying his cushiony chair.

"Okay, I'll be right back," he yelled over his shoulder, rushing to the door.

Hunched over the fifteen-inch computer monitor, Belinda hadn't looked at more than five pictures when she heard Alonzo's iPhone buzzing on the desk. Checking the caller ID screen, she saw the name Paul Williams and decided to pick it up.

"Hi, Paul."

"Ah, Belinda? Did I dial the wrong number?"

"No, no, I'm at the church helping Alonzo with his anniversary project, but he had to step out for a second. What's going on?"

"Well, I was calling to tell *your friend* that I know who's been blackmailing him." Belinda noticed how Paul emphasized your friend, but ignored it. "I need him to meet me at the Jupiter Lanes Bowling Alley in thirty minutes. I'm headed there right now."

"Okay, I'll tell him as soon as he returns. Paul..." She wasn't fast enough; he'd already clicked off the phone. Obviously, he was upset with her for being in Alonzo's office. As much as she appreciated him listening to her yesterday, Belinda didn't think they'd ever be more than friends.

"Why are you talking on my cell phone?" Alonzo asked, returning to his office.

Belinda was searching for the red button. "Oh, it was ringing, and when I saw Paul's name on the screen, I answered," she replied, pressing the end key.

"Okay, I'm glad he called! I've been waiting all day to hear from him!" Alonzo had sparks in his eyes. "What did he say? Did he have good news?"

"Yes, as a matter of fact, he did. He knows who the blackmailer is, but he didn't tell me." Belinda pushed up from his computer chair. "He wants you to meet him at that huge bowling alley on Jupiter Road in thirty minutes."

"Bowling alley? Did he say why he wants to meet at a bowling alley?"

"No, he didn't. He just said he was on his way, and he'd meet you there."

Alonzo reached for his blazer from the coat rack by the office door. "You're coming with me, right?" He stared at Belinda.

She reached for her jacket, too. "Sure, if you want me to."

It was the golden time of day with the sun preparing to set in the west. Alonzo drove into the crowded parking lot of the twenty-four-thousand square foot bowling facility and turned off the ignition.

"This place looks like it's real busy tonight."

"Yeah, I guess a lot of people like to bowl on Friday nights," Belinda said, exiting the SUV.

Walking through the double glass doors, they saw Paul coming to meet them carrying a leather bowling bag in his right hand. They all quickly exchanged polite greetings.

"I guess you're bowling tonight," Alonzo said, eyeing the bag.

"Yep, my bowling team has a tournament scheduled to start in about thirty minutes. So, if you guys will follow me, we can use one of the empty party rooms for a quick meeting."

"Man, this is the largest bowling facility I've ever seen," Alonzo commented, scanning the neighborhood center featuring twenty lanes with state-of-the-art animated computer scoring. Passing by the noisy arcade center, he almost bumped into a little boy rushing to play one of the hottest games in the place.

Paul led them into a small party room enclosed by a glass wall where they had a clear view of the bowling lanes. There were two wooden rectangular-shaped tables in the room with multicolored plastic chairs surrounding each one. Placing his bowling bag on the first table, he asked Belinda and Alonzo to sit down.

"Stay here. I'll be right back," he said, raising his index finger.

Alonzo shuffled in his seat, feeling beads of perspiration forming on his forehead. He pulled a white handkerchief from his coat pocket, and wiped his brow.

"I wish he'd come on and get this over with."

Belinda sighed, crossing her legs. She was ready for this to end, too. Alonzo was going to start sweating buckets of water if Paul didn't hurry up.

In a matter of minutes, Paul opened the door, and held it open for his female guest to enter. "I believe you both know this young lady."

Alonzo and Belinda lifted their heads and dropped their mouths at the sight of the pretty woman with dark blonde highlighted bangs staring at them. She had on dark jeans, a pearl beaded top, and a cropped black jacket covering her model thin body. Belinda didn't immediately remember the name associated with the oval-shaped face she'd only seen once, but Alonzo did.

"Cousin Cynthia," Alonzo began, looking bemused. "What are you doing here?"

Closing the door, Paul ushered Cynthia into a seat beside him.

"It seems this is your blackmailer, Alonzo."

Cynthia slumped in the chair with her eyes cast downward, folded arms across her chest. She opened her mouth like she was going to speak and then closed it tight.

Alonzo bent over in his chair, holding his midsection. He couldn't have felt more pain if Paul had sucker punched him in the gut wearing brass knuckles.

"Why in the world would you do something like this to me? I'm your blood!" Alonzo pounded the table with his fists.

"I know," she said, scooting up in the chair, wiping tears from her cheeks. "I was just so angry with Anna for constantly bragging on you while we were planning the Cousin's Ball and talking about how she was coming to your first anniversary celebration at the church. And my brother, Bernard, was on the committee with us, and she never even acknowledged him one time. Just because neither one of us finished college, she think y'all better than us," Cynthia whined, sniffling.

Inhaling deeply, Alonzo clasped his hands together, said a short prayer, and slowly exhaled. Raising his head, he glared into Cynthia's watery eyes.

"So, let me get this straight. You're telling me this is all about some family jealousy. You went to all this trouble to totally embarrass me and my sister."

"I was never going to go through with it. I just wanted you to cancel the anniversary celebration or something so she would shut up," she said, pouting. "I'm sorry, Cuz, you know I would never do that to you."

Vehemently shaking his head in disbelief, Alonzo shifted his eyes between Belinda and Paul, wondering what they were thinking about his family now. If her plan was to humiliate him, she'd certainly succeeded.

"Well, tell me something. How did you end up with a copy of the video?"

Cynthia murmured, "I knew you were going to ask me that."

Changing positions in her chair, Cynthia continued. "I got it from one of your former college classmates who I was dating up until two weeks ago. His name is Javon Freeman. After I caught him taping himself in bed with another man, and told him how disgusting I thought he was, he brought up your name. He said that if he was a homo then my preaching cousin was one, too. When I finished calling him a liar and a few other names, he said he could prove it. And that's when he searched through his video vault, pulled out a tape, and showed it to me. Before it was over good, he was laughing in my face, telling me I could keep it to remember him by."

Hanging his head in shame, Alonzo covered both his eyes. He never would have imagined that someone from his immediate family would be behind this nightmare. But he should have figured that Javon was the one who'd taped the orgy. Alonzo could see his gapped-tooth smile right now, walking around with a camcorder strap attached to his neck, bragging about how he was going to be a famous movie director.

"So you decided you'd hurt me the way that Anna hurt you?" Alonzo asked, struggling to get the words out past the frog in his throat.

"I'm sorry," she replied, breaking down into tears. Cynthia's whole body was convulsing like she was having an epileptic seizure. Between sobs, she asked, "Can you ever forgive me?"

Alonzo looked over at Belinda like he wanted to ask her, "Can you believe this"

Paul placed his palms on the table, stood up, and said, "If you all will excuse me, I have a bowling game about to start in a few minutes. So, I'm going to leave you all alone."

"Wait a second!" Alonzo called behind him. "Did you bring her here?"

Paul turned around, gripping his bowling bag in one hand. "Yes, I did, and I'm driving her back to Austin tonight after my game."

"Thank you, Paul, for everything," Alonzo said, rising to shake the man's hand.

Belinda steadily rose from her seat. "I'm going to leave you two alone to talk. I'll be waiting outside for you, Alonzo."

Approximately ten minutes later, with the video DVD locked safely in his glove compartment, Alonzo and Belinda were heading back to the church to get her car. It had gotten dark outside except for the full moon shining between the tall buildings high above the city lights.

Breaking through the heavy silence, Belinda touched Alonzo's hand resting on the center console and asked, "How did it go in there after I left?"

Alonzo kept his eyes on the road. Moving his thumb

against hers, he recognized Belinda's touch. "She just kept on crying for a couple minutes. But she finally dried her face once I told her that I accepted her apology."

Belinda blew out a puff of air. "I don't know if I could have done that. Not after what she put you through."

Braking for the traffic light, he said, "I didn't have a choice. She asked for it. If I'm going to be a minister, then I have to practice what I preach. And I preach forgiveness on a daily basis. I'm just glad that it's over. Thank God, I don't have to worry about being shamed in my own church on Sunday."

"I know, now you can finish your anniversary project and work on your sermon."

"Amen, to that!"

Alonzo pulled into his designated space in the church's overflowing parking lot. Glancing at the clock on his dashboard, he announced, "We made it just in time for Friday night prayer service."

Feeling blessed that Paul Williams had saved his life and his church, Alonzo Mitchum prayed harder at the altar than he had in a long time.

29

(Belinda's Dinner)

"Good morning, beautiful. How are you enjoying this gorgeous day so far?" Alonzo asked, smiling like he was glancing at a reflection of himself.

"I'm great. You sound very happy today," Belinda replied, sitting at the breakfast table eating a bite of cheese toast. "Where are you? Are you at the church?"

"No, no, I'm home, and I plan to be here all day. In fact, I'm thinking about making dinner for you today just to show you my appreciation for all of your support."

"That's sweet, but you don't have to do that." Belinda took a sip of hazelnut-flavored coffee.

"I know I don't, and that's exactly why I'm offering to. Now all you have to do is say yes and be over here around five o'clock. We can have an early meal and maybe catch a movie or something later on. How does that sound?"

"It sounds like a plan. What are you cooking?"

"Anything you want me to cook. All you have to do is name it, and I'll gladly make it for you."

"Well, I don't care what you make as long as it's not chicken. I'm so tired of that yard bird. You know, when I was a child, it was my favorite dish. Now, I try my best to avoid it whenever I can."

Alonzo laughed. "I'll try to come up with something edible and see you around five. Let me give you my address real quick."

"Hold on," Belinda said, picking up a pen from the kitchen counter. She scribbled the address on a pad. "Got it,

I'll see you later."

"Who was that?" Mrs. Hines asked, entering the kitchen. She walked over to the refrigerator and pulled out a container of orange juice.

"That was Alonzo—I mean, Pastor Mitchum, calling for me."

"I heard you say Alonzo, and I saw him walking you to your car last night in the parking lot. When are you going to tell me what's going on between you two?"

"Well, let's just say that right now, we're still getting to know one another better. And since he just invited me to dinner at his house, I have to go find something to wear." Belinda stood, scatting away from the table.

Mrs. Hines poured some juice into a small glass, took a quick sip, and yelled, "Okay, wear something nice, but not too revealing."

Belinda heard her mom's request as she closed the door to her room. Making a beeline to her closet, she snatched four dresses off their hangers in five seconds. Belinda was disappointed that she didn't have the latest designer fashion for this season like she normally would, but she'd have to make do with what she did have for now.

Looking down at her raggedy fingernails, Belinda wanted to curse because she couldn't afford to get them or her scaly feet done. Whatever household funds they had left would have to stretch until the end of the month.

Around three o'clock, Belinda started getting ready for a private dinner with Alonzo. After a nice bubble bath, she buffed her fingernails, and painted them and her toenails red. She chose to wear a classic sheath dress in green with a matching jacket, something similar to what she'd seen Michelle Obama wear on television at one of the Presidential events. With a pair of high-heeled, pointed-toed pumps and a sequin evening bag, she headed out the front door.

Belinda parked in the driveway blocking one half of the

two-car garage connected to Alonzo's stunning brown brick home. The vision of loveliness with a small front porch supported by three Roman columns was nicely situated at the end of a cul-de-sac. She thought the stellar three-bedroom home in a gated community was perfectly befitting the charismatic pastor. It wasn't a newly built home, but it appeared to be in pristine condition with lots of space. However, Belinda thought the yard needed a little tender loving care to represent an upscale community.

"Wow, you look marvelous," Alonzo grinned, meeting Belinda at the entranceway of his one-story home. He took her by the hand as she entered and twirled her around.

"Thank you. I dressed to please."

"I tell you what. You're looking like First Lady Obama in that dress."

"I'll take that as a compliment," Belinda said, sniffing the air. "It smells good in here. What did you decide to cook?"

"Ah, let me take your coat, and I'll tell you." Belinda slid out of her dress jacket and handed it to Alonzo. He took a few steps with it in his hand and hung it in the hall closet. "First, we're going to have a Waldorf salad. And then I have to finish making the Memphis-Style steaks with beer and molasses sauce. It's a special recipe that I got from a Food Network show."

"I can't believe you watch that channel," Belinda said, following him through the warmly decorated living room into the open kitchen area. Admiring the way his striped brown slacks hung on his firm derriere, Belinda wondered about his true intentions for their evening together.

"Well, I'm a single man, so I've been trying to learn how to cook from watching Down Home with the Neely's, and I ordered their cookbook." Alonzo pointed to the opened book on the counter amid his individual cups of ingredients.

"What's all this stuff you have on the counter?"

"That's for the beer and molasses sauce," he said, picking

up a large bowl. He stirred the sauce a bit, and then held the wooden spoon up to Belinda's mouth. "Here, taste this."

She opened her mouth, savored the taste on her tongue, and moaned. "That's delicious."

He placed the spoon with the rest of the sauce on it in his mouth, and moaned, too. "Yes, it is."

"So, ah, what all do you have planned for us this evening?" Belinda asked, giving him a daring stare. It was time to start playing her cards.

"Actually, I was hoping that you'd help me finish up my video project for tomorrow. I put together a sample slideshow for you to preview, but I'm not sure if I have enough pictures to do my PowerPoint presentation." Alonzo left the room for a minute, and returned with his laptop computer already booted up. Placing it on the raised counter, he pulled out a high-back, swivel stool, and said, "Why don't you sit up here while I finish making dinner?"

Belinda sat down at the counter, watching pictures fade in and out on the screen while Alonzo went to the other side and started chopping more vegetables. This wasn't quite what she'd planned to be doing this evening, but she wanted to get it out of the way so they could enjoy their meal and get to the movies.

She was almost at the end of the slideshow when the doorbell rang. They both stopped what they were doing, and stared at one another. "Are you expecting more company?"

"No, I'm not," Alonzo replied, tossing the knife in the sink. "But I think that might be the gardener. He was supposed to be here earlier today to mow the lawn and trim the hedges. I wanted all of that done before you got here. Now it's almost dark, and he wants to pop up. So let me go talk to him for a minute."

"Okay," Belinda said, nodding her head.

"I'll be right back," he said, walking out the kitchen. Belinda turned around just as the slideshow was starting over. Pressing the escape button, she decided to exit the program, and return to the desktop. That's when Belinda detected the Internet Explorer icon at the bottom of the computer screen. She thought, "All right, he has Facebook open. Let me sign in and see what Justine and Jesse are up to this evening."

She clicked the icon, opening to his Facebook profile page. Directly to the left of the screen was a picture of Alonzo wearing a long sleeved white shirt unbuttoned, exposing his bare chest. His face was turned to the side with his tongue extended down to his chin. The name beside the picture was one word: Lonz. She couldn't help asking, "What the hell is this? Why is his tongue hanging out like that?"

Sensing that something wasn't quite right about this page, Belinda shifted on the stool, and scrolled further down his wall at some of the messages posted. Her heart rate quickened and her chest muscles tightened as she read one note after the other from various men. It wasn't long before Belinda sadly realized she'd fallen for the okey doke, again. "Oh, my goodness. Alonzo is using the Internet to meet gay men. How stupid is that? And how stupid was I for believing that he'd changed? I should have left his ass alone the second I saw that video on his iPhone," she thought.

Obviously, Alonzo had created an alias and private profile pages which only certain friends could view. Just when Belinda thought she'd seen enough, an Instant Message popped up on the screen from another male friend: Hey, Lonz, see ur online. Missed u. How bout mtg me later so we can do our thang @ my place?

Belinda heard Alonzo enter the house. She counted his footsteps as he swaggered towards the kitchen. Still, she didn't move a muscle. Belinda's eyes remained fixated on the computer screen. Her heart was trying to leap out of her chest, only Belinda mentally willed it to hold on just a little while longer.

"Hey, I'm back. What are you doing?" Alonzo strolled up behind Belinda, looking over her shoulder at his Facebook profile page. Instantly, she felt his body tense behind hers. He breathed in, and then released a puff of hot air around the back of her neck. The room was saturated with silence.

"I'm waiting," she whispered, turning to look at Alonzo.

"I know. I know you are. What do you want me to say?" he asked, placing both hands on his head. Alonzo spun around the room several times like he was in a washing machine on the rinse cycle.

"Just tell me the truth. That's all I need to know," Belinda said, sounding calmer than she actually felt.

"You already know the truth. You know my secret," he whispered. One lone tear trickled down his cheek.

"How long do you think you can keep this secret of yours, Alonzo? You're all over the Internet half dressed with your tongue hanging out, for goodness sakes," Belinda said, raising her voice. Then, she willed herself to calm down again. She felt like a fool, but was through acting like one. This wasn't her man, and they didn't owe each other anything. Belinda just wanted to get away from Alonzo.

"I'm sorry, Belinda. I—I've truly been trying to change." He said, choking the words out, dropping his hands to his sides.

"So have I," Belinda replied, sliding off the stool. Standing her ground in front of Alonzo, with both hands on her hips, she added, "But I don't go around lying and trying to deceive people."

"I'm sorry. Please give me another chance," he pleaded, with tears welling in his eyes. The crack in Alonzo's voice sounded like ice breaking in a cooler.

"No, I'm all out of chances. I can't support you anymore, and I can't be a part of your life anymore, Alonzo. I gave you the benefit of all doubt, and you played me for a fool!" she stated, stomping towards the front door. Belinda stopped at the hall closet, retrieving her coat and bag.

"Please don't leave me," he begged, following behind her, forcing the heavy tears to cascade down his cheeks. "Please don't go, Belinda. I need help. Can't you see I need help!"

Belinda stopped, and spun on her heels. "Well, then, you should get some help, and leave me the hell alone because I can't help you!"

Alonzo rushed to the door and placed his hand firmly against it so Belinda couldn't pull it open. "Okay, okay," he said, holding up one hand. "Please, please, just promise me that you won't tell anyone about this, and I'll move out of your way." He stared at Belinda through watery eyes. With mucus running from his nose, he gasped for air.

Belinda's eyes widened, gazing at him in bewilderment. "You are unbelievable. But I can promise you I won't tell anyone about this. I don't want any association to your name or your church. And I promise that you won't see or hear from me again," she spouted, yanking the door open.

On the way out she thought, "From now on, I'm through with men. I'm done with Alonzo, Paul, and Desmond. All men are good-for-nothing liars and cheaters no matter how nice they appear to be."

30

(Belinda's Soul)

Rolling over in her queen-sized, poster bed, Belinda lifted her head at the sound of the knocking on the door.

"Belinda, it's time to get ready for church. You know, today is the Pastor's anniversary celebration. I heard a rumor that he's planning something special for the congregation. Honey, are you up?" Mrs. Hines asked, excitement ringing in her voice.

"Ah, not really." Belinda touched her forehead, sighing heavily. She didn't want to move.

Mrs. Hines turned the doorknob, easing her head in between the cracked space.

"Are you all right this morning? How was your date last night?"

"I—I can't talk about that right now," Belinda replied, sitting up in bed, gathering the comforter around her waist. "And I'm not going to church today. In fact, I'm not going back to that church again period, Mom. Alonzo Mitchum is the biggest fake in history."

Mrs. Hines contorted her face and stepped further into the room, closing the door behind her. Moving to Belinda's side of the bed, she stood over her daughter, arms folded across her bosom.

"What happened last night?"

"You just—you wouldn't believe it if I told you. I can barely believe it myself. So, please, just leave it alone for now," Belinda begged, lying back against a stack of fluffy satin pillows. She wasn't in the mood to rehash the events from yesterday before ten o'clock on a Sunday morning. "I have to stay home today, Momma. That's all I can say right now. I'll see you when you get back."

Pulling the covers over her shoulders, Belinda turned her back to Mrs. Hines. She closed her eyes, listening to her mother's steps as she exited the room. Belinda was thankful that her mom hadn't asked anymore question because there wasn't any way she was setting a foot in that church today. She just needed some peaceful time to herself to reflect on her life, and start planning how to support herself in the future so she could get her kids back. Then, she went back to sleep.

Belinda slept until noon. She would have slept even longer, but the ringing from her cell phone woke her up. Lifting her head, she reached for the device, and checked the caller ID.

"Hello, Paul." Belinda sat up in bed, propping her head against one hand.

"Good afternoon. I see you didn't make it to church today."

"No, I actually couldn't get going this morning."

"I'm sorry for waking you up, but I just wanted to let you know I didn't call you yesterday because I slept all day. After I drove Alonzo's cousin back to Austin Friday night, I got in touch with some friends down there and ended up not getting home until almost daylight Saturday morning."

Belinda cringed at the mention of Alonzo's name, and wished that Paul hadn't mentioned him.

"That's okay. That's really okay. Listen, Paul," she began. "I need to tell you something. I don't think it's a good idea for us to see each other anymore. I mean, your work is done with us, and we should just leave it at that."

"Where is this coming from, Belinda? I thought we were developing something between us."

Belinda spoke slowly and deliberately. "No, Paul, I'm

sorry that I let things go too far, but there's nothing developing between us, and there never will be. It's past the time for us to part ways. I thank you for all you've done for us, but please don't call me again, okay?"

"Wow! You sound serious. I don't know what happened yesterday, but if that's the way you feel, I have to respect it. You know, I don't want anybody who doesn't want me, and you've made it clear how you feel."

"Thank you for understanding. Good-bye," she said, clicking the phone off. Belinda scooted out of bed, slid on her house shoes, and hurried to the restroom. She hadn't gone all night long.

Feeling worse than she'd felt in a long time, Belinda pulled on a pair of size eight skinny jeans, a knit top, and a pair of low-heeled boots. It was an unusually cold afternoon for late November; the temperature had to be in the upper twenties, so she pulled a leather coat across her shoulders. She needed to get out of the house before her parents returned and the only place she could think of that would give her some solitude was the public library.

Belinda recalled the many hours she'd spent in the prison library reading all types of books after her assault. If it hadn't been for the comfort of those fiction, as well as nonfiction books, and writing in her journal, she might not have made it out of there in one piece. The corner desk had become her favorite space to sit, travel to other places in her mind, and pretend that the prison bars didn't exist for a few hours each day. Since the selection in their facility wasn't the greatest, Belinda found herself reading some of the better books more than once.

Although the downtown library was the furthest from her house, it was one of the only two branches open on Sunday. Belinda chose it for their "popular reading" section, which contained works on a variety of subjects for the general reader. And they offered the best selection of magazines which could be checked out for three weeks, just like the books. The variety of popular interest magazines would help make it worth the trip.

Roaming through the Humanities division, Belinda pulled out several best sellers from popular African American authors who'd captured her interest. She found a comfortable chair in the lounge area while she sifted through fiction, nonfiction, and the latest magazines. Before she knew it, the afternoon had slipped by and the library was preparing to close. Belinda was about to rise from her seat when a colorful book resting on the center table caught her attention. She scanned the room to see if someone else might have left it there, but the area was virtually deserted. She read the title to herself...*SISTAHFAITH: Real Stories of Pain, Truth, and Triumph.* Belinda wasn't sure what that meant and there wasn't time to scan the back cover, but it sounded like something she needed. Clenching the small copy in her hand, she headed for the check-out counter.

Belinda knew her parents would be home by the time she got there. She still wasn't ready to face either one of them even after having a relaxing afternoon at the library. As far as she was concerned, Alonzo Mitchum was the lowest form of scum on earth and his anniversary celebration was the joke of the century.

Somehow, she promised to figure out a way to let her parents know what Alonzo was doing. They couldn't keep attending that church with him as the pastor knowingly deceiving good people like that.

Opening the front door, Belinda entered the foyer and was greeted by the smell of wood burning in the fireplace. She removed her leather coat, hung it up in the closet, and headed to the living room. Her mother was sitting at the end of the sofa and her father was relaxing in the recliner reading the Sunday newspaper. Julia was watching a movie on Lifetime on the sixty-inch plasma television, but stopped long enough to greet Belinda.

"Hi, baby. Everyone missed you at church today. Where have you been?"

"Hi, Mom. Hi, Dad." Mr. Hines looked up, nodded at Belinda, and returned to reading the financial section of the newspaper. They hadn't spoken very much to one another since Belinda found out about the money being squandered. However, he had assured his wife and daughter that'd he come up with a way to earn his money back or do something before losing the house.

"I've been downtown at the library. I see you all are enjoying the fireplace. It sure feels good in here." Belinda sat on the opposite end of the sofa from Mrs. Hines.

"Yes, your father wanted to build a fire as soon as we got home. We miss burning the fireplace everyday during the winter like we did in Michigan. And, you know, it helps with his arthritis."

"I've missed it too. I remember how we used to sit in the living room when I was a child and just watch the fire burning at night. Now, it seems like those days are so far away that they never even happened."

Julia eyed her daughter staring at the fire with a sad look on her face, and asked, "Belinda, are you all right?"

She finally blinked. "Yes, Mom, I'm fine. But I can't go back to that church with you all anymore."

Julia reached for the remote control, turned down the television, and turned towards Belinda.

"Are you going to tell us why?"

"I found out something about Alonzo last night, and I promised him I wouldn't tell anyone. If I break that promise, then I'm no better than he is, and that's not how I want to be anymore, Momma."

"Well, I understand. I don't know what happened between you two, but your father and I heard a rumor a few weeks ago about Alonzo that we never shared with anyone either."

Belinda scooted to the edge of her seat, wondering what her mother was talking about. With curiosity etched across her face, she asked, "What was that?"

"We, ah, we heard something about he used to be gay or he used to hang out with gay men when he lived in Austin. I don't remember exactly what all it was. But he seems like such a nice young man that I didn't pay it any mind. You know how church folk can talk."

Mr. Hines butted in. "Yeah, but sometimes talk turns out to be the truth. I told you any man who's thirty-five and never been married and doesn't have any children is a strange creature. It's not natural."

"Now, George, it's not fair to judge a person based on their marital status. I know a lot of single women over forty who meet that criteria, and they're not lesbians."

"I'm not talking about women, Julia; I'm talking about red-blooded men. Everybody knows that women outnumber men almost five to one, so any man without a wife does not want a wife," George said, rising from his recliner. "I'm going to get me a Coke. I'll be right back."

"Bring me one, too." Julia smacked her lips and sighed. "I still don't know if I can agree with him."

"Daddy's right, Momma. Out of all the people in the world, I should have known that. Why is it that all men are either gay or dogs?"

Belinda reached in her purse, pulling out the library books, and then she pulled out the blue Bible Alonzo had given her. Sighing at the book in disgust, Belinda caught her mother's attention.

"Is that a Bible?" Julia asked.

"It's a contemporary Bible called *The Message*. Alonzo gave me this at my first meeting with him. He asked me to read the Psalms, but the way I feel about him right now, I want to throw this book in the fire. Just knowing that he even touched it makes me want to burn it," Belinda said, her voice ascending. She could feel the anger rising from her stomach making her ill with hateful thoughts. Grasping the book in her right hand, she stomped over to the fireplace.

"Belinda! Stop! You can't burn a Bible," Julia screamed, popping up from the sofa faster than someone half her age. "That would be a sin!"

Spinning on her heels, Belinda faced her mother with tears in her eyes. "I was a fool and believed him." Sniffing, she pinched her runny nose with one hand.

Julia took the book from Belinda with one hand, and led her back to the sofa with the other one.

"Let me keep this book. Now, sit down here and talk to me."

Belinda flopped on the sofa with Julia, maintaining a stoic face.

"I don't have anything else to say. My life is a mess. Every man I try to trust betrays me and leaves me feeling like a fool."

Julia shook her head. "You can't put your faith in man, Belinda, because man will always let you down." She leaned back against the sofa and crossed her legs. "You know, when I first married George, I was so happy I thought I'd hit the jackpot. He was so handsome and ambitious. He wanted to take me away from that little ole two-bedroom house my Momma had, asked me to marry him, and move to Michigan. I'd just graduated from college, but back then, women went to college just to find a husband. Anyway, about two years later, after you were born, I found out that he'd been seeing another woman. I took you and I left. I came all the way back down here with Momma."

"Really? I never knew that. You mean, you actually left Daddy?" Belinda questioned, arching her eyebrows.

"Umm huh, I sure did."

"Well, what happened? What made you go back?"

Julia sighed heavily, thinking she should have shared this with Belinda a long time ago.

"My Momma, God rest her soul, told me I needed to go back to my husband. She said she'd been a single mother struggling all of her life. So, if George was going to take care of me and my daughter and I didn't have to work on nobody's job, then I should go back home, keep my mouth shut, and just look the other way. And that's what I did."

Belinda gave Julia an incredulous stare and shifted in her seat. Facing her mother, she said, "I guess that's how your generation or at least, you, chose to handle things. I couldn't live like that."

"Well, it's no secret that most women tend to marry men like their fathers. And that's what you did, but I think you were determined not to be like me and accept your husband's infidelity. Although you kept your mouth shut, you didn't look the other way. But what price have you paid for that, Belinda? What does it profit a woman to gain the world but lose her soul? Because the daughter I raised would have never tried to hurt another living person. Somewhere along the marriage road, you traded your soul for riches and gold."

Julia's words pierced Belinda ears and heart. Still, her eyes returned to the burning fire, reminding her of all the hostility she'd harvested during her marriage to Desmond. She thought, "Maybe it's time to let it go. I can't keep going on this way, trying to hurt people just because I'm hurting. There's got to be a better way of living. But am I worthy of it?"

Belinda closed her eyes momentarily, releasing a deeply held breath.

"You're right, Mom," she said solemnly. "While I was fighting to maintain my fabulous lifestyle, I was losing my man and my soul to the devil. I hated those women for sleeping with Desmond because I knew he wasn't going to stop cheating, and I wasn't going to leave. So somewhere during my marriage, I ended up becoming all the women I ever hated rolled into one. I completely lost myself. Now, I don't know what I am or who I am."

Before Julia could respond, George returned with two tall glasses of Coke and reclaimed his recliner with one of the drinks in his hand. He didn't bring one for Belinda because George knew she wouldn't want it. Belinda didn't drink any type of soda and often reprimanded them for drinking so much of it.

Julia took a sip of Coke, placed a coaster on the coffee table, and sat her glass down on it.

"Baby, you may not know who you are, but I know who you belong to, and you've got to get some God in your life. You got to get rid of all those demons inside you and learn Him for yourself. Otherwise, you're going to keep making the same mistakes over and over again. You're going to keep hurting yourself more and more."

"But how do I do that?" Belinda placed a hand on her forehead, trying to make sense of it all. "Don't I need to get my life together first?"

"No, no, that's the mistake too many people make. I even made that one myself, thinking that my life had to be a certain way for me to accept Jesus. You were a grown woman before I learned that lesson. But He'll take you just the way you are, Belinda. All you have to do is ask."

Staring at Julia through blurred vision, Belinda felt like the genuine fool of all fools. Her heart was pounding as a spirit seemed to be permeating her entire being. She didn't know whether to jump for joy or start crying in misery, but something had a hold on her. She'd made so many mistakes. Belinda wondered, "Why would God want to listen to a sinner like me? How can He forgive me when I can't forgive myself?"

"I know what you're feeling," Julia whispered.

Belinda snapped at the sound of Julia's voice as if she'd forgotten that the woman was sitting beside her. With tears streaming down her cheeks, Belinda remained quiet as a lamb.

"I know you're thinking that you're not good enough for Jesus. But let me tell you this, baby, you are. Don't be afraid to ask. All you have to do is get down on your knees right now, pray the sinner's prayer to accept Jesus into your life, and you will be saved."

"Will you say it with me, Momma?"

"Of course, I will," Julia replied, easing from the sofa, taking Belinda's clammy hands. They both knelt down on the hardwood floor. With bowed heads, Julia heartily prayed the sinner's prayer, and Belinda softly repeated every word in a trembling voice while choking back tears. They said:

Heavenly Father, I come to you in prayer asking for the forgiveness of my sins. I confess with my mouth and believe with my heart that Jesus is your son, and that he died on the cross at Calvary that I might be forgiven and have eternal life in the kingdom of Heaven. Father, I believe that Jesus rose from the dead and I ask you right now to come in to my life and be my personal Lord and Savior. I repent of my sins and will worship you all the days of my life because your word is truth. I confess with my mouth that I am born again and cleansed by the blood of Jesus! In Jesus name I pray, Amen.

Belinda released her mother's hands. Filled with the Holy Spirit, she collapsed into a heap on the floor. A feeling of indescribable joy flooded Belinda's small body as she continued praying and praising. Belinda's mind finally felt at ease, totally in sync with the universe surrounding her. She knew she was now saved. Belinda was one with God, and He would be her man forever, a faithful and loving husband.

About a minute later, Belinda slowly raised her head at

the sound of an unfamiliar noise. Her eyes bulged in disbelief at the site of her father, lying on the floor in a fetal position in front of the fireplace, crying like a newborn baby who had just gotten whacked on the bottom. He was wailing and calling on the name of Jesus loud enough to be heard throughout the five-thousand square foot home.

Julia Hines hugged Belinda, pulled her closer to her bosom, and whispered in her ear, "It's going to be all right. No matter what happens now, we're all saved."

It was almost midnight by the time the two ladies got Mr. Hines quieted down. Belinda had helped Julia get George peaceably settled into their bed. Her mother was happier than Belinda could ever remember seeing her in all the days of her life. Still, as tired as her soul was, Belinda had a thirst for knowledge. Glancing at the books on her nightstand that she'd checked out of the library earlier in the day, one of them stood out from the rest, *SISTAHFAITH: Real Stories of Pain, Truth, and Triumph*. It wasn't the Bible, but she needed to start her new journey somewhere. It was time for healing, and she needed help.

31

(Belinda's Thanksgiving)

Good morning, Lord, my name is Belinda Hines Taylor, and I've been saved for three days, twelve hours, and thirty minutes.

That's how long it had been since she recited the sinner's prayer with her mother, and that's how she started each day since her first morning of salvation on Monday. Belinda felt like a recovering alcoholic who had to keep reminding God of who she was so He'd continue helping her through each day. Especially considering the way she was struggling against the spirit of depression which was trying to claim her weary soul.

This would be Belinda's third Thanksgiving Day without her children, and she wasn't taking it too well. Looking out her bedroom window, Belinda saw the cold wind blowing through the trees and wished that she felt more warmth circulating inside her body. Although she was satisfied with being a newborn Christian, it had taken a lot of energy to pull herself out of bed and get dressed in a simple denim outfit on this particularly frosty day. However, Belinda kept recalling her mother's words, "Baby, just because you're Christian doesn't mean that you won't still experience some heartaches and pains. It just means that you have a better way of getting past them."

After meditating on that advice, Belinda tried her best to put on a happy face for her parents and a couple of their friends who joined them for the dinner. She spent hours in the kitchen helping her mother prepare the meal, consisting of turkey, cornbread dressing, gravy, whole cranberries, wheat rolls, au gratin potatoes, winter greens, and pumpkin mousse. Still, it bothered her that she didn't have any friends or anyone her own age to hang out with on a holiday. And now with no prospects of a real man on the horizon, Belinda remained in constant prayer. If only she'd had one friend to call on, she'd feel a lot better.

As the chilly day wound down, Belinda excitedly hopped on the Internet and signed into Facebook hoping to communicate with Jesse and Justine. She wondered how they'd enjoyed another Thanksgiving without their mother and what they planned to do over the holiday weekend.

Belinda's home page came up, and she rapidly scanned for updates. There weren't any, so she went to her profile page to pull up one of her two friends because Jesse and Justine were all she had. Belinda saw something that she was totally unprepared for. Her friends count was zero. She couldn't believe. What had happened to her children? Where were they?

An unknown voice deep down in her spirit, beneath the trembling in her belly and the stinging of her toes, whispered one word: Desmond. She asked, "How else could they have disappeared from my friends list?"

From that point, Belinda spent several hours searching for them on Facebook like she'd done that night in Wisconsin, to no avail. She didn't know what to think or how to react to the fact that they were both gone, and there was nothing she could do to get them back. Desmond had probably forbid them to contact her.

Leaning over the computer, Belinda lowered her face into her hands and proceeded to sprinkle the small keyboard with her tears. She had to ask, "When will the pain ever stop, Jesus? What more can Desmond do to hurt me? How can I ever forgive him for this?"

Rocking back and forth, Belinda willed the tears to recede. She needed to be strong, and she needed a clear head if she was going to battle with the devil, Desmond Taylor. He didn't have the right to take away her kids.

It was Friday evening by the time Belinda felt prayed up enough to tell her parents about Desmond's latest treacherous act involving their grandkids. Trying to practice calmness, she spoke using an even-toned voice. It was taking all her strength and willpower to think like a rational woman. Just mentioning the man's name created tightness in Belinda's chest like none she'd ever known. And the idea that he was deliberately preventing their children from any and all communications with her was causing Belinda's head to pound. She felt a migraine coming on if she couldn't get a handle on her emotions real soon.

"Momma, what am I going to do?" Belinda asked, unloading the automatic dishwasher. She was starting to feel warm so Belinda had pushed the sleeves up on her knit sweater. Julia was taking silverware out of the drawer by the stove preparing to set the dinner table.

Julia sighed drastically. "I don't know, baby. I'm about worried to death. We're just going to have to turn it over to the Lord, and let Him work it out."

"Momma," Belinda said, holding a plate in her hand. She wanted to smash it on the floor; instead, she inhaled and exhaled before continuing. "I wish I had your type of faith, but I'm not there yet."

"Keep doing what you're doing, Belinda, because I'm so proud of you," Julia said, pulling her daughter close. "Nobody said the road would be easy."

Easing the plate onto the kitchen counter, Belinda wrapped both arms around her Mom and held them there until the doorbell sounded, startling both of them.

"I've got it!" Mr. Hines shouted from the living room. Belinda heard his footsteps padding to the front door. He had more quickness in his steps since his rebirth.

Slipping out of her Mom's embrace, Julia heard a familiar voice greeting Mr. Hines before the door closed. Cautiously, she stepped around Julia, and headed in the direction of the voices. Belinda stopped abruptly at the sight of Paul Williams' somber face, and instantly knew that something was terribly wrong. She'd told him the last time they'd spoken not to contact her again. He certainly wouldn't darken her door after that unless something was wrong with her immediate family.

"Oh, my God, please tell me that my children are all right!" Belinda screamed, placing a hand over her palpitating heart. She felt her legs weakening beneath the light weight of her body. While holding her breath, the few seconds before he answered felt like an eternity.

"Your children are fine, Belinda," Paul answered, with an unwavering voice.

"Thank you, Jesus." Belinda cried up to the heavens, releasing her breath.

Creasing her forehead, she turned back to Paul, and asked, "Why are you here?"

By this time, Julia had made it to her daughter's side. Without hesitating, she asked, "Why don't we all have a seat and hear what Mr. Williams has to say?"

"Thank you, Mrs. Hines." Paul followed her lead along with Belinda and Mr. Hines.

Once Paul and Belinda were seated on the sofa, Mr. Hines sat in a recliner on one side of them, and Mrs. Hines sat in a chair on the other.

"Okay, Paul, you're scaring me," Belinda began. "What is this all about?"

Paul sighed, like he'd rather be any place in Dallas besides where he was. Even though he'd dreamed of seeing Belinda again, it hadn't been under these circumstances.

"I'm afraid I do have some bad news." Paul rotated his

hands one around the other, trying to get the words out. "Desmond's dead."

The simultaneous gasps that escaped Belinda and Julia's mouth sounded like a sharp drumbeat in Paul's ear.

"Wh—what are you talking about? Are you sure?" Belinda asked, staring at the man as if he was the grim reaper himself.

"Yes, I'm sorry, but I'm sure. A detective on the police force in Madison called me less than an hour ago."

"Oh, my God, Desmond is dead," she said, trying to make it believable. Belinda dropped her head for a second, and then jerked it up. "What happened?"

"Well, apparently, from what Detective Price told me, Desmond spent last night at his girlfriend's house and didn't return home until noon today. His wife confronted him, and they had a violent argument. She ended up shooting him three times in the chest, and he died instantly on their bedroom floor."

Leaping from her position, Belinda asked, "What about Jesse and Justine? Where are my children?"

"Ah, they're being held in police custody until you can get there to pick them up," Paul replied, rising from the sofa.

Belinda turned, staring at her mother's soft features. She wanted to speak to Julia, only the words wouldn't depart from her lips. How was she going to handle this bittersweet news? The man she'd loved for twenty years, and then later wished dead, had died. Now she would be able to see her kids again and hold them in her arms the way she'd dreamed about for so long.

The old Belinda, the one filled with hate after her painful divorce, would have been ecstatic to hear about Desmond's tragic demise. As a matter of fact, she would have thanked the devil for taking him away and been prepared to do a happy dance all over the dog's grave. However, the new Belinda was saddened by the thought that her ex-husband didn't have the chance to turn his life around and get to know God. Silently, she prayed for the father of her children, a man she'd once loved with all her heart. Now, her main concern needed to be for Justine and Jesse, they would need her now more than they ever had.

"You said he was killed at home. Where were the kids when it happened?"

"The detective told me Jesse and Justine were both out of the house with friends."

"Oh, thank God, they didn't have to witness their father's murder," Belinda cried, slumping into Paul's waiting arms. Her legs had finally given out.

"Where's his wife?" she asked, lifting her head.

"She's been arrested on murder charges. I doubt if she's going to be released before the trial," Paul replied, stroking Belinda's back.

Hanging her head, Belinda thanked the Lord for saving her from becoming a murderess and said, "There, but by the grace of God, I could be going to prison for life. I've truly learned my lesson about hurting people over infidelity. A cheating mate is not worth losing your life over, especially when you have children."

Then, another thought entered her mind, causing Belinda's eyes to widen as her heart missed a beat.

"How can I get up there to my kids? I don't even have the money to buy a plane ticket?"

"Don't worry about that," Paul whispered. "I've got two first class tickets for a midnight flight in my jacket pocket. We'll be there before daylight."

Staring into Paul's sympathetic eyes made Belinda's heart sink. She realized now that she'd mistreated the one man who'd ever shown her an ounce of kindness. All he'd done was try to help her, respect her, and be a gentleman. Yet, she'd repaid him with venomousness. There would never be enough words in the English vocabulary to describe the regret she felt. So, Belinda settled for two of the simplest, yet most meaningful words in our language.

"I'm sorry."

32

(Belinda's Beliefs)

Belinda didn't know how she'd made it through the weekend. Everything that happened after she learned about Desmond's death on Friday seemed like a blurry hallucination—perhaps something she'd dreamed and was waiting to see whether or not it was going to come true. What Belinda did know was that her ex-husband would be buried on Saturday and his parents were handling the funeral arrangements. It had been difficult for her to face them in Wisconsin, but Dr. and Mrs. Taylor were already at the police station by the time she and Paul arrived. Belinda was just thankful that her children had not been released into their custody.

She'd spent half the morning enrolling Justine and Jesse into Wilson High School, a nearby facility. Belinda felt awful for not being able to register them in the highest-rated, private institution Dallas had to offer. But given their dire financial situation, she wondered if they'd be changing to another public institution within the next month.

Staring at herself in the bathroom mirror, Belinda buttoned the front of her white blouse and tugged at the collar of her plaid blazer. Seeing how much she'd aged since her release from prison in October, Belinda added a little extra powdered blush to her cheeks.

Belinda couldn't accept that the face staring back at her appeared to be almost ten years older than she actually was, but worry had a way of creating its own special lines. Brushing her relaxed hair back into a chignon, she noticed the gray hairs that seem to have appeared overnight. Belinda leaned in closer to the glass, taking a keen look at the wrinkles around her eyes, which were puffy from crying tears of sadness and joy at the same time. Dabbing on a touch of concealer underneath each tired-looking pupil, she covered up the slightly dark circles. "That will have to do for now," she thought.

Oddly, Belinda would have to face life from now on as a single, unemployed parent with two teenagers and two aging parents to take care of. The tightness around her mouth said it all; Belinda was disappointed with her circumstances. She desperately needed a job, a business, a career, anything that would keep them from losing their house.

At least, the kids had taken the move to public school well, much better than Belinda would have expected. She was thankful for the two-hour session they'd had with the grief counselor in Wisconsin right after their father's death. It had actually helped them.

Belinda had slept in the full-sized bed with Justine last night, holding her daughter's shaking body until she fell asleep. They'd been apart for so long that it felt like the motherly thing to do. Justine sprayed Belinda with the anger she felt from being separated for over a year.

"I thought you abandoned us," she spat. Justine's words stung Belinda's ears like a bee in the darkness.

Hugging Justine nearer to her bosom, Belinda listened to her daughter describe what their life in another state had become like without her, the shock of losing their father, and the swift move back to Dallas. Being actively attentive to her emotions, Belinda patted Justine's back, and whispered, "Things are going to get better," because that was her silent prayer for them.

They both shed tears of sadness over the death of Desmond, as well as tears of joy over their reunion. Justine even explained that their disappearance from Facebook was a result of Desmond finding out that they'd made contact with Belinda, but none of that mattered now. They were together, and they'd never be separated from each other again.

Jesse tried to be a man about the situation by pretending not to be affected by his father's death. He chose to sit alone in his bedroom listening to his iPod, telling Belinda over and over again that he was alright. But the Wisconsin counselor had recommended that both children get further counseling and Belinda was in agreement with her. If the school couldn't provide it, she'd have to find it another way. She hadn't stuck with counseling after her prison episode, but now she could see how it could be helpful following a traumatic event such as this. She prayed that Desmond's parents would at least help her with that.

Justine and Jesse seemed genuinely excited about the concept of attending "regular" school this morning, especially the part where they didn't have to wear uniforms or loafer shoes.

"You mean we can wear our afterschool clothes to school?" Justine asked, a smile inching across her lips.

"That's almost too good to be true," Jesse added. "I get to dress like a real man for my senior year." They bumped fists like the president and first lady.

Belinda grimaced on the way to the kitchen, wondering if they'd take moving into a two-bedroom house on the other side of town as well as they had adjusted to attending public school. Heading towards the sink, she picked up the morning newspaper Mr. Hines had left on the counter per her request.

"Good morning, Momma. The coffee smells good. And I really need it."

"Good morning, baby. I guess you got the kids enrolled into school okay." Mrs. Hines was sitting at the eat-in kitchen table, having a strong cup of coffee.

"Yes, I think they're going to be fine. I can't believe they were actually happy to get into the public school system." Belinda poured herself a cup of coffee and sat down beside Julia.

"For what it's worth, I think they're going to do well. The change of environment will probably do them good, too. What do you have planned for the rest of the day?"

"I'm about to look through these employment ads to see what types of jobs are available. Then, I'm going to get online and do a nationwide search. I've got to do something if there's nothing available for me in Dallas. I'd hate to move, but since Desmond's parents are the beneficiaries on his life insurance policies, they refuse to give me a dime unless I give them full custody of both kids. And we both know that's not about to happen as long as there's breath in my body. We'll all be huddled together in one tiny bedroom in grandma's rental house before that happens."

"I know that's the truth. I don't understand how some people can be so nasty to their own blood. We just have to keep praying and keep believing that the Lord will make a way somehow for the children's sake. As long as we can all stay together, that's all that matters to me."

"I hear you, Momma. I'm praying and trusting that I'll find a well-paying job right here in the city." Belinda looked around, noticing how quiet the house was and asked, "Where's Daddy?"

"He went down to the golf course over an hour ago. I think he's trying to get in as much golfing as he can before we have to start moving. He's going over to make sure that the renters are out of the house later on today. And then, we can give it a good cleaning tomorrow."

Saddened by the thought that her worst nightmare would come true, Belinda dropped her head and said a silent prayer. She hadn't believed in prayer very much before getting saved, but God had brought her through just the same. Now that she prayed faithfully, she believed that He'd make a better way, as long as she put forth the efforts to be a better Christian. If she did her part, she was confident that God would do His.

"Would you like to ride with me to the post office, baby? Your Auntie Karen sent me a package for my birthday next week, and I wasn't here to sign for it Saturday."

"Sure, Momma, just give me a minute to pour another cup of coffee," Belinda replied, rising from the table.

"Okay. I'm going to get my purse out of my bedroom," Julia stood, heading down the hallway. "Grab me a can of Coke on your way out."

Shaking her head while popping open the refrigerator, Belinda wanted to scold her Mom for drinking soda before noon, but decided to keep her mouth closed. She didn't have the energy to worry about that today.

Belinda snatched the red and white soda can from the refrigerator, and joined her mother in the car.

"So you want to tell me how things went between you and Paul this weekend?" Julia asked, pulling away from the curb.

"He's the most thoughtful man I've ever met. But I've blown it with him." Crossing her thin legs, Belinda stared out the passenger's side window at the beautiful homes in the neighborhood. As much as she regretted having to move in with her parents, she was going to miss their luxurious living abode. Squinting at the man driving a golf cart in the distance, Belinda wondered if it was her father.

"Why do you say that? The man obviously cares about you. He was by your side the entire weekend."

"I know, and I probably would not have made it through the last few days without him, especially trying to handle Desmond's parents. You should have seen the way they glared at me at the police station. You would have thought that I pulled the trigger instead of his wife."

"Well, Belinda, he seems to be a forgiving man. All you have to do is ask for a second chance. If it's meant to be, then he'll be willing to give it a try."

Staring at Julia, Belinda asked, "Do you really think so?"

Julia chuckled at the question. "Judging from the look I saw in his eyes, he'd be more than happy to hear from you. Just give him a call and see what happens, baby." Julia patted Belinda's left hand and smiled.

Nodding her head, Belinda continued thinking, "Am I ready for another relationship? Do I even want to try? My only concern right now is strictly for my children. I've wasted years on a man who didn't love me. Maybe it's time to just think about myself."

Julia seemed to have read her daughter's mind. "Don't let one or two men harden your heart against love because that's just what the devil wants you to do. God wants us to have companionship, that's why He invented the institution of marriage."

"I know, Momma. I'm not bitterly against it. I'm just not sure anymore if it's for me," Belinda replied, staring out the window as they approached the red-bricked post office building.

There was a long line of customers so they had to wait nearly fifteen minutes to be served. Julia handed the blonde-haired clerk a green slip of paper and received a small, brown, paper-wrapped box in return. Like a child on Christmas morning, she held the package to her ear and shook it as she stepped away from the counter.

"Okay, you have your package. Is that it?" Belinda asked, holding the glass door open to exit the building.

"Ah, well, I might as well check my P.O. box while I'm here, and see what type of junk mail I have this week," Julia replied, laughing. She dangled the keychain in her hand.

Belinda still held the door for a couple more people to

exit before releasing it. She stepped back inside the building, waiting on Julia to check her box.

"It sure is crowded in here today. You'd think that they were giving away candy or something."

"Yeah, this post office is always like this. That's why I don't like coming down here." Julia opened her small mailbox, pulled out a couple of catalogs, and one envelope. She walked outside with Belinda, clutching the mail in one hand and her car keys in the other. Once she was inside the car, Julia handed the mail to her daughter.

"Here, hold on to my mail for me."

Extending a hand, Belinda took the mail. Her fashion-trained eyes went directly to the latest Neiman and Marcus catalog. As Julia pulled into traffic, Belinda scanned the book, salivating at all the high-priced apparel she used to be able to afford without a second thought. For the remainder of the ride back home, her eyes were glued to those pages. Belinda didn't notice the sunny day, or the road construction, or the new three-story mall being built because she was too busy daydreaming.

Once they were home, Belinda placed the mail on the kitchen counter. Mrs. Hines walked in behind her and opened the small package she'd received from her sister. It contained a necklace, a birthday card, and a money order for a hundred dollars. Julia was touched by her sister's gift.

"Oh, isn't this precious. She sent me a locket," Julia said, opening it up. "Look, baby, it's a picture of me and Karen as little girls."

Leaning over, Belinda looked at the black and white pictures of two little girls on opposite sides of the locket, and smiled.

"You two were so pretty." Then, her eyes went to the envelope lying on the counter. Belinda wrinkled her brow. "Momma, why do you have a letter from the Coca-Cola Company?"

"Oh, that's probably my annual statement from them," Julia replied, nonchalantly. Placing her handbag on a stool, she walked towards the refrigerator.

"What do you mean? You own stock in Coke?" Belinda asked, eyes bulging. She didn't have any idea that Julia had knowledge of the stock market.

"Well, it's not much, but I bought some of their stock before you were born," Julia said, pulling a bottle of water from the refrigerator. She opened it and went back to the stool beside Belinda.

"You never told me about this," Belinda said, holding the envelope in her hand. "Aren't you going to open it?"

"No, baby, I never open those. I haven't opened one of those statements in over thirty years." Julia took a sip from her bottled water.

Belinda stared at her mother incredulously. She couldn't wait to hear her explanation for this because it certainly wasn't making sense to her.

"Okay, I have to ask why you would own stock in one of the most popular companies in the world and not open your statements?"

"Well, I bought that little piece of stock my senior year in college in nineteen-seventy," Julia began, closing one eye, trying to remember the exact year. "Anyway, I was taking a general finance class. The assignment was to choose a company and study their stock report for a whole month. So, since I loved Coke and they had these real popular commercials on the TV every day, I picked them. When the month was over, I decided to make a small investment in the company, just to see what would happen."

"Do you remember how much you invested?"

Julia tilted her head to one side, staring upward, trying her best to recall the old days.

"I was on scholarship and didn't have much money, so it couldn't have been more than a hundred dollars. Anyway, I followed the stock for a couple of years, but it hardly made any money. Then, after I married your father, I didn't need the money so I stopped opening the statements. Whenever I picked them up from my private mailbox, I filed them away in my special place every year so George wouldn't see them."

"Where did you keep them?"

"I put them in one of my hat boxes on the top shelf in my closet. He would never think to look up there for anything."

"Why'd you hide them from Daddy?"

Julia shrugged. "It was just something that I had before I got married, and I wanted to keep it to myself. My mother always told me to keep a separate account or put something aside for me. So, I guess this was my something."

Belinda was shocked. She couldn't respond at first. Belinda's heart was beating so loud in her ears that she didn't even hear the entire response. Then, she couldn't open the envelope fast enough.

Without waiting for Julia's permission, Belinda ripped the paper apart and stared at the statement balance in disbelief. She turned, screaming at the top of her lungs in her mother's face. Belinda jumped off the stool, waving the envelope in her hand.

Julia stood, watching Belinda scream and run in circles around the room. Julia crisscrossed her arms over her chest, held her head back, and praised the Lord. She knew beyond a shadow of a doubt that He had answered her prayers. Julia didn't know the value of her Coca-Cola stock, but she knew it had to be a mighty blessing for her child to carry on like this.

"Momma," Belinda said, taking Julia's trembling hands. She'd finally calmed down enough to speak and allow the tears to flood her grateful eyes. "You're worth twenty million dollars!"

"No! No! You're kidding me!" Julia released her

daughter's hands and placed one hand over her palpitating heart like she was about to experience the big one. "I can't be worth that much money."

"Yes, you are. Look at this," Belinda said, placing the statement beneath Julia's nose. "That's a lot of zeros."

"I—I need to sit down," Julia stammered, reaching out for the back of a chair. She eased herself down into the soft seat, leaned back, and exhaled.

The front door slammed close and both ladies turned to see Mr. Hines gracing the doorway. With his hands jammed inside his pockets, he seemed scared to move any further. Belinda ran towards her father screaming louder than a contestant on the *Price is Right*, "Daddy, you're not going to believe this!"

33

(Belinda's Prayer)

Belinda stretched up to the sky, welcoming the morning light on her gleaming face. She'd spent the evening celebrating with her parents and children at one of the finest downtown restaurants. They didn't tell Justine and Jesse about the good fortune that had been bestowed upon their family. The kids assumed that this was just a night out to commensurate their return to Dallas. But it was so much more than what they could ever imagine.

When Mr. Hines volunteered to drive his grandchildren to school this morning, Belinda gleefully consented and dashed back into her bed. She'd already called Attorney Smith and made arrangements for them to meet at her office later this morning to review the stock paperwork and request an extension on the foreclosure procedure.

All and all, her life was really looking up. Belinda felt good about herself for the first time in a long time, and it wasn't just because of the money they had now. It was because she'd finally found herself. Belinda was better than the woman she used to be; she was happy being saved. And as such, she had regrets regarding how she'd treated certain people in her life. But the main person on her mind right now was Paul Williams. She'd dreamed about him last night. While smiling and reminiscing about her dream, Belinda sat up in bed, leaned against a stack of pillows, and dialed Paul's number.

"Hi, Paul, I'm calling to thank you again for helping me this weekend. I don't know what I would have done without your help."

"You're welcome. I told you that you don't have to keep thanking me. And tell your father I said not to worry about trying to pay me back for anything. It's all on me, all right?"

Belinda grinned to herself thinking, "This guy really is a special sweetheart."

"Paul," Belinda began, lowering her voice. "I was also calling to ask you for your forgiveness. I'm sorry for the way I treated you, like you were beneath me or something. I was wrong for that."

Paul laughed. "Ah, I never took it personal. But I can tell you this, Belinda. I've already forgiven you for that. I could never hold a grudge against a pretty woman like you."

Belinda loved Paul's outgoing personality. He was always pleasant, and made her laugh like she was doing now.

"You're flirting with me, just like you did in my dream last night."

"Oh, so you dreamed about me last night, did you? Well, tell me more, please."

Belinda imagined Paul scooting to the edge of his seat to hear what she was about to say. With joy in her heart, Belinda went on to tell Paul about her vivid dream.

"Well, we were at this party, or it might have been an evening wedding reception. Anyway, we were outside and the place was beautifully decorated with bright flowers everywhere. We were standing on the veranda away from the other guests. You were holding a flute filled with champagne and telling me how pretty I looked in my white sleeveless dress. I can still see the smile you had on your face."

"Well, that's not hard to imagine because I'm always glad to see you. In fact, I'd love to see you again real soon."

"I was hoping you'd say that. Thanks for forgiving me."

Later that day, after the meeting with the attorney, after

the teenagers returned home, after the family had eaten dinner together, Paul came by to check on his lady friend, bearing gifts of flowers and chocolates. Belinda checked her appearance in the foyer mirror before opening the door. She made sure her tangerine sweater was pulled down neatly over her Guess brand, dark rinse jeans. Then, Belinda met him at the door with a super smile showing her pearly whites.

"Come on in," she said, accepting his tokens.

Ushering Paul past the living room where her parents sat, and then past the kitchen, they entered the den. They both flopped down on the two-piece sectional and relaxed against the cushiony seats. The conversation was flowing smoothly when Paul said, "You know you have a powerful testimony, don't you?"

Belinda whispered, "Yes, I do, but I've got a long way to go before I'm ready to testify in church."

"I don't know about that. You might surprise yourself with what you can do. Anyway, ah, I'd like to invite you to come with me to my church on Sunday. I'll even pick you up and drive you there myself," he said, patting his chest.

"I'll consider that," Belinda replied, tucking one foot underneath her thigh. "But I have a lot of amends to make in life before I get to that point. I don't know how I'm going to do them all, I just know I've got to do something."

"Well, if you really mean that, then I've got an idea. Why don't you write down the name of every person that you'd like to make amends with, and say an individual prayer for each of them?"

Belinda thought for a second and realized that it wasn't a bad idea. She'd been thinking about writing each person a letter asking forgiveness, and then not mailing it. But praying seemed like an even better recommendation.

Reaching for the paper and pen on the coffee table, Belinda started making a list of Desmond's mistresses and a few other people whom she'd harmed over the past twenty years. About twenty minutes later, she had over twenty names. Paul helped Belinda pray for each name on the list. When they were done, she turned to him and said, "Thank you for praying with me, Paul." Belinda sighed heavily, looking at him. "But I have one more person who's been on my mind who I'd like to pray for."

Paul nodded for her to continue.

"Her name is Yvette Riley. She's younger than me, but she was my cellmate in prison. She was the first person, besides my mother, who ever prayed for me, and I'll never forget that. I wonder what she's doing right now?" Belinda propped her chin up on her fist.

"Well, if you're that curious, why don't you give her a call and find out. You got her number, right?"

Belinda was instantly filled with excitement. She placed both feet on the floor, left the room for a minute, and returned with her cell phone.

"I saved her number as soon as I got this phone. I don't know why I never called her. I guess I didn't want to be reminded of that part of my life. Now, I know that whole experience helped change me."

Paul relaxed onto the cushiony sofa, leaning over on one elbow, listening to Belinda speak into the phone. Apparently, someone had just answered.

"Hi, Yvette, this is Belinda Taylor, do you remember me?"

"Hello, Belinda. Of course I remember who you are. Where are you?" Yvette's husky voice boomed across the telephone line.

"I'm at my parents' house right now. I've been out for awhile."

Yvette squealed into the phone. "Girl, that's wonderful. How come you're just now calling me?"

"Well, it's a long story, but I'm a different person now. I

have my kids back with me, and I finally accepted Christ into my life. So, I wanted to call and thank you for being one of the first people who ever prayed for me. You'll never know what a difference you've made in my life."

"Girl, you're welcome. I'm just overjoyed to know that you're trying to live right. God knows how hard it is to make it out here, especially when you have three kids to take care of."

Belinda noticed a distinct change in Yvette's voice, she suddenly sounded a little sad.

"Yvette, what's going on? Did I call you at a bad time?"

"I have to be honest with you, Belinda. It's a blessing that you called me when you did because I was just sitting here thinking about writing another bad check, knowing there's a good chance that I'll go back to jail if I do. But, honestly, I only have eighty cents left in my checking account, all the food stamps are gone for the month, and my kids are hungry. What else can I do?"

Belinda's heart started bleeding from the sound of the hopelessness in Yvette's voice. She picked up the pen and paper from the coffee table again, and said, "Yvette, give me your address. I'm coming to visit you right now."

Paul, being a true gentleman, offered to drive Belinda to Yvette's duplex on the south side of town.

"That's not a safe place for a woman to be driving alone," he said, helping Belinda climb into his Nissan SUV.

On the way there, she told Paul about everything that had transpired with her family over the last couple of days, including the Coca-Cola stock windfall. She laughed at his reply.

"Wow, that's good news. I hope you didn't tell your Daddy what I said about not having to pay me back."

"Of course, I didn't, crazy man," she teased.

"You know, I'm just saying," he grinned, rubbing his chin.

Belinda asked Paul to do her a favor before making it to Yvette's house.

"Would you stop at the grocery store and let me get her a few groceries? She said her kids were hungry, and that's an awful thought."

"Sure," Paul replied, pulling into the supermarket. "Let me have the address so I can put it into my GPS," he requested, turning off the car engine. He waited for Belinda to go inside and return to the truck carrying two plastic bags.

They continued their ride in silence, listening to smooth jazz on the radio, both lost in their own thoughts, until Paul turned onto a dark street.

"We're almost there," Paul said, listening to the animated voice of the GPS telling them that their destination was coming up on the right.

Belinda held her breath as Paul crept past each building.

"There it is," Belinda said, pointing to the double unit building. They were arguably in one of the poorest neighborhoods in Dallas. Paul pulled up, parked directly in front of the door, and grabbed the grocery bags.

Before Belinda could knock on the door, Yvette swung it opened and pulled her into the warmest embrace Belinda had ever felt. They exchanged happy greetings as Yvette invited them inside.

Stepping across the threshold, Belinda almost covered her nose at the odor penetrating her nostrils. She fought hard to maintain a straight face as they entered the cramped living room. It smelled like food had gone bad in the refrigerator or meat had been left out to spoil. Belinda took the two bags from Paul, handed them to Yvette, and said, "I bought you all some bread, mayonnaise, mustard, cheese, and sandwich meats."

"Girl, thank you." Yvette grabbed the bags, headed to the tiny kitchen table, and screamed for the kids to join her.

Belinda couldn't move out of the way fast enough to keep from getting trampled by Yvette's three healthy-sized kids.

"Now, y'all know better than that. Apologize to Ms. Belinda right now."

Hugging each child, Belinda said, "That's okay, let them go ahead and eat."

Yvette busied herself in the kitchen fixing sandwiches while Paul sat in the living room, and Belinda stood in the kitchen doorway surveying the rest of the house and thinking, "This place is a mess. How can she live under such horrible conditions? One of the doors is hanging off the kitchen cabinet, the floor has sticky stuff on it, the sofa and loveseat is dirty, the carpeting is beyond filthy, and the paint is peeling off the walls."

They didn't have any chairs to sit in, so the children stood around the kitchen table waiting on their food. One by one, they each received a well-made sandwich.

"I'm sorry about the way it smells in here," Yvette said, avoiding Belinda's eyes. "The refrigerator went out day before yesterday. Everything we had in it got spoiled. I called the landlord, but he hasn't been over here to look at it yet."

"You explained things to him, and he still didn't come?"

"Yep, and it'll be a miracle when he does get here. Girl, we got a list of stuff that needs fixing around here. You can see that for yourself," Yvette said, flapping her hands at her sides. She sighed, and returned her attention to the kids. "When y'all finish eating, y'all can watch TV in the back room," Yvette said, placing both hands on her narrow hips. They all yelled with joy, stuffing more bread in their mouths.

Belinda couldn't stop the aching in her heart for Yvette and the sweet kids gobbling down their food. She had to do something to help someone who had helped her in a time of need. Silently, Belinda thanked God that her family wouldn't have to move from their five-bedroom home located on the golf course, but there wasn't any sense in grandma's house going to waste either. Suddenly, Belinda had the answer that would help a friend and allow her to be a true friend. Stretching her lips from cheek to cheek, Belinda asked, "Yvette, how would you like to move with your children out to the country? My grandmother's rental house is vacant, and we'd love to have you all as tenants."

Yvette's screams of joy helped to soothe the aching in Belinda's heart. Now if she could ever get the ringing out of her ears, Belinda would be just fine.

34

(Belinda's Journey)

Belinda and her children started attending the Abundantly Blessed Church with Paul on a regular basis while her parents chose to stay home and attend The Potter's House via television every Sunday morning. Abundantly Blessed was a modest-sized, non-denominational church with close to three-hundred members. With an unconventional female pastor, Melissa Thomas, at the helm of the ministry, Belinda felt revived after listening to her message each Sunday.

After four months of attending the lively church, volunteering to help with the elderly, and assisting with church school classes, Belinda began to feel a calling on her life. She hadn't heard the voice of Jesus speak in her ears, but Belinda could feel her heart changing. Something was moving in her spirit and the more she studied the Bible and meditated on the Word, the more she began to feel like she could make a difference in someone's life.

On Easter Sunday, after preaching a prolific message regarding the importance of service in the church, Pastor Thomas asked Belinda to meet with her outside at a picnic table underneath one of the elm trees. It was a gloriously sunny day for an egg hunt. The soaring temperature was perfect for the ladies to show off their new sleeveless dresses. While the older children hid the eggs, the younger children sat at the picnic tables enjoying fruit punch.

"Ms. Belinda, thank you for meeting with me. I promise I won't take up too much of your time." Pastor Thomas sat down at the end of the table. Belinda slid onto the bench seat to the left of her.

"That's fine, Pastor, I'm not in a hurry to leave. My kids are out hiding eggs," Belinda responded, smiling nervously at the Pastor. She wasn't sure what this was about, but just the idea of being asked to meet with Pastor Thomas was unnerving.

"First, I'd like to thank you for being an active participant in our church for the past few months. It's been a pleasure having you here every Sunday, and your volunteer efforts are sincerely appreciated." Pastor Thomas pulled her long micro braids to the back. She tied them in a knot on top of her head, leaving some to hang down her back, giving Belinda an opportunity to study her freckled face up close.

"Why, thank you," Belinda responded, sounding taken aback. "I truly enjoy coming here and hearing your inspiring messages."

"Well, we're glad to have you. But what I want to ask you about today is how would you feel about leading one of our women's groups next month?"

"Ah, what type of group is it?"

Pastor Thomas sighed, clasping her hands together on top of the wooden table.

"You know, we have a suggestion box in the vestibule. And lately, I've gotten quite a few requests for counseling with battered and abused women. So, I'm thinking about starting a women's support group just for that, and I thought you might be the person to lead it for me. Of course, I'll be around to assist you in any way that I can, but you'd be the leader."

Now it was Belinda's turn to sigh.

"Whew!" she said, releasing a breath. Then, she chuckled. "I really wasn't expecting that."

"Well, sometimes our blessings come unexpectedly," Pastor Thomas responded quickly. "From what you've shared with me about your background, I think you'd be able to help some of these women get their lives back on track. You know, some of them are really young and most of them have children, but they don't have the backbone or the self-esteem required to get out of these destructive relationships. And it saddens me to see our women this way."

"I see what you're saying, Pastor. And I have been feeling like there's more I could be doing to help someone in the church. So, if you don't mind, I'd like to have a little time to absorb this idea and give it some thought."

Pastor Thomas patted Belinda's hand before responding.

"Oh, sure, take all the time you need. It's not definite yet. It's simply something that I see as a growing need in the church. And if we get the group going, we can open it up to other women in the community that might not otherwise cross our doors. So, please, think about it and get back with me when you're ready."

"Okay, I'll do that."

"Thank you. Now, if you'll excuse me, I've got some work to finish up in my office. If you want to talk about it some more before you leave today, that's where I'll be for at least the next hour." Pastor Thomas said, checking her watch. She gave Belinda a confident smile as she walked away.

Belinda remained in her seat, wondering what had just happened. "Could this be what God has been calling me to do? Can I possibly help these women in some way? Desmond never battered me, but I think his infidelity could be considered a form of abuse. Can I relate to these women with that in mind?"

Belinda had some tough questions to answer before accepting the Pastor's challenge to lead the battered women's group. She had to search her soul to examine her deepest motives, as well as evaluate how she might personally respond in a ministerial role. She had to pray—grapple with her true thoughts and emotions. But most importantly, she had to listen to what God was trying to tell her because He was definitely trying to tell her something.

It only took Belinda a week of fervent prayer to reach a decision. Coupled with the support of her family and a yearning in her heart to help other women, Belinda was ready to make a commitment to serving the church. She spoke with Pastor Thomas the following Sunday after morning worship to give her the good news. Belinda was happy and excited about leading the battered women's support group one night a week in the church's basement.

The way Pastor Thomas responded to her announcement, Belinda knew she'd made the right decision.

"Oh, thank you, thank you, Sister Belinda!" Pastor Thomas said, hugging her tightly. "I knew you'd come to the proper conclusion. These women are going to love you."

Belinda agreed to meet with the support group on Thursday evenings at seven for one hour. At the first meeting, she stood up in a navy wrap dress and introduced herself the way she began her daily praise.

"Good evening, my name is Belinda Hines Taylor, and I've been saved for five months, fifteen days, nine hours, and..."

Epilogue

A year later

"So, that's my story of how I made it from the jail house to the church house. Now you all can see why I consider myself blessed beyond belief. Because I know some of y'all don't believe this really happened to me, but I'm a witness to the truth." Belinda held the microphone, pacing back and forth in a gold textured, two-piece skirt suit. The congregation was standing on its feet clapping and praising God in tongues.

"Before I take my seat this evening," she began, returning to stand behind the podium. She looked down, turned a few pages in the Bible, and then looked out at the members. "I want to leave you with the single most important thing I learned along my journey to Christianity. It is in Exodus, chapter twenty, and it is called the Ten Commandments. I'm going to go through them real quick just to remind you of what they are because they are the essential elements for daily living. The first commandment is, I am the Lord your God, you shall have no other gods before me; the second commandment is that you shall not make yourself an idol; the third commandment is that you shall not make wrongful use of the name of your God; the fourth commandment is to remember the Sabbath and keep it holy; the fifth commandment is that you shall not murder; the sixth commandment is that you shall not commit adultery; the seventh commandment is that you shall not steal; the eighth commandment is that you shall not bear false witness against your neighbor; the ninth commandment is you shall not covet your neighbor's wife or anything that belongs to your neighbor, and the last one I want to mention, as well as practice right now, is to honor your father and mother," Belinda said, closing the Bible, searching the audience for her parents.

"I want my family members to stand so I can introduce them to you all, especially the visitors that we have today, and then I'm going to take my seat." Belinda smiled proudly, waiting for them to stand.

"Okay, this beautiful lady is my mother, Julia Hines." Belinda waited for the audience to finish clapping between each introduction.

"This distinguished man is my father, George Hines."

"Standing beside him is my cute daughter, Justine."

"Next to her is my gifted son, Jesse."

"And the handsome man on the end is someone the Lord sent to me, especially for me, and I thank him every day for doing that. He's been a faithful member at this church, and now he's my fiancé, Paul Edward Williams."

The end

Other Titles from Barbara Joe Williams

The 21 Lives of Lisette Donavan: Anthology (2012)

A Man of My Own (2012)

A Writer's Guide to Publishing & Marketing (2010)

Moving the Furniture: 52 Ways to Keep Your Marriage Fresh (2008)

Courtney's Collage (2007)

How I Met My Sweetheart: Anthology (2007)

Falling for Lies (2006)

Dancing with Temptation (2005)

Forgive Us This Day (2004)

Email her at: amanipublishing@aol.com

Visit her website at: www.barbarajoe.webs.com

CPSIA information can be obtained at www.ICGtesting.com
Printed in the USA
LVOW071744290313

326724LV00004B/484/P